ACCLAIM FOR JEREMY BATES

"Will remind readers what chattering teeth sound like."
—*Kirkus Reviews*

"Voracious readers of horror will delightfully consume the contents of Bates's World's Scariest Places books."
—*Publishers Weekly*

"Creatively creepy and sure to scare." —*The Japan Times*

"Jeremy Bates writes like a deviant angel I'm glad doesn't live on my shoulder."
—Christian Galacar, author of GILCHRIST

"Thriller fans and readers of Stephen King, Joe Lansdale, and other masters of the art will find much to love."
—*Midwest Book Review*

"An ice-cold thriller full of mystery, suspense, fear."
—David Moody, author of HATER and AUTUMN

"A page-turner in the true sense of the word."
—*HorrorAddicts*

"Will make your skin crawl." —*Scream Magazine*

"Told with an authoritative voice full of heart and insight."
—Richard Thomas, Bram Stoker nominated author

"Grabs and doesn't let go until the end." —*Writer's Digest*

BY JEREMY BATES

ISLAND OF THE DOLLS

World's Scariest Places 4

Jeremy Bates

ISLAND OF THE DOLLS

PROLOGUE

The bullfrog sat on a big green lily pad in the middle of the rotten-smelling pond. Its throat expanded like a balloon as it made a rusty croaking sound.

Eight-year-old Rosa Sánchez took another careful step toward it, then another, doing her best not to disturb the scummy water. She had taken off her sandals, and the mud on the bottom of the pond squished between her toes, feeling both good and gross at the same time.

The frog shifted its fat body on the lily pad so it seemed to stare right at her, its bulging eyes glistening.

Rosa froze, one foot in the air, stork-like.

The bullfrog croaked.

"Look away, frog," Rosa mumbled in Spanish. "Look away."

It didn't, and Rosa, thinking she might topple over, get her clothes wet and stinky, set her lead foot down. Something sharp—a rock or a pokey bit of branch—jabbed the underside of her heel. She ignored the pain, keeping her eyes on the bullfrog.

It continued to stare back at her, its eyes unblinking. The air left the sack in its throat, and the bullfrog shrunk nearly in half. Still, it was a big sucker. And it was so close...

Rosa took another step and thought she might be able to grab it now if she was quick enough. She stuck her hands out before her and tilted forward slowly.

The bullfrog sprang. Rosa's hands clutched its slimy flanks.

1

But she was too slow. It plopped into the water and disappeared from sight.

Rosa's momentum, however, kept her moving forward. One uncoordinated step, two, then she dunked facefirst into the water. She closed her eyes but forgot to close her mouth and got a big gulp of what tasted like sewage. Her hands sank into the muddy bottom of the pond, then her knees, yet she managed to arc her back and keep her head from going completely under.

She made a noise like she was crying, though she wasn't crying, she was eight years old, a big girl, and big girls didn't cry when they fell in water. Still, she *wanted* to. She was soaked, a foul taste was in her mouth, and she couldn't get back to her feet. The mud sucking at her hands and knees was too slippery—

Now her head did go under. Water gushed into her ears, her nose, but at least she'd kept her mouth closed this time. When she burst back through the surface, she crawled, moaning, toward the bank, grabbing at tall grasses, roots, anything she could reach, until she was up on dry ground.

Rosa flopped onto her stomach, her eyes burning with tears. Then she sat up. Her clothes clung uncomfortably to her thin frame. And she stank like a toilet. Worse than a toilet. It reminded her of the smell when her big brother Miguel found the dead rat in the wall of their house, and told Rosa to take it out to the street.

Miguel. He was going to murder her. He was already mad at her for walking too slow when they got to the island and went looking for a spot to make camp. Then he got even madder because he wanted to kiss his girlfriend, but he couldn't do that with Rosa around. That's why he told Rosa to go do something. Rosa didn't want to at first. The island scared her with all of the dolls hanging from the trees or sitting on the ground, just staring at her with their painted faces and glass eyes. However, you didn't say "no" to Miguel, not unless you wanted to get a slap across your head, and so Rosa went, not planning to go far...and then she saw the pond. At first she wanted to muck around in the water a bit. She didn't know there would be bullfrogs. But there sure were; they were everywhere. She spotted three right away. Yet she wasn't careful then, and they all hopped off their lily pads and vanished beneath the water before she got close enough to catch one. It took her another fifteen minutes before she found the big fatty.

And now it was gone too, and she was dripping wet, and Miguel was going to call her names and slap her across the head—

A scream shattered the quiet.

Rosa jerked her head about.

That had been her brother's girlfriend, Lucinda.

Did Miguel jump out from somewhere and scare her, as he always liked to do to Rosa? Or did one of the dolls hanging from the trees come to life and attack her? That's what Miguel kept telling Rosa: the dolls were alive but they were just sleeping, and when you weren't looking they would—

Another scream.

Not Lucinda. Deeper, male.

Miguel?

Rosa didn't know, because she'd never heard her brother scream before, or at least not for years. Miguel wasn't afraid of anything.

Rosa got to her feet, her soaked clothes forgotten.

Her eyes scanned the trees ahead of her, searching for movement, for Miguel to be sneaking from bush to bush—and that's what this all was, wasn't it? A joke, not on Lucinda, but on Rosa. Miguel got Lucinda to scream, then Miguel screamed too. As soon as Rosa went to investigate, they would jump out and scare her.

Rosa waited. The forest was silent. No wind. No crickets. Nothing.

"Miguel?" she said.

No reply.

Rosa picked up her sandals and began to walk back the way

she came, toward the source of the screams. She knew Miguel was going to ambush her, but that was okay, because it would only be scary for a second, then everyone would be laughing. And that was better than how Rosa felt right now. Like she was sick, like she wanted to throw up.

Rosa left the glade with the pond. Trees closed tightly around her. She had to duck branches and watch where she stepped. The late afternoon seemed suddenly dark. She didn't remember it being this dark earlier. Was that because the branches were blocking out the sun and sky? Or had a cloud passed before the sun?

"Miguel?" she said, though not very loud this time.

Because what if something else heard her?

Like what?

The dolls?

They couldn't do anything to her. They were only dolls. Even if they came to life, she was a lot bigger than them.

But they got Miguel and Lucinda.

No they didn't! Rosa told herself severely. Miguel was joking around. He was going to jump out any second now.

He didn't jump out.

The forest remained silent and dark.

Maybe she should return to the pond and wait there for Miguel to grow bored of his game and come and get her? Then again, what if Miguel or Lucinda really were hurt? What if they needed her help?

Rosa continued forward, pushing through the thick foliage. She began to move quickly, heedless of the scratching branches and the sharp rocks and other deadfall beneath her bare feet. Then she was running. All she could hear was a thumping in her head and her loud breathing. Every tree looked the same, and she wondered if she was heading in the right direction. But she didn't stop. If she turned back, she would probably only get more lost. Besides, she was pretty sure the camp was right ahead. It couldn't be much farther.

She ducked around a tree—and ran into several dolls hanging from a low branch. She cried out and fell on her butt. Looking up, she recognized them from earlier: grimy, peeling, sinister.

That meant the camp was not very far away.

"Miguel!" she shouted. She could no longer suppress her fright.

"Rosa!" His voice came back, strangled, weak, filled with terror. "Go! Run!"

Rosa got to her feet. A sob caught in her throat, tight, painful.

"Miguel!"

"*Run*—" He was cut off abruptly.

Rosa hesitated a moment longer, then she turned and ran.

XOCHIMICO, MEXICO

2001

JACK

1

I woke up covered in my own blood. It had congealed between the right side of my head and the pillow, and I had to peel the damn pillow away, as if it were a crusty bandage. I held the pillow in front of me, staring in disgust at the brown splatter on the white slip. All the while I was trying to remember what had happened the night before.

I'd been having dinner with my fiancée, and her brother and his girlfriend. What a ball that had been. Listening to Jesus talk about himself all evening. That was Pita's brother's name, Jesus. Ironic how the one guy I'd ever met named after a god had an ego of a god to match. His girlfriend, Elizaveta, was far too good for him. Smart, down-to-earth, attractive. I didn't know how he landed her. Actually I did: money. Pita's and Jesus's father, Marco, turned a mom-and-pop restaurant and pub into a multi-million-dollar brewery, and after Marco died of a brain aneurysm the year before, twenty-nine-year-old Jesus stepped up to the top position.

Setting the stained pillow aside, I touched the cut on my head, igniting a sharp pain that until then had been dormant. The cut ran from the outside of my eyebrow straight to my hairline. Dried blood crumbed beneath my fingertips and fell to the bed like red dandruff.

Recalling what happened, I cringed in embarrassment.

We'd been sitting on the back deck, the four of us. Dinner was finished. Jesus had been smoking one of his expensive cigars and going on about a skiing trip to Chile he and Elizaveta had gone on the previous winter. I was only half listening until he launched into some ridiculous story that had him back-country skiing outside the ski resort's boundaries, which he reached by helicopter. I chuckled loudly. It wasn't that I didn't believe him. Pita once told me she and Jesus had gone on skiing trips every year when they were younger. So I assumed he was a decent enough skier. It was the bragging. Making sure to mention the chartered helicopter, the difficulty of the off-piste terrain, his entourage, which included a famous Mexican singer.

I wasn't nitpicking or being overly critical of Jesus. Everything the guy said and did was orchestrated to make him look good, to make people want to admire him, to see him as the apotheosis of success. Yet at the same time it was all layered in humility, like he was just one of the guys. His efforts were so transparent he became a caricature, a joke. You couldn't help not laughing at him sometimes.

Jesus asked me what was funny. I told him nothing, please continue. The back and forth escalated, the insults becoming sharper, Pita and Elizaveta telling us to stop. Then the asshole took a cheap shot, bringing up the accident that ended my racecar driving career, saying I didn't have the guts anymore to break the speed limit.

I could have taken a swing at him. I should have. Instead I went inside to take a leak. I didn't return to the deck. I went to the second floor, to the balcony that overlooked the deck and the adjacent swimming pool. I climbed atop the railing so I stood precariously on the headrail, yelling that I was going to jump into the pool below, challenging Jesus, the fearless alpine skier, to do the same.

It was probably a good thing I slipped. Roughly ten feet separated the balcony and pool, and had I jumped, I might not have reached the water. But that's what happened, I slipped —or lost my balance, it was all a blur—falling backward and cracking my head on something. I have no idea what. All I remember was the exploding pain—loud was how it felt—then the gushing blood, then everyone gathered around me. They wanted to call an ambulance, but for some reason I didn't want them to. I guess I didn't want to spend the night in the hospital. Then I was in the shower. I seem to recall standing there for a very long time, watching pink water swirl down the drain.

Grimacing, I pushed myself off the bed now, to my feet. I felt momentarily lightheaded, likely due to a loss of blood. I was in the guest bedroom. Not surprising. Pita wouldn't have let me sleep in our bed bleeding like I'd been, even if it was my house. And what had she been thinking letting me go to sleep with a serious head wound? I know I said I didn't want her to call an ambulance, but she should have done so regardless. I might not have woken up at all.

Light streamed through the window, all too bright, almost audible, like a horn. I wondered what time it was. I stepped into the pine-paneled hallway and went to the bathroom because I heard running water.

I knocked on the door lightly, then opened it. Steam fogged the mirror. Pita stood beneath the shower spray, her mocha-colored back and butt to me, her hands massaging either shampoo or conditioner into her dark hair.

"Hey," I said, the word coming out brittle. My throat was as dry as if I'd eaten a handful of saltine crackers.

When we first began dating some five years before, Pita would have turned all the way around, showing off her body. Now she only turned her head slightly so she could see me sidelong. She lowered an arm across her breasts.

"You're alive," she said in her Spanish-accented English.

"Barely," I said.

"So does that mean you're not coming anymore?"

"Coming?"

"Don't you remember anything from last night?"

That irked me, but I said, "Where are we going?"

"You really don't know?"

"I wouldn't have asked if I did."

"Maybe if you didn't drink so much—"

"Forget it, Pita."

I was about to close the door when she said, "Isla de las Muñecas," and went back to washing her hair.

2

Man, I really had been black-out drunk. But a light switched on inside my head, the darkness shrouding my memories cleared, and the rest of the evening came back in snippets. Isla de las Muñecas. Island of the Dolls. That was the reason Jesus and Elizaveta had come by. We'd spent most of dinner discussing the details of the excursion. We'd agreed to leave at 10 a.m. Jesus and Elizaveta would pick up Pepper, then come by my house. Pita and I would follow them in my car to Xochimilco, where we would embark on a two-hour boat ride to the island.

Pepper was a host for a Mexican copycat of The Travel Channel, a basic cable show that featured documentaries and how-to programs related to travel and leisure around the country. He caught a break at the beginning of his career when he got a regular gig as a presenter on episodes featuring animal safaris, tours of grand hotels and resorts, lifestyle stuff—and in the process became a bit of a mini celebrity. Nevertheless, it wasn't until last year that things took off for him due to a documentary he hosted on El Museo De Las Momias, or The Mummies' Museum. The story went that after a cholera outbreak in the nineteenth century the city cemetery in Guanajuato was filling up so quickly that a local tax was imposed demanding relatives to pay a fee to keep the bodies interred. Most relatives couldn't pay or didn't care, the bodies were disinterred, and the best preserved were stored in a building. In the 1900s, entrepreneurial cemetery workers began charging tourists a few pesos to check out the bones and mummies—and the place has since become a museum displaying more than a hundred dried human cadavers, including murder victims, a Spanish Inquisition victim in an iron maiden, criminals buried alive, and children laid to rest dressed up as saints. Most were so well preserved that their hair, eyebrows, and fingernails were still intact, and nearly all of their mouths were frozen in eternal screams, a result of the tongue hardening and the jaw muscles slackening following death.

The documentary proved to be a huge hit, so Pepper pitched The Travel Channel an ongoing series titled *Mexico's Scariest Places*. They liked the idea, and Pepper's next project took him to La Zona del Silencio, or The Dead Zone, a patch of desert in Durango that got its moniker after a test missile launched from a US military base in Utah malfunctioned and crashed in Mexico's Mapimi Desert region. The missile was carrying two containers of a radioactive element. A big US Air Force recovery operation lasted weeks—and made the region a pseudo Area 51 ripe with myths and urban legends regarding mutations of flora and fauna, lights in the sky at night, aliens, magnetic anomalies that prevented radio transmissions, the whole works.

Pepper has since done several other episodes in the series —most of which focused on haunted mansions and shuttered asylums and the like—but the Island of the Dolls had always been his golden egg so to speak. Problem was, the island was private property. The owner had recently died, and his nephew was now in charge—and he repeatedly refused to allow Pepper and his film crew access to the island. The Travel Channel, for their part, gave Pepper the unofficial go-ahead for the documentary, telling him if he got footage, great; if he got busted doing so, they didn't know anything about it.

That was where Pita and I came in. Pepper didn't want to go to the island alone, and we didn't have any affiliation with the television network. I had been looking forward to the trip until Jesus got wind of it a few days ago and, in his blusterous fashion, insisted he and Elizaveta come as well.

Pita was rinsing her hair now. Milky white soap streamed down her back. I asked her, "We still leaving at ten?"

"Yes," she said without looking at me.

"What time is it now?"

"You have half an hour to get ready."

I groaned, wondering if I could pull myself together in time.

"You don't have to come," she told me, turning enough I could see the side of her left breast.

"I already told Pepper I would."

"I'm sure he would understand—your head and everything."

"Would you mind?" I asked cautiously, wondering whether I was walking into one of her traps. I would agree with her, only for her to pounce, accuse me of never wanting to do anything with her, of disliking her brother, something along those lines. Her machinations would have been amusing had they not always been directed at me.

"I think you should rest, Jack," she said. "That's what I think. But it's up to you."

3

Jesus and crew arrived forty minutes later in Jesus's brand new Jaguar X-Type. The vehicle suited him: all show, little substance. Because under the prancing cat hood ornament, and leather and wood interior, it was nothing but an all-wheel-drive Ford Mondeo. Jesus likely didn't know that. He would have purchased it because it was the type of car a young, affluent guy should be driving.

While Pita went out to greet everyone—wearing a chambray shirt with roll-tab sleeves and cutoff jean shorts that showed off the bottom curve of her ass—I went to the garage and loaded our daypacks into my three-year-old Porsche 911. It was parked next to a junked '79 Chevrolet Monte Carlo. I used to own the same make and model as a kid in Vegas. I'd worked in an auto-repair shop for three years to save enough money to buy it. When I turned eighteen and got my racing license, I began racing four nights a week at the local tracks. I consistently finished middle to back of the pack, but I nevertheless became a fan favorite because of my name. The race track announcers thought Jack Goff sounded like a joke and took every opportunity to mention it over the PA system to the delight of the crowd. Soon nobody was calling me Jack anymore. It was always Jack Goff. Announcers, interviewers, fans, whoever. It had that two syllable cadence—and of course innuendo—that made you want to say the whole thing.

I never won a checkered flag with the Monte Carlo, but it was my first race car, and I had some of my fondest memories in it. That's why I bought the junker to restore a few months ago. It was a pet project, a way for me to fill in the days now that I was finished racing.

I got behind the wheel of the Porsche and rolled down the driveway until I came nose to nose with the Jaguar. Elizaveta, in shotgun, her face hidden behind a large sunhat and sunglasses, flashed me a smile and a wave, which I reciprocated. Jesus had his window open, his elbow poking out, as he spoke with his sister. His hair as always was impeccably neat, the sides short, the top parted to the left and slicked back. He wore Aviator sunglasses and a day's stubble he no doubt considered fashionable. The glare of the sun on the windshield prevented me from seeing Pepper in the backseat, and I was wondering if I should get out to say hi when Jesus and Pita finished their chat.

Jesus finally acknowledged me, tipping a grin and tooting

the Jaguar's horn. I squeezed the steering wheel tighter and wondered why I had decided to come. But I had little choice. As I'd told Pita, I'd already committed to Pepper. I would be copping out if I gave him some excuse, especially given my head didn't hurt that much. In fact, my hangover bothered me more than the gash. I felt heavy, unmotivated, blah—but okay enough for a daytrip. Besides, Jesus's company or not, I was still interested in seeing the infamous Island of the Dolls.

Cranking up the volume of some Mexican song heavy on the bass, Jesus reversed onto the street, swung about, and started off. Pita hopped in next to me in the Porsche.

A couple of minutes into the ride she began humming to herself. She'd pulled her thick wavy hair into a ponytail, away from her face, which was sculptured with faultless features. Long-lashed, coyote-brown eyes (which she liked to say were hazel); a straight nose so unremarkable you didn't notice it, which was a plus when it came to noses; full lips more playful than pouty; angular cheekbones, and a gently rounded chin.

Pita's hums transformed into words, a Spanish song I recognized from the radio. She sang it softly under her breath. She had a throaty singing voice.

"What's up?" I asked her.

She glanced at me. "What do you mean?"

"You're in a good mood."

"I'm not allowed to be in a good mood?"

"I just mean...what were you and God talking about?"

"Don't call him that."

"I don't to his face."

"He calls you Jack."

What she meant was, he didn't call me Jack Goff. And she was right; he didn't. Not to my face anyway. I said, "What were you and your brother talking about?"

"Nothing."

"You were chatting for five minutes."

"He's my brother, Jack. We were just talking."

"About the weather? The trip?"

"What does it matter?"

"I'm making conversation, Pita."

"No, you're making it sound like we were conspirating or something."

I didn't correct her mispronunciation. She sometimes got certain English words mixed up or wrong altogether. Conspirating/conspiring was one I'd never heard before though.

"How's Pepper?" I asked, changing topics.

"Excited."

"Does he still want to interview you?"

"Yes, he will give me what he wants me to memorize on the boat. He wants you to say some things too."

"I'm not going on film."

"He really wants you to."

"Why doesn't he ask Jesus?"

"Because Jesus is too well known."

"And I'm not?"

"We're not in America anymore, Jack," she said. "I'm talking about Mexico. People here know my brother. They don't know you."

It was true. I only stood out in this country because I was white, and because of my height. That anonymity was the initial appeal of moving down here. Having said that, my exit from racing had been a pretty big deal, and I could only imagine ESPN getting their hands on a copy of Pepper's "Island of the Dolls" episode and airing a clip of me with the headline: "NASCAR Rookie of the Year, Jack Goff, Turned Paranormal Investigator for Mexican TV."

"I'm not going on film," I repeated.

Jesus stopped at a red light. I pulled up beside him. I was staring ahead at nothing in particular, going over the directions to Xochimilco in my head, when I heard the Jag's engine rev.

I looked past Pita and saw Jesus grinning at me. He revved the engine louder and longer.

"Is he serious?" I said.

"Don't you dare think about racing him," Pita said.

"I'll cream him," I said, grinning myself.

Jesus started blipping the throttle, making the Jag go vroom vroom and sound sporty.

I depressed the clutch, shoved the Porsche into gear, and brought the engine up to 5k RPM.

"Jack!" Pita shouted above the noise. "You're not racing him!"

"The road's clear."

"Jack—!"

Jesus jumped the start before the light changed. I dumped the clutch and nailed it. The tires let out a brief squeal, the revs went to redline. My head snapped back. Jesus's head start had given him a fender length on me, but I gained it back on the shift to second.

We remained side by side through to third gear. I wasn't worried because I knew I would out-per-mile him when I hit fourth.

And sure enough, by the time we were both in high gear, I'd put a car length on him with no trouble.

"Slow down, Jack!" Pita said.

Given I was doing ninety in a forty zone, and now two car lengths ahead of Jesus, I figured I'd proven my point. I let off the throttle.

Instead of backing down, however, Jesus ripped past me.

"Little prick," I grunted, gunning it again.

"Jack!" Pita said.

We were approaching an onramp to the freeway that ran east-west across the middle of Mexico City. Jesus hit it without slowing. I did too.

Pita was still shouting over the roar of the flat-6—only now she sounded more scared than angry, her shrieks punctuated with "Stop!" and "We're going to die!" But there was no way I was backing off. Not until I put the poser in his place.

Jesus and I moved into the left lane, passing traffic at more than a hundred miles per hour. I parked myself on his ass, rid-ing his slipstream.

I veered slightly to the right, to see ahead and to make my move to overtake—when I noticed one of the cars we thundered past had lights on top and "Policia" written down the flank.

A moment later the cop swung into the left lane behind me, siren wailing.

"Jack, you have to pull over! You're going to get us arrested! Pull over! Jack!"

Jesus overtook a red sedan in front of him, swinging back into the left lane. I stuck with him for the next five hundred yards, whipping around several more vehicles.

"Jack!" Pita all but wailed. "Please!"

And I conceded.

Speeding down the far side of an overpass, I glanced in the side mirror, didn't see the police car, and locked up the brakes, squeezing in between two freight semis in the right lane to the tune of bovine air horns and flashing high beams.

Several long seconds later the cop blasted past me none the wiser.

Jesus's problem now.

4

When we reached Xochimilco an hour later, I followed signs that read "los embarcaderos"—the piers—to Cuemanco, one of nine locations that offered access to the ancient Aztec canal system. It was where we had agreed to meet the others. I parked in a busy parking lot, retrieved our daypacks from the trunk of the Porsche, and handed Pita hers. She took it silently and started toward the strip of ramshackle buildings that separated the parking lot and the waterfront. I fussed through my bag for a minute, checking the sparse contents. It wasn't necessary. I knew what I'd packed. But Pita and I needed a bit of space.

After we had evaded the cop, Pita had spent the next ten minutes yelling at me in a mix of English and Spanish, saying I was crazy, I could have killed them, all because of my ego. I didn't argue with her. She was right. Street racing was stupid and reckless. So I listened stoically to her tirade, which seemed to incense her all the more. Eventually, however, she ran out of fury and called Jesus on her cell phone. As it turned out, he ended up pulling over and paying off the cop. I didn't pick up any more details than that, and Pita refused to speak to me, let alone elaborate, after she hung up.

Nevertheless, the outcome was what I'd expected. This was Mexico after all, and just about every cop could be bought. Some actively searched out bribes. I'd learned this firsthand my first week in the country. A cop pulled me over on some empty stretch of road and told me I'd been speeding, which I hadn't been. He took my driver's license as a "guarantee" and said I could either get it back on the spot if I paid him one hundred fifty American dollars, or I could follow him to the police station, where I would have to pay two hundred fifty. It was clearly a scam, I got pissed off, and tried to swipe my license from his clipboard. He accused me of being *aggressivo* and doubled the fine. We continued to argue until I gave up. I paid him one hundred sixty—all I had on me—which he was more than happy to accept.

I closed the Porsche's trunk with a heavy thud, slung my daypack over my shoulder, and went to the docks.

5

The boardwalk along the canal was filled with people and a general air of festivity. Gondola-type barges called *trajineras* lined the bank for as far as I could see. Most were the size of a large van, featuring a roof for shade, open-aired windows, and tables and chairs for picnicking. They were painted a spectrum of colors, ornately decorated, and for some reason bore female names.

I scanned the crowd for Pita—I had little trouble seeing over all the dark-haired heads—but I didn't spot her anywhere. I wasn't too concerned. I had my cell phone. If I didn't bump into her sooner or later, I could call her, or she could call me.

I started along the boardwalk. Merchants called to me from their market stalls, hawking wares that ranged from handicrafts and T-shirts to embroidered clothing, linens, sandals, and other souvenirs.

A walking vendor fell into step beside me. He was short and wore white pants and a white shirt over his padded frame. Smiling, he asked what I was looking for.

"My friends," I said.

"You want watch? Rolex? You want Rolex?"

"No, thanks."

"What you want? Marijuana? Pills? I get you anything."

I shook my head, pulling away from him.

"Hey, man!" he called after me. "Girls? You want girls? I give you my sister! Cheap!"

Another fifty yards on I came to two old women selling banana-leaf tamales. I realized I hadn't eaten anything all morning, and I bought two, one stuffed with chicken and salsa, the other with refried beans.

I found a bench to sit on and dug into the tamales. Two of the best things about living in Mexico, I believed, were the weather and the food. It was pretty much spring-like year round with zero humidity, and the greasy street meat was made with crack or something it was so addictive.

I gave the last bite of my second tamale to a flea-riddled mutt that had been eyeing it hungrily, and I was thinking about getting a third when the vendor who tried to sell me his sister spotted me and came over.

"My man!" he said, sitting next to me. "How's the tamale?

Good, yes? You like Mexican food?"

"I'm not a tourist," I told him. "I live here."

"You live here? Where?"

I wasn't going to tell him my neighborhood, as it was one of the pricier ones in Mexico City, so I simply told him the name of the general borough.

"So what you do?" he asked.

"Listen, I don't want to buy anything."

He smiled. "No problem. No problem. But where're your friends? Maybe they want a watch? I have Cartier too. Anything they want."

I stood and continued along the boardwalk again. The tout caught up to me.

"So you and your friends going down the canals, huh?" he said. "You need a boat? I get you good price."

"My friend already organized one."

"Your friend, huh?" I felt him looking at me like he didn't believe me, or like I was brushing him off, which I was.

"Yeah, my friend. He's filming that island with the dolls. He's organized everything. The boat. The tickets. We don't need anything."

"You go Isla de las Muñecas?" he said.

I realized I'd said too much, and I was planning to ignore the tout, keep walking, but the expression on his face caused me stop. I couldn't tell if it was fear or anger.

"What?" I asked.

"You go Isla de las Muñecas?" he repeated.

"No," I said. "We're not going *to* it. We're going around it." I made a curlicue gesture with my finger. "Take some pictures, come back. Just tourists, okay?" I started away, but his hand seized my wrist tightly.

"You don't go there."

"Let go of me."

Passersby were looking curiously at us, and I was starting to get angry myself. I tried pulling my arm free from his grip. He wouldn't let go.

"Why you film there?"

"Let go of me."

"Why you film there?"

"Last warning."

"You go," he said, lowering his voice to a threatening whisper, "you die."

I stared at the guy, wondering if maybe he was crazy. Perspiration had popped out on his forehead. The cheerfulness was gone from his face, replaced with tension. He black eyes held mine.

My cell phone rang, breaking the terse moment. I yanked my arm free and took the phone from my pocket.

"Yeah?" I said, moving again, blending into the flow of traffic on the boardwalk.

"Where are you?" It was Pita.

"I just got something to eat."

"Everyone's waiting for you."

"Everyone's here? Where? I didn't know where you went."

"About four hundred meters east of where we parked. You'll see a restaurant with a green awning. The *trajinera* is out front."

"I'll be there soon."

We hung up.

Stuffing the phone back in my pocket, I glanced over my shoulder, expecting to see the nut job staring after me.

He was gone.

1950

1

María Diaz was born premature at thirty-two weeks via an emergency caesarian section. She weighed three pounds thirteen ounces. She passed all the typical tests and was deemed a perfectly healthy baby. When she was one week old, however, her heartrate skyrocketed. Her parents rushed her back to the hospital, where she suffered twenty-two seizures over the next twelve hours. As epilepsy was not well understood then, her pediatrician assumed hemorrhaging in the brain and confidently told her parents she wouldn't survive the night.

María was now four years old. She knew nothing of what happened during that eventful first week of life, of course. Like most four year olds, her knowledge was largely restricted to her immediate environment, which included her house and the street out front of it.

Currently María stood before a shelf in the house's playroom, deciding which dolls would participate in her morning tea party. Her first choice was Angela, who was dressed in a lacy blue dress and bonnet. She was a Rock-a-bye Baby, which meant at nighty-night time you had to rock her until her eyes closed and she fell asleep. María carried her carefully to the small table and set her in a chair. She flopped forward, her heavy rubber head clonking the tabletop. "No more sleeping," María told her sternly and sat her upright. She waited to make sure Angela wouldn't move on her own again. Satisfied, she returned to the shelf. Eight dolls stared back at her, but there were only two available seats at the table. After some contemplation, María decided on Miss Magic Lips. She was wearing her pink dress with glitter-net trim, and she was smiling, showing her three front teeth, which meant she was happy. When she was unhappy she pressed her lips together and cried.

Not wanting to make a third trip to the table, María also grabbed Teddy, who wore nothing but an apricot-colored sweater. He was a bear and not a doll, but he was a friendly bear and got along with everyone.

At the table she sat Miss Magic Lips to the left of Angela, and Teddy to her right. They were better behaved than Angela, and neither of them tried to go to sleep. Pleased, María went to the chest in the corner and mussed through the toys for the necessary saucers, tea-cups, and kettle. She set the table, then said, "Thank you everyone for coming to my tea party. Who wants some tea?"

"I do!" Angela said, though it was really María speaking in a higher pitched voice.

"Here you go, Angela," María said, reverting to her normal hostess tone. She poured imaginary tea into her cup. "Who else?" she asked.

"Me!" Miss Magic Lips said.

"You're happy today, Miss Magic Lips," María observed, pouring tea into her cup.

"I want a cupcake," Angela said.

"I don't have any cupcakes."

"Can you bake some?"

María looked at the pink stove by the wall and said, "Well, maybe. But Teddy still needs his tea. Right, Teddy?"

"Yes, please."

She filled his cup.

"Can I have honey with it?" he asked.

"I only have sugar. Is that okay?"

"Yes, please."

She picked up an imaginary cube of sugar and dropped it in his cup.

"I want a cupcake!" Angela said.

María sighed and went to the oven. She turned some knobs and said, "Okay, they're baking."

Back at the table, she took her seat opposite Angela, poured herself a cup of tea, then raised it to her lips. "Oohh. It's very hot! Be careful every—"

She never finished the sentence.

2

María's mother knelt before her, a worried expression on her face. María blinked, slowly, torpidly, like a housecat after it had been fed. When did her mother arrive? Was she here for the tea party too? She was speaking to her. "Answer me, María," she said. "Are you okay? Can you hear me?"

"I'm having a tea party, Mom," she said.

"I see that, sweetheart. But just now, what were you thinking?"

María frowned. "That the tea was hot."

"That's all?"

She nodded. "Why?"

"You didn't answer me when I came in the room. You were staring off into space."

"I was thinking the tea was hot."

"That's all?"

"That's all."

Her mother seemed relieved and hugged her.

"Are you here for the tea party?" María asked into her shoulder.

Her mother released her. "No, honey. It's lunchtime. I made you tortillas."

"I *love* tortillas."

"Then let's go eat."

"What about my tea party?"

"You can finish it later. Your dolls won't mind, will they?"

"Angela might. She doesn't like waiting."

"That's part of learning how to become a little lady. Sometimes you have to be patient."

"Angela," María told her, "you have to be patient."

Angela stared back at her.

"Be good while I'm gone," she added. Then she followed her mother from the playroom to the kitchen for lunch.

JACK

1

I saw Pepper first, then Elizaveta. They were standing next to a tree on the bank of the canal.

"Jack!" Pepper said, opening his arms wide. "*Bienvenidos Xochimilco!*"

He was smiling broadly at me, and I couldn't help smiling back. He was one of the merriest people I knew with a cherub face and sparkling eyes to match his go-happy personality. He was also one the most fashionable people I knew. Today's statement was a banana-yellow Oxford shirt open at the throat, a purple blazer draped over the shoulders, a polka dotted handkerchief poking from the blazer pocket, fitted purple slacks creased and rolled up at the cuffs, and a white belt and matching loafers, sans socks.

We embraced, patting each other on the back.

Pepper always liked people commenting on his outfits, so when I stepped away I said, "I like the jacket, just on your shoulders like that. Very Ralph Lauren."

"Jack," he said, clearly thrilled with the compliment, "the chicest way to wear a coat is not to, don't you know that?"

"Hi, Eliza," I said, pecking her on the cheek. She smelled

of flowers and still wore the sunhat and oversized sunglasses. Combine those with her pink top, white shorts, bangles, wedge heels, and leather shoulder bag, and she and Pepper could have just come straight from lunch at the St. Regis.

Elizaveta slapped me lightly on the chest, then waggled her index finger. "You are crazy," she said in her Russian accent, which was slightly masculine, broad and bold. She dropped the cigarette she was smoking and toed it out. "Do you know that? Very crazy."

"So I've been told already."

"You want to kill us?"

She was trying to be mad at me but failing. She clamped her lips against a silky smile.

"Jesus challenged *me*," I said. "Did you get mad at him too?"

"Very mad. I think he's crazy too." *Very med. I zink ees crazy too.*

"Where is he, by the way? And Pita?"

"They went to restroom." Elizaveta frowned in concern at the bandage on my forehead. She took off her sunglasses to see it better. She had emerald-green eyes, aristocratic features with prominent cheekbones, thin lips, and long dark hair. While she was likely white as a snowflake when she'd lived in Saint Petersburg—or "Sankt Peterburg," as she would pronounce it—her skin was now brown from the tropical sun.

She'd been in Mexico for four years or so. She worked as a governess for a wealthy Russian family, homeschooling their two daughters. Her employer, a consultant for a Mexican state-owned oil company, ran in the same circles as Jesus, who she met at a neighborhood picnic. Jesus spent several weeks wooing her before they started dating roughly one year ago.

Sometimes I thought Elizaveta and I would have made a good couple had I not been engaged to Pita, and she not seeing Jesus. She was smart, fun, cheeky—my type, I suppose. I felt guilty when I caught myself contemplating the two of us together, but they were thoughts, that was all, I couldn't control them. I had never cheated on Pita, and I never would.

"Is your head okay?" Elizaveta asked me, frowning at the bandage on my forehead.

I lifted my baseball cap and ran a hand through my hair. "I'm fine," I told her.

"What happened?" Pepper asked.

"He tried jumping from balcony to swimming pool last night and fell," Elizaveta said. "See, he is crazy."

"I agree with Eliza," Pepper said. "Anyone who chooses to drive a car around a track filled with other cars at two hundred miles an hour has to be crazy."

I switched the topic and said, "So this place is pretty spectacular. I had no idea it would be so busy."

"Weekdays aren't," Pepper said. "But weekends, yes, especially Sunday."

"So which one is our boat?"

We turned to face the canal, the gondolas lining the bank. With their garish colors and kitsch decorations, they were the amphibious equivalent to the Filipino Jeepney. Pepper pointed to the one directly before us. "Lupita" was painted on the back arch.

"What's up with the female names?" I asked.

"Some refer to someone special," Pepper said. "Maybe a wife or a daughter. But some, I think, are just the name of the boat."

"I never knew there was anywhere so green in Mexico City."

"We call Xochimilco the lungs of the city. Xochimilco means 'flower fields.' Wait until you see some of the *chinampas*. They are beautiful."

I frowned. "Chin what?"

"The island gardens that separate the canals. The Aztecs made them."

"To grow flowers?"

"And other crops. There used to be many more *chinampas*, but after the Spanish invasion, and the lakes dried up, these canals are all that remain."

I looked at Pepper skeptically. "Lakes?"

"Oh my, Jack," he said. "Didn't you know Mexico City was once surrounded by five lakes?"

"I had no idea."

"You Americans," Elizaveta said.

"You knew?" I asked her.

"Of course. I am Russian, and Russians are not ignorant Americans. I learn about the country where I choose to live."

I rolled my eyes. "So where did the lakes go?" I asked Pepper, still not sure he wasn't having me on. "How did they just dry up—?"

"There he is!" a voice called from behind us, cutting off my question. "Mr. *Days of Thunder* himself!"

I turned to find Jesus and Pita approaching—along with Jesus's new best friend, Nitro.

2

To say Nitro and I didn't get along was a gross understatement. The animosity between us started because of a screen door. One of Pita's friends threw a party a couple of months back, and as expected at any decent party, there had been a copious amount of boozing going on.

Around 2 a.m., after most guests had left, roughly ten of us remained behind. Pita's friend was renting the penthouse unit in some old Art Deco building. We'd moved to the patio to take in the city views. At one point I went inside to the kitchen to get another beer, and when I returned to the patio I walked straight into the screen door, knocking it off its track. I picked it up and set it aside, given I wasn't in any condition to figure out how to replace a screen door. No harm done, I thought. But Nitro seemed to take the whole thing personally. He started railing on about me in Spanish. I didn't know what he was saying, but it was clear he was insulted. I asked him what his problem was. He told me to fix the door. I told him to mind his own business. He got up in my face, reeking of testosterone, so I clocked him. He came back at me like a loosed pit bull. We pin-balled around the patio, toppling plants, smashing bottles and glasses, breaking a glass coffee table—in other words, causing much more damage than a dislodged screen door.

When people pulled us apart, Nitro had a busted lip, and I had a black eye. Pita and I took a taxi home, and I figured it was the last I'd see of the guy. But the fight seemed to have endeared him to Jesus, because Jesus began inviting him everywhere after that. He even showed up to Pita's birthday party in July. I did my best to ignore him when we crossed paths, but he was as adept as Jesus at pushing my buttons, and we've come close to blows on a few more occasions since.

Looking at Jesus and Nitro now, you'd think they were complete opposites. Jesus was his typical preppy self with a tweed jacket over a white button-down shirt, khaki chinos, and oxblood penny loafers. Nitro, on the other hand, was dressed like me in a tank top and shorts and flip-flops—the difference between us being his arms were brocaded with ink and his hair was tied back in a ponytail.

It was Nitro who'd called me "Mr. *Days of Thunder*."

"You know, chavo," Nitro went on, "for a race car driver—a *former* race car driver—Jesus totally left you in his dust on the highway."

"Who got pulled over?" I said.

"Who wimped out?"

"You really need to get over that screen door, Muscles," I told him. He didn't react to the pejorative nickname, but I knew it got to him, which was why I used it. "You know what I don't get?" I added. "It wasn't even your place."

"Jack," Pita said. "Drop it."

But I didn't want to. This trip was getting to be too much. First, Jesus invites himself. Then he invites Nitro—and no one bothers to tell me?

"Anyone else coming I don't know about?" I asked.

"We mentioned Nitro was coming last night," Pita said.

"Not to me you didn't."

"I'm sure we did," she said.

"We did," Jesus assured me with bullshit sincerity. "Maybe you just don't remember—?"

"Guys! Guys!" Pepper interjected brightly. "What does it matter? We're all here, and we're going to have a great time. That's all that matters." He flourished his arm toward the *trajinera*. "Now all aboard!"

3

A long yellow table ran down the center of the gondola. Fourteen chairs accompanied it, giving everyone plenty of room. Pepper and I sat across from each other near the bow while Jesus and Nitro sat near the stern. Pita and Elizaveta settled smartly in the middle of the boat, acting as a buffer between Nitro and me. The boatman or oarsman—or whatever you called the guy who steered the gondola with the long pole—was two boats down, playing cards with two other boatmen. He was middle-aged with a grizzled moustache and wiry salt and pepper hair. Dark salt stains dampened his shirt around his neck and beneath his arms. When he saw us boarding, he jotted across the boardwalk, disappearing into the crowd, returning a few minutes later carrying a large bucket of ice filled with beers, sodas, and an assortment of juices. I asked him how much for the lot. He told me three hundred pesos, which worked out to twenty pesos a drink, or roughly one dollar. I passed money to Pita, who passed it to Jesus, who paid the guy. Then Jesus plunked the bucket on the table. Elizaveta and Pepper each took a soda, Jesus and Nitro and me a beer. Pita declined everything. She was on some strict diet, and I rarely saw her indulge in anything that contained more calories than a stick of celery.

The boatman expertly guided us away from the crowded dock and into the waterway, then we were on our way.

4

The canal was crowded with other flat-bottomed gondolas like ours, most filled with Mexican families, couples on dates, and Caucasian tourists. A flotilla of merchants in smaller canoe-like boats tooled between them all. Their wares were similar to their brethren's on the docks: jewelry, candied apples, corn, toys, ponchos, flowers. Jesus waved over a floating *tortería* restaurant and ordered a variety of sandwiches. While we were eating—despite the two tamales I'd consumed earlier, I was still hungry—a boat carrying a Maríachi band in *charro* outfits sidled up next to ours, serenading us for the next while at what worked out to be a few bucks a song.

Soon we pulled away from the congestion and moved deeper into the ancient network of maze-like canals. The floating gardens Pepper mentioned earlier replaced the historic buildings and markets and general hustle and bustle of Cuemanco. Tall semi-evergreens lined the banks. Many had developed multiple trunks that formed expansive canopies of dark green pendulous foliage. A few were absolutely monstrous, as thick as a living room in diameter, and I suspected they had been planted by the Aztecs hundreds of years before. Complimenting these were coral-red flame trees and purple-blue jacaranda and colorful flowering plants such as bougainvillea, poinsettia, oleander, and hibiscus.

As we glided down one channel after another, I glimpsed old farm-houses, flower nurseries, and other cottage industries. Birds and farm animals grazed on green pastures. Kids swam in the water, men and women toiled in fields, and older folks sat stoically on rocks or logs or other makeshift seats, not doing much of anything. Pita and Elizaveta waved at them. A few waved lazily back.

Pepper, I realized at one point, was saying something to me. I blinked, looked at him. The warm sun and pastoral scenery had lulled me into a hypnotic state.

"What did you say?" I asked him, tilting a beer to my lips.

"Where do you go sometimes, Jack?" Pepper said in his ebullient manner. "I asked you if you can now see why the Spanish dubbed Xochimilco, 'The Venice of the New World.'"

"It's nice," I said.

"You'd never know these canals were a mass grave."

I frowned. "What are you talking about?"

"A mass grave," he said. "During the revolution, the army dumped the bodies of hundreds of opposition fighters into the canals."

"You're kidding?"

He shook his head. "Not long ago many skeletons were discovered all throughout the channels."

We were floating over dead people? Suddenly the place was not so Eden-like.

I said, "You should mention that in your documentary."

"I intend to.

I sipped my beer, thinking about this, letting it gather weight in my mind, when Pita flicked the cigarette she'd been smoking into the water. She was chatting with Elizaveta, telling her how she and Jesus used to come to these canals at nighttime when they were younger. They'd rent a large gondola with their friends and turn it into a floating nightclub with music, dancing, drinking.

Pita, and Jesus for that matter, were colloquially referred to as "Juniors"—the sons and daughters of Mexico's elite ruling class, whose wealth was only matched by their sense of entitlement. Pita and Jesus weren't so bad—they actually worked (Pita was the PR specialist for the family brewery)—but I couldn't stand some of their friends. They were the type who bragged about having four hundred pairs of shoes, or two hundred suits—and keeping them stashed away in swanky homes abroad.

I considered sliding Pita my beer bottle, telling her to put her cigarettes out in it instead, but that seemed like a jackass thing to do, especially given the fact we were still fighting. She'd think I was starting something, and she'd continue tossing her butts in the water, to make a point. Lately she'd become adept at making much of nothing.

I shifted on my too-small chair to get more comfortable. My headache was returning. Maybe it was the onset of one of my migraines, or maybe it was just the heat, or the beer, but a locust-like thrumming had started in my frontal lobe, beneath the vertical gash that likely required stitches. I massaged the area around the bandage with my fingers.

"Jack, look there," Pepper said. He was pointing past me to a glade in the trees along the bank, where a twenty-foot Aztec pyramid stood. It appeared to be a stage prop, painted in bright shades of purple, pink, and green. "That's the set for a show that has been put on there for the past ten years," he added.

"What kind of show?" I asked.

"It's called 'La Llorona.' It's based on a famous legend in Mexico of the same name. Basically, a beautiful woman drowns her children to get revenge on her husband, who cheated on her with a younger woman."

"Hell hath no fury—"

"Yes, yes, Jack," Pepper said. "Anyway, this woman, she's so filled with guilt, she ends up killing herself. But she's held up at the gates of heaven. She's not allowed to enter until she finds her children. So she ends up trapped between this world and the next, doomed to search for her kids for all eternity."

"Hence the reason you should never murder your kids to spite someone." I swatted at a fly buzzing around my head, missed it, and said, "So why's it called 'La Macarena'—?"

"'La Llorona,' Jack. That's Spanish for 'The Weeping Woman.'"

I furrowed my brow. "Does this legend have anything to do

with the Island of the Dolls? You mentioned the hermit who used to live there, Don Juan—"

"Don Javier Solano."

"He found a body of a little girl in the canal?"

Pepper nodded. "The locals around here believe there is a connection, definitely. Because on nights when the *chinampas* are shrouded in fog, La Llorona is believed to roam about, kidnapping other children who resemble her missing children, drowning them in the hope she can take them to heaven instead of her own."

"I don't know if you can really pull the wool over God's eyes like that, you know, with Him being omniscient and everything."

"It's a legend, Jack. But that's what the locals think happened to the little girl."

"La Llorona drowned her?"

Pepper nodded again. "You know how superstitious Mexicans are."

I did. And this didn't apply to only the poor and uneducated. Superstition seemed to be built into the collective unconsciousness of the entire country. Pita, for instance, was about as Americanized as you could get, but she one hundred percent believed in ghosts.

"What about you, Jack?" Pepper went on. "Are you superstitious?"

"Hardly."

"I'm not surprised," he said. "You look like an atheist."

"What does an atheist look like?"

"Like you. They have a hard edge. How should I say this...always looking a bit pissed off."

"I'm not always pissed off."

"I didn't say that, Jack. I said, *looks* pissed off. I know you're a very nice guy."

"Thanks, I guess." I finished the beer, set the empty bottle aside. "So I still don't see how all the dolls work into the story? Why did this guy, this Solano, begin stringing them up all over his island? Were they some sort of offering to the drowned girl's spirit?"

Pepper nodded. "She began contacting him at night, communicating with him in his dreams. She told him she was lonely. So the dolls were his gift to her, to keep her spirit at peace."

"This might sound like a stupid question, Peps, but where did he get all these dolls?"

"Didn't your teachers ever tell you there's no such thing as a stupid question?"

"Only because they were the ones always asking the stupid questions."

"An atheist *and* a pessimist—oh joy." Pepper beamed a smile at me. "To answer your question, Jack, Solano got most of his dolls from Mexico City. He would go there occasionally to search the trash heaps, or the markets. But then later in his life, about ten years ago, Xochimilco was designated a national heritage site. A few years after that a civic program to clean up the canals was implemented, and the island was discovered. At first the locals thought Solano was an old crackpot and steered clear. But then a few of them began to trade him dolls for produce he grew."

I swatted at the fly that kept taunting my slow reflexes and thought about what Pepper had told me—and I had to admit I was now more curious than ever to see the island.

"Pretty cool, Peps," I said. "Sounds like you have one hell of a documentary on your hands."

"I agree, Jack. I think it will be my best one yet. And with the way Solano died recently, it all just comes together."

I raised an eyebrow. "How did he die?

"Didn't I tell you?"

"You only told me he died, which is why we're able to trespass on his island."

Pepper folded his hands on the table and leaned forward conspiratorially. "He drowned in the same spot where he found the girl's body, fifty years to the day."

"Bullshit!" I said.

"It's true, Jack."

"What did the police say?"

"They couldn't determine anything. Solano had been dead for too long. The fish and salamanders got to him long before they did."

5

I dreamed I was in a gondola with Pita. Not in Xochimimco. Maybe Venice, though I had never been to Venice before. It was dusk, what daylight remained was washed out, otherworldly. A mishmash of old buildings decorated with friezes and columns and broken pediments lined the banks of the wide canal, though they all seemed deserted.

I had the sense we had been in the gondola for a very long time, hours, days even. Pita kept telling me we were almost there, and by "there" she meant heaven. She was excited to see her younger sister, Susana, who'd died when she was five years old. Susana and Pita had been playing hide-and-seek with some other neighborhood kids. Susana climbed into the fountain out front their house and drowned in the shallow water.

Pita never talked to me about Susana. She'd mentioned her when we first began dating, but that was it. Now, however, she seemed more than happy to talk about her sister, and she began listing off all the things they were going to do when they were reunited. When I mentioned that Susana might still be five years old—how do you age if you stop existing?—Pita went quiet, contemplative.

I was grateful for the reprieve. I had enough on my own mind. Specifically, I was worried I wouldn't be allowed into heaven because I was an atheist. I kept wondering what I would do if Pita got in and I didn't. She would probably tell me it was my fault for not believing in God. She would do the whole I-told-you-so routine. She would leave me there, outside the gates, on my own. And that's the last thing I wanted: to be stuck by myself in limbo, if that's where we were right then.

The daylight continued to fade quickly, as if time was being fast-forwarded. The air cooled, becoming frosty with the prescience of death.

As if on cue, a corpse appeared in the water, starboard. It floated face up, a few feet from the gondola. The eyes were ivory orbs, sightless. Skin was missing in places, revealing vellum-hued patches of skull.

I pointed out the body to Pita. She looked the other way, playing ostrich, believing if she didn't acknowledge it, then it wouldn't exist. But then another body appeared, then another. Soon they filled the canal for as far as I could see in the gloom. Heads and limbs bumped against the hull of the gondola as we cleaved through them, but instead of slowing down, we seemed to be speeding up, as if the dead were ushering us along.

I was telling Pita this couldn't be the way to heaven, it was too morbid, too sad, when a thundering roar, like a waterfall, sounded in the distance. It was accompanied by a thick, wet mist, which wrapped around us, blinding us.

Pita began to scream. I turned to face the boatman, to tell him to stop, to take us back.

The boatman was a skeleton, its empty orbits gazing past me, its mouth fixed in a permanent rictus, its impossible arms pushing us forward with that long pole, rhythmically, inexorably.

Pita had stopped screaming, and it took me a moment to realize why. She had become a doll. Life-sized, but definitely a doll, molded from polymer clay, painted bright colors, with glass eyes and synthetic hair.

I tried to stand, to jump ship, to swim through the corpse-infested water to safety, yet I couldn't move, and I wondered whether I was a doll too.

Suddenly the mist parted and a black disc on the surface of the water appeared. Doom filled me as I knew this was a one-way trip, I was seconds away from dying, and there was nothing I could do to prevent it from happening.

The gondola plunged over the edge of the void, into a bottomless abyss, and I was falling, falling, falling.

6

I woke up and knew I was still dreaming because now I was in the ER room of the Florida hospital where I'd been airlifted to by helicopter after the racing accident. My heart wasn't beating. I was in cardiac arrest, effectively dead in both brain and body. Then I began to float, or my consciousness began to float, up toward the ceiling of the room, and then I was looking down, watching the medical staff work the defibrillator on my bare chest, watching them inject me with a cold saline solution to hopefully save my brain and organs, hearing their discursive conversations, hearing "Hotel California" on the stereo, hearing the lyrics about checking out but never leaving.

Everything was just as it had been when this happened to me for real eleven months before...and then the dream took on a mind of its own. A hole opened in the ceiling, and I found myself being pulled into it, down a tunnel of white light. Yet this wasn't the comforting white light you hear about from people who'd had near-death experiences. There was no feeling of overwhelming transcendent love, no sense of connectedness to all of creation. Instead there was only terror like I had never experienced and never knew existed, terror that stripped me to my bones. Because there was a presence in that white light. It was waiting for me. I couldn't see it, hear it, or smell it, but it was there, and it was waiting. And it wasn't God, or at least not the benevolent one to which Christians and Muslims and Jews prayed. It was pure evil. And when I reached it, when it enfolded me in its embrace, it would never let me go. I would spend all eternity—the afterlife, heaven, hell, whatever you wanted to call it—in absolute, unrelenting pain.

7

I came awake with a start. *I wasn't dead.* I was in the gondola in Xochimilco, seated at the long picnic table, my head on my arms.

I sat straight, still waking up, and rubbed my eyes. I was shaken from the nightmare, disorientated. The first part of it —when I was in a gondola, and maybe a doll—wasn't too bad. That was almost fun in a trippy sort of way. But the second part, when I was dead in the ER, floating down the tunnel of white light, toward whatever it was that awaited me, that was not fun at all.

I'd been having similar dreams two or three times a week since the accident. Sometimes I'd just float around the ER watching the doctors and nurses work on me. Sometimes I'd leave the ER and zip around the hospital, invisible to the patients and staff. Sometimes I'd watch my physical body wake up in the ICU, and I'd freak out because I realized there was no getting back into it; I was going to be trapped outside of it forever, doomed to haunt the hospital. And then there was the dream I'd just had, which was the worst by far.

The tunnel. The white light. The thing in the light.

I shuddered—and berated myself. I didn't believe in out-of-body experiences. I mean, I think something weird happened to me in the ER. I had a top-down view of my body while on the operating table after all. But I didn't think this was my spirit stepping outside my body, preparing to travel to the other side. It was more along the lines of neurons in my brain dying, doing whatever weird shit they do when they die. Maybe even some sort of astral projection.

The day, I noticed, had become overcast, tinged with the scent of ozone. The clouds were unusually low and dark. I picked up the beer bottle before me but found it empty.

"Welcome back," Elizaveta said to me, cocking her head waggishly. *Velcome beck.* She still sat next to me, though everyone else had moved to the gondola's stern, where it appeared Jesus and Pepper were discussing something of importance with the boatman.

"Why'd we stop?" I asked, looking down the table for an unopened beer.

"The boatman thinks there will be tropical storm," she said. "He doesn't want to leave us on island, because maybe he cannot come back, get us."

It was Mexico's rainy season, which meant almost daily afternoon showers. They were brief but intense, capable of filling streets with rainwater in a matter of seconds. Tropical storms were a different matter altogether, reaping destruction and often lasting days.

"Didn't anyone check the forecast before we came?" I reached for the metal bucket and tilted it to see inside. Two sodas and one orange juice floated in water that had once been ice.

"Did you, Jack? But do not worry. Probably he only wants more money. Jesus will fix everything."

"Perform one of his miracles?"

"You know, Jack, he hates—he *hates*—when you compare him to that Jesus."

"That's the thing," I said. "There should only be *that* Jesus. Nobody calls themselves Buddha."

"He didn't choose this name. So you should stop making jokes. Besides, Jack," she added, "you should know what it's like having unfortunate name."

Giving up on finding a beer, I pushed the bill of my cap a little higher and prodded the bandage on my forehead with my fingers. The headache had receded, but it was still there, hiding, ready to pounce if I moved too quickly. "How long was I out for?" I asked.

"A long time," she said. "And you snore."

"No, I don't."

"I heard you." She made exaggerated snoring noises.

"I don't snore," I insisted.

"How would you know if you were sleeping?"

"I just know."

"Don't be ashamed. Everybody snores."

"Do you?"

"No."

Just then Jesus dug his wallet out of his pocket and withdrew several bills from the sleeve. He handed these to the boatman, who took them with reluctance.

"See," Elizaveta said happily. "I told you Jesus would fix it."

"Hallelujah."

She gave me a severe look. I pretended not to notice and said, "I'm going back to sleep. Wake me up when we get there."

"When we get there?" Elizaveta seemed amused. "Look behind you, Jack. We are already here."

8

I wasn't sure what I was seeing at first. My brain didn't register the dolls. There were too many; the sheer number overwhelmed me. But then I was seeing them, registering them, because there they were, everywhere, an entire midget army clinging to trees and dangling from branches. There must have been hundreds of them—and these were only the ones lining the bank. "Holy shit," I said.

"I know," Elizaveta said.

The gondola started moving, the boatman pushing us forward with that long pole of his through the overgrown wetland flora. Pita retook her seat and began talking with Eliza-veta. I kept my attention fixed on the island.

The dolls were every shape and size and color. They were clothed, naked, broken, weatherworn, grungy. And opposed to the beatific dolls that had lined every shelf in my sister's bedroom up until she was eight or so, the decrepit state of these made them appear to be demonic. Like they'd been to hell and back and couldn't wait to return.

I was still trying to get my head around the uncanny spec-tacle when the gondola bumped against a short pier with a jolt. Then everyone was getting to their feet, gathering their stuff, preparing to disembark.

1952

1

María woke to her mother shouting at her from the kitchen: "María, get up! You don't want to be late for your first day of school."

María buried her face in her pillow.

"María! Get up now!"

Reluctantly she poked her head out of the covers. The blinds were open. It wasn't dark, but it wasn't light either.

"María!"

María forced herself out of bed. She took off her pajamas and dumped them in the laundry basket. Then she pulled on the clothes her mother had laid out for her: a beige dress, white underwear, and white socks. She scooped up Angela, who had been sleeping with her, and went down the hall to the bathroom. She peed, then brushed her teeth. She'd had a bath the night before in her mother's bathwater, so she didn't have to have another one this morning.

"I don't want to go to school," María confided in Angela, speaking around the toothbrush in her mouth. She listened to Angela's reply, then said, "I don't want to leave my mom. And I don't want to meet my teacher." She listened again. "Of course you can come. You're my best friend." She spit, rinsed, then went to the kitchen.

Her mother stood at the sink, washing dishes. She was starting a new job as a seamstress today, and she was wearing her uniform. She glanced over her shoulder. "Eat up, sweetheart. We have to leave soon."

María sat down at the table, but she only ate a few of the beans before her. She didn't touch the sweet roll or piece of tamarind.

Then, out of the blue, she began to cry.

"Oh, baby," her mother said, drying her hands on a dish towel and crouching before her. "What's wrong? Are you worried about your first day of school?"

She nodded.

"Just remember, it's everyone's first day. Everyone feels just the same as you."

"What if nobody likes me?"

"Don't think that. You'll meet plenty of friends."

"Do you promise?"

"Cross my heart. Now go put on your shoes."

María went to the door, took her book bag from the hook on the wall, and she slid her feet into her Mary Janes.

Her mother frowned at her. "Angela has to stay home today, sweetheart."

María clutched the doll tighter. "I want her to come with me."

"You're five years old now, María. You're a big girl. And big girls don't take their dolls to school."

"I want her to come!"

"No one else will have a doll."

"I don't care!"

"Some of your classmates might tease you."

"I don't care!"

"María, please..."

"I want her to come! I want her to come! I want—"

"Okay! Okay!" Her mother shook her head. "If you want to

take her, take her. But don't say I didn't warn you."

2

The school was a huge two-story yellow-brick building with a playground on one side and a farm on the other side. The sight of it made María's heart beat faster. She wanted to turn around and go home, but she knew her mother wouldn't allow this, so she followed her through the iron gate, up a set of steps, and to the office where a gramophone was playing music.

Her mother spoke to the woman there, signed some papers, then led María through a maze of hallways that smelled of floor wax and wood polish and chalk. Some of the classroom doors they passed were open. The students were seated at wooden desks, and they all seemed to be older and bigger than her.

María hugged Angela more tightly.

They climbed a set of stairs and stopped in front of a classroom. Her mother knocked on the door, even though it was open. "Good morning, Mrs. González," she said. "I'm Patricia Diaz, María's mother. I'm sorry we're late. This is María."

The teacher consulted the clipboard in her hand and said, "That's all right. Come in, María."

María stared up at her mother, begging her with her eyes not to leave her.

"It's all right, sweetheart," she said, bending over and stroking the top of her head. "Go on and meet everyone. I'll be back at two-thirty to pick you up at the front doors." She turned and walked away.

"María?" Mrs. González said. "Come inside now, please."

María shuffled hesitantly into the classroom, taking in the new sights: the paintings of animals on the walls, the large blackboard, the bookcase filled with books, the globe mounted on a metal meridian.

Her classmates were all looking at her. They weren't seated at desks like the bigger kids but at small tables in groups of four.

"You can sit right here, María." The teacher indicated an empty seat at a table near the front of the room.

María went to it, wishing everyone would stop staring at her.

Before she could sit down and become invisible, Mrs. González said, "Please remain standing, María. We're introducing ourselves. Can you introduce yourself to the class, María?"

She shook her head.

"You can tell us your name, can't you?"

"María," she said quietly.

"I can't hear her!" a student said.

"Please speak more loudly," the teacher said.

"María," she said.

"I still can't hear her."

"That okay, Raúl." Then, to María: "What else can you tell us?"

"Nothing," she said.

"Surely you can tell us something?"

She shook her head.

"How about we ask you some questions then. All you have to do is answer them. Does anyone have a question for María?"

A boy stuck up his hand. "Why are you so small?"

Everyone laughed.

Mrs. González cracked her meterstick against a desk. "Quiet, children. Everybody grows at their own pace. María may end up being taller than all of you in a few years."

A girl raised her hand. "Why do you have a doll?"

"She's my friend," María said.

"I still can't hear her!"

Another hand. "What does your dad do?"

"He's a construction worker."

"What does he build?"

"He puts up street lights."

Another hand. It belonged to a funny looking boy with large teeth and eyeglasses. "Do you want to be my friend?"

"Okay."

Someone shouted: "He loves you!"

"Do not!"

"He wants to *marry* you."

"Do not!"

The class began making eewwing noises.

Mrs. González cracked her meterstick again. "That's quite enough, children. Quite enough. María, you can sit down now."

Thankfully, she sat.

3

After everyone introduced themselves, Mrs. González explained the rules of the classroom the students were to follow for the duration of the schoolyear, then she read a story from a picture book. At lunchtime María ate the lunch her mother had packed her and drank the milk that was delivered to the class in small bottles. Most of the kids spent the break playing games and making friends. María was too nervous to join them and remained quietly in her seat. When two girls asked her why she was sitting by herself, she told them because she wanted to. Then Mrs. González rang a brass bell with a wooden handle, and everyone returned to their chairs. She set a large piece of paper displaying the outline of a house on each table. She also distributed packs of crayons and explained what sharing meant. Finally she instructed each group to color their house. There were two rules. The first was to color inside the lines. The second was to only use up and down strokes.

María chose a green crayon and began coloring the grass out front the house. The girl sitting beside her—María couldn't remember her name—started yelling at her, saying she was doing it wrong. Mrs. González came over and asked what the problem was.

"She's doing it wrong," the girl said, pointing at María's green scribbles.

"Did you understand my instructions, María?" Mrs. González asked.

"Yes."

"What did I say?"

"Color the house."

"Yes, but what were the rules I mentioned?"

She couldn't remember.

"You must color only inside the lines, and your strokes must be vertical. That means up and down." She demonstrated with her finger. "Do you understand now?"

María nodded and went back to coloring, now using up and down strokes. When a boy at her table finished with the brown crayon, she snatched it up and began coloring the front of the house.

"Teacher!" the girl beside her said, sticking her hand in the air. "She's doing it wrong again!"

Mrs. González returned and said, "What did I tell you, María?" She sounded angrier this time.

"Color the house."

"Yes, but what were the rules?"

"I don't know."

"I've explained this twice now"

Tears warmed her eyes, then spilled down her cheeks.

The girl beside her said, "She's crying!"

Another student: "She's a baby!"

"She's stupid!"

"She's a stupid baby!"

Bawling, María threw her crayon down and raced out of the room.

JACK

1

Pita stepped onto the island first, followed by Jesus, then Nitro, then Pepper, then Elizaveta, and finally me. Almost immediately the boatman pushed away from the pier. He didn't look back.

"Why doesn't he just wait around for us?" I asked.

"Because he is afraid of island," Elizaveta told me.

"Of course," I said sardonically. "The ghost."

"This is *so* weird," Pita said in awe. "I mean, look at all the dolls. They're everywhere."

I was looking. And they were everywhere, literally. They adorned not only the trees but fence posts, railings, clotheslines, even the collection of ramshackle huts—*especially* the huts. They were almost buried beneath the dolls.

"They're like...dead babies or something," she added.

"Hey, I like that one with no shirt," Nitro said. "She got curves just the way I like them." He made a slithering motion with his hands.

I said, "Can't get any living, breathing women, Muscles?"

"Shut up, Jack Goff."

"Ugh," Jesus said, pointing to a doll nailed to one of the

pier's timber piles. "Are those maggots?"

We shuffled closer for a better view.

"They're ladybugs," I said.

"They're not ladybugs, Jack," Jesus grumbled.

They weren't, I realized. But they definitely weren't maggots. They were black, beetle-like, with red diamonds on their backs. However, I could see why Jesus might have thought they were maggots from a distance. They were a squiggling mass that covered much of the doll's torso and half its face. They were clumped together particularly thickly over the doll's right eye. In fact, I think the eye might have been missing, and they were spilling out of the empty cavity in the head.

Pepper produced from his bag an SLR camera with a big lens and told us to give him some room so he could take a picture.

We started down the dirt path. After a brief congress in Spanish, Jesus, Nitro, Pita, and Elizaveta turned right over a crude bridge. I continued straight ahead, glad to be on my own.

Birds chirped and squawked all around me from hidden roosts, while cicadas put up a wall of cryptic noise. The heat had left the afternoon, and now I found myself almost cold. The forest was still and dark. I walked slowly, swatting absently at flies and turning my head this way and that, as if it were on a swivel. Dolls decorated nearly every tree. Most appeared to be secured to the trunks with nails or wire, though some were tied to branches by their hair.

I shivered. I couldn't help it. Dolls in general were inherently creepy. Their inexpressive eyes and knowing smiles, their lifeless limbs and outstretched hands that seemed to be beckoning to you. Yet these rejects took the cake. Even in the gloomy light of day they were menacing. The sun had bubbled and scabbed their "skin," while the rain had eroded much of their paint, leaving behind waxy skull-like faces the color of bone meal. Pita's description had been quite apt: they really did look like dead babies—horribly mutilated dead babies with black-rimmed eyes and tufts of wasting hair. And aside from their state of dissolution, many were decapitated or missing arms and legs, while others were nothing more than butchered torsos, or disembodied heads impaled on broken boughs.

As I progressed through their ranks, I found it rather unnerving to have so many sets of soulless eyes trained on me. They might be nothing more than glass orbs, unseeing, lacking consciousness or menace, yet I couldn't shake the sensation of being watched, of the dolls twisting their heads and limbs unnaturally to follow me after I'd passed them by.

I stopped beside a sagging timber hut with a corrugated iron roof. The majority of the dolls attached to the warped wood were the porcelain-faced variety—these had dominated the island thus far—but among them I was surprised to see a Cabbage Patch Kid, a troll doll, and several nude Barbie dolls.

Footsteps sounded behind me. I turned just in time for Pepper to snap a picture of me.

"That better not be for your documentary," I said.

"It's only a photograph, Jack. It's for my private collection."

"Private collection? You sound like you have a trunk full of body parts somewhere."

He assumed feigned hurt, hand on hips. "You know me, Jack, I'm a pacifist."

Actually, I didn't know Pepper was a pacifist, and the revelation surprised me. I'd always considered anyone who felt bad about stepping on a bug once in a while a bit of an oddball—unless, of course, you went out of your way to step on bugs, and if that were the case, you had a whole different set of problems.

I said, "So you've never flushed a spider down the toilet?"

"What are you talking about, Jack? I *hate* spiders. I kill them all the time. I'm opposed to violence. People-against-people violence."

"I thought pacifists were opposed to violence categorically

because of the karmic consequences and all that."

"You're thinking of Ghandi, Jack. You can definitely be a regular pacifist and kill spiders." He stopped next to me and studied the wall. "Wow, Barbies!" He raised his camera, adjusted the focus, and snapped consecutive shots. "What do you think happened to that one? I've seen a few like it." He indicated a doll that appeared charred, as if it had been set on fire.

"Maybe it came to life and Solano had to torch it."

"Oooh, Jack, that's good. I have to remember that."

"Get a photo of that pissed-off one too." I pointed to a doll with an onion-domed head that seemed to be scowling at us, one plump arm outstretched.

Pepper aimed the lens inches from the evil thing's face. The camera clicked.

I adjusted the doll's arm so it was now reaching above its head.

Pepper seemed shocked I touched it. "What are you doing?"

"Take some more photos. You can tell people it moved on its own. It will make good TV."

He was nonplussed. "The documentary will make good TV regardless."

"Even if nothing spooky happens?"

"Patience, Jack. We only just got here. Let's wait and see."

"For what? *Night of the Living Dead*—only with dolls?"

He huffed. "Okay, fine. You don't believe in spirits, or an afterlife. I'm not going to try to persuade you otherwise. You are too stubborn."

I raised my eyebrows. "I'm stubborn?"

"You're the most stubborn person I know."

"I beg to differ."

"See, you won't even admit I might be right."

"Because I'm not stubborn."

Pepper sighed melodramatically. "Yeesh, Jack."

"Tell me, Peps," I said, "in all your TV shows, all your investigating, have you ever seen a ghost, really?"

"Not in the sense you might be thinking."

"What sense is that?"

"Not a white sheet that goes 'boo.'"

"So what have you seen?

"Things that cannot be explained. I've recorded cold spots, abnormal ion counts in the atmosphere, photographic anomalies—"

"With your *Ghostbusters* equipment."

"*Scientific* equipment, Jack. Electromagnetic field detectors, infrared cameras—"

"I hate to point out the elephant in the haunted room, Peps, but if any of that stuff actually worked, wouldn't it have proven the existence of a ghost already?"

"There's no more scientific evidence to support the existence of black holes than there is to support the existence of spirits. But you believe black holes exist, don't you?"

"You're talking apples and oranges."

"Why, Jack? Parapsychology is not a pseudoscience, or at least it shouldn't be classified as one. There are plenty of respected institutes and universities investigating paranormal phenomena. There was a particularly important experiment done a couple of years ago. A person with a terminal illness volunteered to die in an air-tight glass box. At the moment he passed away the glass, which was thirty centimeters thick, cracked in numerous places. The amount of energy needed to accomplish this would be tremendous." Pepper paused dramatically. "Now with this in mind, remember what Einstein said. All the energy of the universe is constant. It can't be created or destroyed. It just gets transferred to a different form. So what happens to the electrical energy in you and me, the energy that makes our hearts beat, when we die? It continues, just in another form. And that form is..."

"Ghostly," I said.

"Right, Jack."

"Well, whenever you get more proof of this than cracked

glass, or a fleeting electromagnetic field, let me know, will you? Beers on me."

"I figured for someone who's had an out-of-body experience, you would be a little more open-minded to what may lie beyond this life."

"Neurons firing, Peps. Hallucinations."

"Look, Jack. We might not yet have the means to conclusively prove spirits exist, but that doesn't mean they don't exist either."

"What about clothes then?" I said. "If our energy gets converted to a different form after we die, why do our clothes, a manufactured convention, come with us? You know, the manifestation of the butler in the old British mansion. Why's he always wearing a petticoat and bowtie?"

"Close your eyes and picture yourself. What are you wearing?"

"What I'm wearing now."

"You're not naked?"

"Sorry to disappoint you."

I opened my eyes. Pepper was smiling triumphantly at me.

"See, Jack," he said. "When you see yourself, you see yourself clothed. The same could be said for ghosts. If they have any control over the energy which they're comprised of, then it's quite likely they would manifest themselves how they saw themselves as a living person, wearing clothes."

I shook my head. "I don't get it, Peps," I said. "Why do you want to prove ghosts exist so badly?"

"Why? Because it would prove your life continues beyond this one, Jack! It would change the way we think about everything. It would be revolutionary."

"But you're presupposing that there being an afterlife would be a good thing."

"How could life everlasting not be a good thing?"

I thought of my dream earlier. "Because what if that life everlasting was eternal suffering? Would you really want to know that's what awaited you?"

"You mean hell?"

"Call it what you want. But, hell, fine, why not. Would you want to prove the existence of hell?"

"Well, sure, because if there's hell, then there's heaven."

"Maybe not, Peps," I said. "Maybe there's only hell, and that's why death is so mysterious, so unknown. Maybe it's not supposed to be understood or unraveled. Maybe it's so cloaked in secrecy because what lies beyond is so terrible that life would cease to be livable if we knew what awaited us after we died."

"Damn, Jack!" he said. "How do you ever get out of bed in the mornings?"

"Because life is what it is. There's either something waiting for us after we die, whether good or bad, or there isn't anything. Overthinking, even proving, what might be or not be won't change a thing." I clapped him heartily on the back. "On that note, let's go see what's lurking inside this hut."

2

Unsurprisingly, there were no ghosts inside the hut. There were, however, dolls. Best guess, a hundred, probably more, crammed into an area the size of a small bedroom. For a moment I thought of those carnival midway booths with prizes overflowing the walls and ceiling—only these weren't cute stuffed animals or toys. They were like all the other dolls we'd already seen: decrepit, sad, mottled, cobwebs spun inside their mouths and eyes sockets. Yet they were different too. They all had their heads and limbs intact, while many were bejeweled with necklaces, bracelets, and strange handcrafted headgear. The result was an incongruous mixture of neglect and love.

I said, "Seemed Solano had special affection for these particular guys."

Pepper was moving from wall to wall, camera stuck to his eye, taking close-up shots of several of the most disturbing dolls. "Look at this one, Jack," he said excitedly. *Click, click, click.*

I joined Pepper at the support post to which the doll was attached, wrinkling my nose at the almost sickening musty smell that permeated the air. At some point the doll had been painted flesh-colored, but now most of it was covered in a gray grime that made me think of a necrotizing disease. Clumps of tangled black hair fell in front of its face, though it was parted almost deliberately so one black eye could peer out. A dozen colorful bracelets encircled its wrists, while a stethoscope dangled from its neck.

"Oh, and this one," Pepper gushed, moving on to a doll whose bald head was studded with nails and nose rings and anything else that could pierce the plastic. *Click, click.*

I said, "I wouldn't have guessed Solano as a *Hellraiser* fan."

"Hey, is that a shrine?" Pepper was already moving on once more. *Click, click.* A step backward to frame the shot better. *Click.* "Can you take a picture of me in front of it?"

"Don't you want to get all this stuff on film?"

"I like to take photographs first, to get a feel for the locale."

He passed me his camera, then crouched next to the shrine, which featured two wood-carved cranes atop a hand-painted sign that read "XOCHIMILCO." Beneath this sat what might have been the most bizarre doll yet. She wore some sort of hat from which dangled ribbons, rosaries, and large hoop earrings. She also wore sunglasses, a necklace with a large silver pendant, and a white and pink dress with two teddy bears embroidered on the chest.

"You guys make a good pair," I said, squinting through the camera's viewfinder and taking several pictures. "Any idea what her deal is?"

Pepper took the camera back and twisted his lips in a thoughtful expression. "I can't say for certain, but I would guess she was Solano's favorite. Maybe it was the first doll he found?"

"She doesn't look old enough."

"Since when do dolls age?"

"They do here, on this island. Some look like they're a hundred years old."

"Maybe the spirit of the little girl chose it to serve as her medium."

"To speak to Solano? I thought you said she spoke to him in his dreams?"

"And perhaps she spoke to him through certain dolls too."

"Are you making this all up as you go?"

He feigned hurt. "Please, Jack. Can you at least try to keep an open mind?"

"I am, Peps. It's all going in one side and coming out the other." I indicated a large wood-framed photograph hanging on the wall to the left of the shrine. "So is that the great Solano himself?" It showed a man with thinning black hair, kind black eyes, an unkempt handlebar mustache, and a wispy goatee. He was smiling, revealing yellowed teeth. He wore a sleeveless jacket beneath a poncho. "Looks like a nice enough guy."

"Nobody said Solano wasn't nice."

"Just crazy."

"Spiritual—"

"...MA-MA..."

I started. Pepper seemed as surprised as me.

I said, "Which one—"

"...MA-MA..."

The voice was loud, whiny, effeminate.

Pepper began backing up toward the door.

"Where are you going?" I said.

"A doll just *spoke*, Jack!"

Ignoring him, I moved along the wall, trying to figure out which doll was speaking—

"...MA-MA..."

My eyes paused on a clown doll directly before me: brown

shaggy hair, white face, pink nose, pink dimples on the cheeks, pink lips.

Was it smiling at me?

The kid inside of me that had once been afraid of the dark and wondered what slept under my bed wanted to follow Pepper's lead and get the hell out of the claustrophobic room. Nevertheless, the rational adult wouldn't allow it.

It was just a doll. An inanimate chunk of plastic. Battery-powered, programed to speak every now and then.

I reached for it, to turn it around, to peel off its pajama top, to check for the on/off switch and battery compartment—

A thunderous *bang!* shook the wall, accompanied by an ear-splitting shriek.

I cried out, stumbling backward. I collided into a support beam and fell down, dragging several dolls with me. At the same time laughter erupted from the other side of the wall.

Embarrassment burned me from the inside out. I pushed myself to my feet, scooping up the dolls on the floor. I'd snapped the strings holding them in place, there was no way to reattach them to the beam, and I was still cradling them in my arms when Nitro and Jesus appeared in the doorway to the hut, both grinning like pigs in shit.

Nitro said, "You scream just like a little girl, Jack Goff!"

Jesus assumed a straight face that barely disguised his look of hauteur. "I hope you're okay, Jack," he said with the proper air of civility. "You didn't hurt yourself, did you?"

I dumped the dolls at the base of the support beam and went to the door. "Funny, dickheads," I told them. "Now how about getting the fuck out of my way?"

Jesus stepped aside. Nitro seized my forearm as I passed him. "You just going to leave those dolls there on the ground, chavo? That's disrespectful."

"Let go of me," I told him.

He squeezed tighter. "You got to learn some manners, my friend. You can't just go around busting everything—"

I shoved him hard enough he nearly fell over. I would have

gone after him but Jesus grappled me from behind, pinning my arms to my side.

I ran him backward, crushing his body between mine and the doorframe. His hold on me slackened, though he didn't let go.

Nitro, recovering, eyes storming, charged. I spun around, using Jesus as an unwitting shield. Nitro's fist whizzed past my right ear.

Then Pepper leapt into the skirmish, shouting, telling us to break it up.

"Jesus!" Pita said a moment later, appearing from nowhere. "Nitro! Stop!"

Jesus released me. I turned back around, tensing to attack Nitro, but Pepper and Jesus were in the way.

Nitro was pushing against Pepper, letting Pepper hold him back.

"Jack, Nitro!" Pita shouted. "What the heck is going on?"

Nitro ran the heel of his hand over his mouth. "Your boy-friend got scared and spazzed out, that's what."

"Don't touch me again," I told him quietly.

"Or what, chavo? You gonna sissy-push me again?"

I shoved Jesus and Pepper out of the way and lunged at Nitro. He threw a punch that deflected off my chin, dazing me. Nevertheless, I got my shoulder into him. We smashed through a railing and tumbled down a gentle slope. We struggled all the way to the bottom, flipping back and forth. Nitro was strong, all muscle. But I was bigger, probably had thirty or forty pounds on him, and when we came to a stop I got my weight on top of him—only to realize I didn't know what to do next. He pissed me off, but I wasn't going to smash in his face. That's when I heard Pita and Elizaveta. They were talking frantically. Something had happened.

I got off Nitro. I expected him to leap at me. He didn't.

I climbed the slope, clawing at long grasses and ferns. At the top I saw Jesus sitting on the ground, Elizaveta and Pita and Pepper crouched in front of him.

"What happened?" I asked, going over.

"He twisted his ankle," Elizaveta told me.

They'd rolled up Jesus's left pant cuff. Elizaveta gently pulled off his penny loafer. He wasn't wearing socks. There was a large red bump where there shouldn't be on his ankle.

Elizaveta probed it with her finger. Jesus hissed in pain.

"Sorry," I said. "I didn't mean to—"

Pita glared at me. "You pushed him over."

"He was in the way."

"In the way of what?"

I shrugged. "Nitro."

"Nitro—right. Why were you attacking Nitro? What's wrong with you, Jack?"

"With me?" I said. "Are you serious? Nitro—"

"You heard her, chavo," Nitro said. He'd climbed the slope behind me.

"Fuck you, Muscles."

Pita said, "You've gone over the board, Jack."

I blinked. "Over the board?"

"You know what I mean."

"Over the board?"

Her face flushed. "Jack!"

"Why don't you take a hike, Jack Goff?" Nitro said.

I faced the joker. He was grinning, his barrel chest puffed out like a turkey's. His eyes drilled into mine, black, taunting. He wanted to start something again because he knew everyone was on his side.

I walked away.

3

I'd met Pita some five years ago when I was twenty-three. Her father, Marco Cuhna, had put together a self-sponsored racing team to compete in the '96 Busch Series Grand National Division, NASCAR's minor league circuit, and he wanted me to be his driver. I'd come a long way from the back-of-the-pack kid racing the Monte Carlo on local tracks. The previous year I'd won the American Speed Association rookie title, while the current season I'd finished fourth in standings with two wins. Nevertheless, the big corporate sponsors didn't want to touch me. I wasn't fit enough to compete at a more elite level, they said. I bumped too much on the track and drank too much off it. In other words, I wasn't the whitewashed, polished driver you could put on the front of a Wheaties cereal box. Yet none of that bothered Marco Cunha. "They're stupid," he told me simply during our first meeting. "They want someone with perfect hair, perfect teeth, perfect personality. Why? Who watches NASCAR? I tell you, Jack. Beer-drinking, blue-collar young men. And they want someone they can root for. An underdog, a hothead, an anti-establishment figure." He smiled. "So now you tell me, Jack. Know anyone who fits that bill?"

Driving the No. 11 Conquistador Brewery Chevrolet, I finished the '97 season sixteenth in the point standings with zero wins. Not exactly statistics to celebrate, but Marco had faith in me, and I had become sort of family, as by then Pita and I had begun dating seriously. She was in her final year at UCLA and came one Sunday to watch me race at Irwindale Speedway. She, Marco, and I went for dinner afterward, and when Marco retired to the hotel, she and I stayed out partying well into the morning, parting with a goodnight kiss. After that, we kept in touch via telephone every now and then until she graduated in June—then she was accompanying her father to every race. I hadn't wanted a girlfriend. I was too busy. A typical day had me putting in fifteen hours at the racetrack. Pita, however, was persistent, she was always around, and she was a lot of fun. At first we were spending one or two nights a week together. Then it was three or four. Then it was every night, falling to sleep together, waking together. She didn't know much about stock car racing, but she learned quickly.

Moreover, she was a people person by nature, and she fell in love with the glamor of the industry. The buzz of the press conferences, the socializing at the press dinners, the race day parades and post-race functions. What she didn't like so much were the pit lizards, or groupies, who always seemed to know where I hung out away from the track. Pita was a confident, attractive woman, but seeing these girls throwing themselves all over race car drivers drove her crazy, and it was the source of our first few fights. So to prove to her I wasn't interested in any of them, I proposed to her in Charlotte, South Carolina, on a clear night in the center of an asphalt oval.

The following season I recorded my first win at the Chicagoland Speedway and finished seventh in the point standings. Sadly, that was the year Marco died from a brain aneurysm and Jesus took over as Chairman and CEO of Conquistador Brewery. His first order of business was to disband the racing team and sell the operation. He argued the costs of sponsoring a race car outweighed the publicity generated, as the company's three varieties of beers had yet to receive a significant boost in sales. I didn't know what a "significant boost" entailed, and I didn't care much. Aside from not wanting to be under Jesus's thumb—we'd enjoyed a healthy dislike for each other pretty much right off the bat—I had a slew of new offers from other teams.

In the end I signed with Smith Motorsports for the '99 season and began racing fulltime in the Winston Cup Series, NASCAR's top-level circuit. I earned my first career pole position for the Daytona 500, but then crashed at the Las Vegas Speedway, finishing forty-first. However, I rebounded with consecutive wins in the Coco-Cola 600 and Pocono 500. All said, it was a breakout season. I won four races, two poles, twelve top five's, and fifteen top ten's. I also took NASCAR's Rookie of the Year—and just like that I became a household name. I was being interviewed by *Motor Week Illustrated*, *Sports Illustrated*, *SPIN Magazine*. The guys on SportsCenter were always talking about me (and cracking jokes about my name). I received two lucrative endorsement deals, I bought a private bus to travel in, a gated house in Vegas, the Porsche. It was all beyond my wildest imaginings.

Then the accident happened, and everything changed.

4

It took me close to twenty minutes to reach the far side of the island, which made the island larger than I'd originally guessed. My beer-filled bladder felt ready to burst, so I unzipped and aimed at a patch of elephant ear plants, careful to avoid the backsplash. My urine was bright yellow due to dehydration. I hadn't brought any water, and I wondered if anyone else had. Jesus, probably. He was so obsessive compulsive it wouldn't surprise me if he organized in advance which ties and cufflinks to wear for each day of the week.

I shook, zipped, then slipped the daypack off my shoulders. Mosquitos and other bugs had joined the cloud of flies hovering around my head, all of them buzzing and biting, causing me to repeatedly smack myself. Then a kamikaze fly shot up one of my nostrils. I snorted and waved my arms angrily, my hands striking a couple of the annoying fuckers.

I opened the pack's main pocket and withdrew a liter bottle of vodka. Yup, I had my priorities right. Forgot the water but remembered the booze. I twisted off the cap and took a small sip, ladylike, to acclimatize my palette. Then I took a long belt. The vodka burned a trail down my throat and hit my stomach with a warm punch. As an afterthought I glanced the way I'd come, to make sure nobody was coming looking for me.

Nobody was.

Bottle in hand, I wandered from the shadows beneath the deciduous and coniferous trees to the marshy edge of the bank. There wasn't a patch of blue left in the sky, and it was no longer a question of if it would storm but when. I wondered what this meant for us. Would the boatman return early to pick us up? Or would he wait out the storm...which could last...how long? One day? Two? Surely he wouldn't leave us stuck on the island for that long? On the other hand, if the rain and wind and flooding were bad enough, he might not have a choice.

Oddly I found I wouldn't mind being stranded on the island. I'd always been a nature person. When I was five years old my father sold the patent to one of his inventions for a good chunk of cash and bought an RV to travel the country. Most of what I remembered from my childhood involved national parks and campfires and breakfasts at interstate McDonald's. I didn't attend grammar school. My parents homeschooled me —or RV-schooled me, I guess you'd say—though this involved less arithmetic and history and more hunting, fishing, and basic survival skills. Only when I was old enough to attend high school did my parents settle down in a trailer park in Vegas, where they still lived today.

So, sure, as far as I was concerned, roughing it for a day or two on the island would be a bit of an adventure. Pepper and Elizaveta were good company. Pita and I would likely make up by nightfall. I'd have to put up with Jesus and Nitro, unfortunately, but whatever. And this place would be something else at nighttime, wouldn't it? The Island of the Dolls in the dark— how you were supposed to see it.

Three dolls to my left caught my eye. They were tied to a tree, one at chest level, the other two much higher. How Solano got them up there, I didn't know. I doubted he had a Craftsman ladder tucked away somewhere. Then again, living fifty years on an island by yourself, you had time to build yourself a ladder.

The doll at chest level was one of the more normal looking ones on the island as it hadn't yet been disfigured by the elements. It had a button nose and chubby cheeks and a frisky smile. Actually, it sort of resembled Pepper. It even had short black hair, which I thought I could style into a pompadour.

I took another drink of vodka and decided Pepper might like a souvenir of the island. I set the bottle at the base of the tree and withdrew my keys from my pocket. Attached to the keyring was a Swiss Army knife I'd purchased at La Merced, a public market on the eastern edge of Mexico City's historic center. I used to go there to buy chili peppers and other vegetables, and to stuff myself with the street food. There was one particular stall that sold what might have been the best quesadillas and tostadas in the world. Nevertheless, I hadn't been back to the market in a while because I got tired of the underage prostitutes propositioning me at ten bucks a pop.

Anyway, I bought the pocket knife because, given how much I'd started drinking over the last year, always having a bottle opener handy was a no-brainer.

I opened the knife's sharp blade, gripped the doll, and was about to cut the string securing it to the tree when its eyes blinked open.

I started, looking around for Jesus or Nitro. They weren't anywhere in sight, of course. This was not another prank. I'd caused the eyes to open when I gripped the doll. I'd disturbed the pendulum inside it, or whatever mechanism was responsible for controlling the eyelids.

I used my fingertips to close the doll's eyelids, the way you might close the eyelids of a recently deceased person. As soon as I ceased contact, however, they flipped up again, so the doll stared at me with its disturbingly lifelike eyes.

Cutting the little monster free, I stuck it in my pack, collected the vodka, then started back the way I'd come.

5

I chose a different route back which I believed would reveal more of the island while offering up a whole new freak show of dolls. I wasn't disappointed, as Solano's obsession seemed contained by no boundaries. As the forest closed around me, the canopy and understory blocked out much of the sky to create a syrupy, shadowed world. Birds cawed and chirped and beat their wings far above my head. Cicadas whirred louder than before, an angry, palpitating sound that could suddenly and inexplicably stop before starting up again. Bugs bit my legs and arms and neck, and the sensation of being watched returned, making me feel suddenly alone, isolated.

Jack, a doll to my right whispered. Its voice was like the rustle of leaves, so close and clear I turned my head despite myself, my eyes searching the cluster of dolls wedged into the various crooks of a tree. *Are you lost? You're going to die—*

"Shut the fuck up," I said, to hear my voice, a real voice.

I took a belt of vodka and pressed on, following the well-beaten path. For a while I tried to pick out a doll to give to Pita—a peace offering of sorts—but I couldn't find any that resembled her. For starters, about ninety-nine percent of the dolls were Caucasian, which I found strange. China had Chinese dolls. Japan had Japanese dolls. Weren't there any patriotic doll makers in Mexico?

Eventually I came across one doll with black hair that could pass as Pita if you ignored the pigmentation. Nevertheless, I left it where it was because it was seriously evil-looking, and if I gave it to Pita, she would likely accuse me of making fun of her.

When I was roughly halfway back to the side of the island where we'd disembarked, I came to a dilapidated cabin. Unlike the hut Pepper and I had investigated, this was much larger and featured a porch with an actual swinging door.

I tried the door, expecting it to be locked. It opened, and I stepped inside. The main room was dark and carried the forgotten smell of wood rot and age. There was a contrary feel to it, perhaps because there were no windows, though gaps between the corrugated iron roof and the timber walls allowed for some natural light.

When my eyes adjusted to the murkiness, I found myself in what you might call a living room. There was no TV or stereo or anything resembling modernity. But there were two rattan chairs, a table, and a bookcase, all of which appeared to have been rescued from a trash heap. More junk littered the floor, or at least what I considered to be junk, though Solano would have likely begged to differ. Some of the detritus included glass bottles, tires, an umbrella, a lunch box, a handsaw, a hammer, even a very old car seat.

And of course there were dolls—a riot of them, thirty, forty, more. Most were like those outside, discolored and blistered and boiled from the tropical sun. They were affixed to the walls, a cornucopia of creepy, crawly, bump-in-the-night abominations, and once again the sight of so many of them filled me with a niggle of trepidation and sadness.

I wondered why they made me feel like this, and some Freudian mumbo-jumbo I read once came to mind, something regarding an inherent contradiction. Dolls are inanimate objects, they're lifeless, but because they look like us, they appear alive—and when something that's not alive appears *too* alive its familiarity turns to unfamiliarity, our brains reject it as unnatural, and our feelings for it sour toward revulsion.

A roundabout way, I guess, of saying dolls are just plain spooky.

I crossed the room to the table where one doll sat alongside what might have been a shoebox. The wooden floorboards creaked beneath my weight. My heartbeat thudded in my ears, likely because even though Solano was dead, I felt as though I was trespassing, invading his privacy—which was exactly what I was doing.

I peered in the shoebox.

I wasn't sure what I'd been expecting to discover—spare doll parts?—but certainly not makeup. Yet that's what I found, loads of it, far more than any woman would ever need. I selected a metallic tube of lipstick, removed the cap: Fire-truck Red. I dumped it back in the box and examined the doll. Its face was painted with eyeliner, eyeshadow, blush, and lipstick. Moreover, it was in much better condition than its outdoor cousins. Limbs intact, dressed in clean clothes, free of cobwebs and filth. The word "groomed" came to mind.

I picked up the doll. Its eyes were dark, reptilian, almost calculating, its earlobes pierced with bronze hoop earrings, its fingernails sporting vermillion nail polish. I sniffed its hair —a pleasant citrus scent.

Did Solano bathe the thing?

I wished Pepper were here to see it, because it was proof I was right. Solano had been a crazy bastard. Maybe even a raving lunatic.

I pictured him sitting at this table at nighttime, an old man worn down by time and aged by the weather and hardship of living off the land, working by candlelight, brushing the dolls hair, or carefully applying blush to its cheeks, or lipstick to its lips, or polish to its nails, mumbling incoherently to it as he did so, maybe asking how her day was, or what she was going to do tomorrow, or, hell, had she met any Ken dolls lately.

Yet why? What had he been thinking? That it was a flesh-and-blood child?

Did he fuck it?

This question startled me. He wouldn't, couldn't—it was a *doll*, for Christ's sake. Then again, some people had pretty sick fetishes, and he was lonely as a cloud out here, no human company...

I was tempted to lift the doll's dress, pull down its knickers, see if Solano had altered the space between its legs in any way. But I didn't. I didn't want to know.

The sight of a gaping hole would make me sick.

Suddenly I didn't want to touch the thing any longer, and I set it back on the table. I moved on to an adjoining room, the floorboards once again creaking beneath my weight. I poked my head into what turned out to be a kitchen. I wrinkled my nose at the smell of something rotten. Dishes were piled on the top of a roughly hewed counter. Alongside these were a knife, a spoon, and a fork. Staples such as pasta, salt, rice, and sugar occupied a single shelf. A basket on the floor was filled with dry corn which Solano likely ground into flour. There was no sink or stove because he wouldn't have had running water or electricity. I assumed there would be a fire pit nearby where he would have boiled water from the canal and cooked his food. Pepper mentioned the locals traded him dolls for produce he grew. I hadn't seen a vegetable garden anywhere, but then again I had only seen a small slice of the island.

My eyes swept the floor, the shadowed corners, for a dead mouse or small animal, something that had crawled in here to die and was responsible for the stench. I didn't see anything.

Back in the living room I went to one of the two rooms I had yet to explore. It was a Spartan bedroom: bed, dresser, window, that was all.

The door to the second room was closed. I gripped the doorknob and was about to twist it when a sneeze originated from the other side of the door.

I froze, dumbstruck.

Please, Jack—first a doll opening its eyes, then another talking to you, and now one sneezing?

But then what had I heard?

I pushed open the door, half-expecting a Chucky doll to scuttle toward me on its small child's legs, a big knife gripped in one hand.

The room was empty save for a bed and a dresser.

"Hello?" I said, regardless.

No reply.

I didn't want to check beneath the bed. It was something a child would do, to assuage their paranoia and superstition. Nevertheless, I knew I couldn't avoid doing so, because I'd heard something after all. I hadn't imagined that.

I touched a knee to the floor and looked.

6

The little girl was on her belly, hands at her sides, fingers splayed on the floor, like a sprinter about to bolt from the starting blocks—or come straight at me. Matted black hair obscured much of her face. She wore an embroidered cheesecloth top and pastel-colored jeans.

When I regained my wits, I cleared the lump in my throat and said, "Hi." This sounded not only lame but, given the circumstances, sinister as well, what a stranger says to lure an unsuspecting child into his car. "I'm Jack," I added.

The girl didn't reply. I guessed she was seven or eight. She had a round face with small features that suggested she would one day grow up to be an attractive woman.

I wondered if she could be Solano's daughter. Had he had an affair with a local woman and been charged with raising the illegitimate child? Or was it more sinister than this? Had he kidnapped her and held her prisoner here until he died? If so, how long had she been on the island? Her clothes weren't in tatters, but they weren't clean either.

I opened my mouth, then shut it. I wasn't good with kids, wasn't one of those people who could converse with them using falsetto voices and fake laughs.

I thought about getting Pita, but I discarded this option immediately, knowing the girl would be gone when I returned.

"What are you doing under there?" I said—then realized she likely didn't speak English. "Er... *Que haces...haciendo?*"

The girl swallowed. Her eyes darted to the door, then back to me. She was going to make a run for it. And what would I do? Let her go? Grab her? Close the door, trap her in the room, and shout for help?

No, no shouting. Jesus and Nitro would never let me live that down.

"Umm... *Puedes entender? Mi español... mal...*"

The girl said something so softly if I hadn't seen her lips moving I might not have believed she'd spoken.

"*¿Qué?*" I said.

"Yes," she said louder, but still not much more than a skeletal whisper.

"You understand me?"

She nodded.

"So you speak English?"

"We study it at school."

I hadn't known English was studied in Mexican schools at such a young age, and I said, "Where's your school?"

"Balcones de San Mateo."

"Is that in Mexico City?"

"Naucalpan."

Which was north west of the city. "So what are you doing way down here on this island?"

"I—" She bit her lip. Tears shimmered in her eyes, then spilled down her cheeks.

"Hey, hey," I said. "It's okay. It doesn't matter." I lifted my baseball cap with one hand and ran the other through my hair. "What's your name?"

"Rosa," she said.

"Okay, look, Rosa. Why don't you come out of there?"

"I don't want to."

"You can come meet my friends."

"Your friends?"

"Yeah, I'm here with..." I had to mentally count. "Five of them."

She sniffled, then rubbed her leaking nose and eyes with the back of her hand. "Are they nice?"

"Two of them are tools. But the other three are nice."

"Tools?"

"Like, uh... Do you know what a dork is?"

She nodded.

"Well, they're like that. Dorks. One's called Muscles."

"Is he strong?"

"He thinks he is."

"Maybe he can protect us?"

"Protect us?"

She bit her lip and didn't say anything.

"Is there somebody else on this island, Rosa?"

She remained silent.

"Come out, Rosa," I said. "Come meet my friends. You can't stay under there all day."

"What's the other dork's name?"

I laughed. I couldn't help it. Rosa smiled hesitantly, as if unsure what was funny.

I said, "God."

"No it's not!"

"What a stupid name, right?"

"He can't call himself God."

"Hey, I agree totally."

"What about your other friends? Do they have stupid names too?"

"Their names are Pita, Pepper, and Elizaveta."

"Those are better."

"I agree."

"Why are *you* here?"

"The island? One of my friends—Pepper—he works for a TV show."

Rosa's eyes widened. "Really?"

I nodded. "Do you know what a documentary is?"

"Not really."

"It's like a real-life movie. You know, like those animal shows and stuff? Only Pepper's shows are about ghosts."

She seemed surprised. "He knows about the ghost?"

I frowned. "What ghost?"

"The ghost on the island. The ghost that..." She bit her lip again.

I studied her silently. I had a dozen questions, but there would be time to ask her them later. Right now I needed to get her out from under the bed, to the others. They'd know how to talk to her, get her to open up. I said. "Are you hungry, Rosa?"

She nodded.

"We have water. I think we might even have a candy bar. Do you want a candy bar?"

She nodded again.

"Okay. But you have to come out of there first."

I offered my hand to her. After a long moment, she took it.

7

We walked side by side, holding hands. I would have felt awkward doing this with a child back in the city, and I felt equally uncomfortable now. But the girl—Rosa—didn't want to let go. She really was spooked by something. Which was what I was trying to figure out. What was the ghost she thought she'd seen? Shadows playing tricks with her eyes? A glimpse of a doll in the dark? A figment of her imagination?

Moreover, why was she on the island in the first place? Someone brought her here from Naucalpan obviously, but who? And where were they now? The island wasn't big enough that you could lose someone on it. Sound carried out here precisely because there was little sound of anything to begin with. All Rosa had to do was yell and whoever she came with would hear her.

Which meant something had likely happened to her guardian. But again I was stumped. Because if the person slipped and cut their head open on a rock, or had a heart attack or some other serious medical emergency, you'd think Rosa would tell me. Yet the fact she was mum on this, as well as the so-called ghost, led me to conclude the two were related. Something happened to Rosa's guardian, and for whatever reason Rosa believed a sinister spirit was responsible.

"You don't believe me."

Her voice startled me. "Huh?" I said, even though I knew what she meant.

"You don't think there's a ghost on the island."

"Did you actually see one?"

"No..." She frowned, struggling with what to tell me. Then

she blurted, "It killed my brother."

I stopped. She did too. She looked up at me, and she seemed so small, so afraid.

I said, "Your brother brought you here to see the dolls?"

"To show his girlfriend the dolls."

His girlfriend? I crouched next to Rosa. "How many people did you come here with?"

"Just them. My brother, Miguel, and his girlfriend. He wanted to show her the dolls. We made camp, and then…then he wanted to be alone with Lucinda, and he told me to go away."

"Lucinda is his girlfriend?"

She nodded. "So I went away. I found a pond. I was trying to catch frogs. And then I heard my brother scream, and he never screams."

"What happened to him?"

She scrunched up her face, fighting more tears. "I don't know."

"You don't know?"

"He told me to run. He sounded like…"

"Like what?"

"Like he was dying."

"What about his girlfriend? What happened to her?"

"I don't know. I ran away until I found that house." She pointed back toward Solano's cabin. "I fell asleep on the bed. But when I woke up, it was dark, and I was scared, so I hid underneath it."

"You've only been here for one day?"

She nodded.

I stood, took her hand again. One day, I thought. Which meant if what she was telling me was the truth, and if someone had indeed attacked her brother, then the person could still be around. I recalled the feeling of being watched earlier. The dolls—or a living person? I looked past Rosa, then over my shoulder, my eyes searching the trees.

"Come on, Rosa," I said. "Let's get to the others."

1954

It was a warm spring day. María, now in the third grade, spent recess walking in the field behind the school. She held Angela in her right hand, the doll's feet dragging on the ground. Her mother often tried to stop her and Angela from being friends, but she would always throw a temper tantrum, yelling and crying, until her mother gave in.

She passed a group of kids in her grade playing a game with a ball. The boy with the ball threw it up into the air and all the other kids ran. When the ball came down he caught it and yelled a country name, and all the kids stopped. Then he went after the closest one and threw the ball. It hit a girl on the head, and everyone cheered.

María continued on. She didn't understand the rules. Besides, it didn't look very fun. She was much more interested in her present activity: collecting leaves. She didn't know why they fell off the trees, but she liked to pick them up in case the trees ever needed them back.

Eventually she came to the wooden split-rail fence that separated the school from the farm. On the other side of it was an open-air stable that consisted of a corrugated iron roof on posts. A black horse and two cows stood inside it. The horse saw her and came over.

"Hi, horsey!" she said. "What are you doing today?"

"I like horses," Angela said.

"I do too. But I don't like how they smell."

"That's manure."

"I know. Horses don't have toilets like we do, so they go on the ground."

"Do you like cows?"

"Yeah, but they smell even more than horses."

She continued her conversation with Angela and didn't notice the two girls in her grade approach until they were right behind her.

"Hi, María," Lydia said. She was a bit fat and mean, and María tried to avoid her if she could. A few days ago Lydia told her she was going to tie María to a chair and kill her mom and dad in front of her. "What are you doing?"

"I'm petting the horse."

"I'm petting the horse," Devin repeated in a dumb-sounding voice. She was tall and thin and had dark skin. "Why are you so stupid?"

"I'm not stupid."

"Yes, you are," Lydia said.

"No, I'm not."

"What's it like to be stupid?"

"I'm not stupid."

"You are. You're a stupid head. You're a stupid head who carries a doll around. Everyone thinks so."

María's eyes became hot and wet.

"Are you going to cry?" Lydia said.

"No."

"Go on, crybaby. Cry. That's what crybabies do."

"I'm not a crybaby."

"What's in your hand?" She grabbed the stack of leaves María had been holding.

"Those are mine!"

"Why are you carrying leaves?"

"They're mine!"

Lydia ripped the leaves into little bits and threw them up in the air, so the wind scattered them about.

"Ewww!" Devin said, covering her mouth with her hands.

She pointed at the horse.

Lydia shrieked in amusement.

María turned to see the horse, but she didn't know what she was supposed to be looking at.

"Is that…?" Devin said.

"Gross!"

"So gross!"

Lydia whispered in Devin's ear. Devin listened, then began nodding and giggling.

"Look, María," Lydia said, pointing. "The horse has five legs."

María noticed the fifth leg for the first time. It was pink and crusty and peeling. Also, it was shorter than the other four. It didn't even touch the ground.

"Do you see it, María?" Lydia asked.

"Yes."

"It needs help."

"Huh?"

"You need to pull it down so it touches the ground."

"I don't want to."

"If you don't, the horse will fall over. It will die. It will be your fault."

"I don't want to touch it."

"We'll tell Mrs. Ramirez you killed the horse."

She looked at the leg. Maybe she could just pull it quickly. Then the horse would be okay, and Lydia and Devin would leave her alone.

She stepped to the fence.

"Go on!" Lydia urged. "Pull it down."

"I can't reach it."

"Climb under the fence."

María hesitated.

"Hurry up! Climb under the fence."

María went down on all fours. Leaving Angela on the ground, she crawled beneath the fence rail. Then she was right next to the horse.

"Grab it!" Lydia said.

"Pull it!" Devin said.

María grabbed the horse's leg. It was smooth and thick and warm. She pulled it. But instead of going down it went up, breaking free of her grip, disappearing into some kind of sheath.

María looked back at Lydia and Devin, confused.

They were bent over, laughing so hard tears came to their eyes.

María smiled hesitantly, wondering what she had done that was so funny, and wondering if maybe they would be nice to her now.

JACK

1

I heard them before I saw them. Pita was speaking in Spanish in a long monologue. By the sound of the choppy, unnatural cadence of her speech, she was reciting what she'd memorized for the documentary.

Sure enough, when the trees filtered away, she was standing before the hut that contained the shrine, over-enunciating her words and gesturing to the dolls attached to the wall, as though she were an action reporter covering a breaking news event. Pepper stood ten feet away, his video camera perched on a tripod. He was watching Pita on a small LCD screen. Nitro was behind him, arms folded, legs slightly apart, his back to me. Jesus sat against a tree, the leg with the sprained ankle stretched straight before him.

When Pita saw Rosa and me she did a double-take. She stopped midsentence, her mouth ajar.

The others turned, confused, surprised.

Rosa shied behind my legs and gripped my hand tighter.

"Who the fuck is that, chavo?" Nitro blurted.

Jesus and Pepper were both saying something to me. I didn't have time to reply to either because Pita had come hurrying over. She unclipped the microphone from her collar, squatted next to me, and starting spurting off Spanish to the girl.

Rosa mumbled something back. Pita frowned. They exchanged a few more words.

"What?" I said.

Pita looked up at me. "She says she doesn't want to speak Spanish because you can't understand."

"Sounds logical to me."

"What did you do, brainwash her?"

Rosa pressed tighter against my legs. I peeled her off me and crouched so we were at eye level. "What's the matter, Rosa? Remember, they're my friends."

"I don't like the dork," she said.

"Dork?" Pita was indignant. "Me?"

Rosa pointed past her to Nitro. "Him."

Nitro guffawed.

"That's okay," I said. "Nobody likes him. But you can talk to Pita. She's nice."

"What are you doing here, honey?" Pita asked. "Where are your parents?"

"They're at home."

"So who are you with?"

Rosa threw her arms around my neck and buried her head into my chest. I hesitated, then patted her on the back. "Where's Eliza?" I asked.

Pita looked around, as if just noticing she was gone. "I don't know."

"Nitro," I said, "go find Eliza. She shouldn't be on her own."

"Fuck you, Jack Goff."

"Do it!"

For a moment I didn't think he was going to, he was going to stand there in stupid defiance. Then Jesus gave him a godfather nod.

Scowling, Nitro wandered off into the trees.

To Pepper I said, "Do you have any more of those candy bars

you had on the boat?"

"Lucky I have a sweet tooth," he said, nodding. "I have one more." He went to his bag, retrieved the candy bar, and brought it to Rosa. "Here you go."

Rosa raised her head from my shoulder. She took the candy bar and said, "Are you Pepper?"

Pepper beamed. "Have you seen my show?"

"Jack told me your name," she said.

"And did he tell you Nitro was a dork?" Pita asked.

"Who's Nitro—? Oh, you mean Muscles?"

Pita shot me a look.

"Nice, Jack," Jesus said.

"Here," I said to Rosa. "Let me do that." I unwrapped the candy bar, then handed it back to her.

She took a small bite, then another, and another, all the while chewing quickly.

"The poor thing's ravenous," Pita said.

"Rosa," I said, easing her away from me and standing. "Can you give us a sec? I'm going to tell them what you told me, okay?"

She nodded without taking her eyes from the candy bar.

I moved a dozen yards away, indicating for Pita and Pepper to join me. Jesus got up and hobbled over on his good foot. When we were out of earshot, I said, "I found her beneath a bed in what I think must have been Solano's house."

Pita frowned. "What was she doing?"

"Hiding from you?" Jesus said.

"Not me exactly," I said. "She told me she came here with her brother, Miguel, and her brother's girlfriend, Lucinda. Yesterday, by the sound of it. Anyway, she says she was catching frogs or something when she heard her brother scream. He told her to run, and she did. She hasn't seen him since."

They stared at me like I'd just told them I'd been abducted by aliens.

"That's what she told me," I insisted.

"My God, Jack!" Pepper said. "Do you think she's telling the truth?"

"Why would she lie?"

Pita said, "Maybe she's mad at her brother so she made up this fantasmal story?"

"Fantasmal?"

"Jack!"

I shrugged. "I don't know. She seems genuinely frightened. Besides, wouldn't her brother have gone looking for her? The island is big, but not that big. Wouldn't we have crossed paths with him by now?"

"We didn't know the girl was here," Jesus pointed out.

"She was hiding. If her brother was looking for her, he'd be calling out and stuff."

"Okay, hold on a minute," Pepper said. "We're jumping ahead. We need to slow down. What happened to her brother? What made him warn her away?"

I hesitated. "She thinks a ghost attacked him."

"A ghost?" Pita's eyes widened. "You mean, the ghost of the little girl who haunts this island?"

"Come on, Pita," I said.

"Come on, what?"

"This is serious. Something's happened—"

"I am being serious, Jack."

"You think a ghost attacked Rosa's brother?"

"Why not?" she said defiantly.

"She's entitled to her opinion, Jack," Jesus said.

I looked at Pepper for support. He might like to debate the existence of ghosts and spirits and whatnot, yet he was a pragmatic guy, and I didn't think he really believed what he preached. It all went part and parcel with his act.

Nevertheless, he was looking at his shoes, unwilling to back me. He knew how religious Pita was, how superstitious. He wasn't going to reveal himself as a false prophet, rain on her parade.

"Okay, whatever, ghost, no ghost," I said. "Bottom line, we know one-eighth of fuck all right now. We're just speculating.

So what's important, what we have to do, is find Rosa's camp. We can figure out what happened then."

"Easier said than done, Jack," Jesus said. "This island has to be a couple of hundred acres easily. And it's all jungle."

Pita had taken her mobile phone from her pocket and was holding it up in the air. "No reception," she said.

"I could have told you that," Pepper said. "We're in the middle of nowhere. There isn't a radio tower for kilometers."

"Rosa?" I called. "Do you think you can find the way back to your camp?"

"I don't know." She looked about helplessly. "I don't think so."

"How did you guys get to the island? Did you take one of those gondolas?"

"*Trajineras*," Pita said.

"*Trajineras*," I amended.

Rosa shook her head. "We took a canoe."

"So if we found the canoe, do you think you could find your camp?"

She nodded. "Easy."

2

Nitro and Elizaveta returned a few minutes later—Elizaveta had gone off to take some pictures with her small digital camera—and we gave them a quick rundown of everything Rosa told us. Like the rest of us, Elizaveta was visibly agitated by the possibility a murder had occurred on the island. Nitro's reaction, however, was the exact opposite: he seemed pumped, like a Hardy Boy keen to tackle a new mystery. He even went so far as to scavenge a stick to defend us with.

We didn't want to split up given a killer might be lurking about, but we didn't have a choice. Jesus's sprained ankle made him immobile. So in the end we decided to divide the group in half. Elizaveta and Pita would stay behind with Jesus, while Nitro, Pepper, and I (with Rosa guiding us) would set off along the bank to circumvent the perimeter of the island in search of the canoe.

Nitro and his stick took vanguard. Pepper and I came next with Rosa between us, holding our hands. We followed a strip of land that ran between the tree-line and the water. The ground was mostly hardpan and scrub, occasionally overrun with huge ferns and waist-high vegetation, but it was relatively easy-going. The dolls were strung up in greater concentration here, along the waterfront, than anywhere else on the island, though no one mentioned them. The fun and games were over; our little day trip had suddenly become very serious business.

The weather continued to worsen, and quickly. A wind picked up shivering foliage and small twigs, and it started to rain lightly. The clouds blocked out the sun completely, so everything was lit in a premature, felt-gray twilight, more dusk than midafternoon.

"Great," Pepper said, holding out his free hand to verify it was raining.

"Maybe it will blow over," I said.

"I checked the forecast this morning," he said. "The meteorologist didn't say anything about rain today. I swear."

"What channel do you watch?" Nitro asked him.

"Canal de las Estrellas."

"Switch to El Trece. The weather girl on that one..." He whistled. "Major smoking hot front, you know what I'm saying?"

"Do you have a girlfriend, Muscles?" I asked him.

"What's it to you, Jack Goff?"

"I take that as a no."

"Take it whichever way you want, brother."

"Maybe the ponytail's the problem," I went on. "You should have left it in the nineties."

Nitro laughed. "We go to a bar babe-hunting, you and me,

I'll outscore you ten-zero, you better believe that."

"Babe-hunting?"

"The girl I'm pounding right now, she's vaginamite."

"Vaginamite?" The guy really was a douchebag—a prurient douchebag.

"Fucking right, Jack Goff."

"Watch your language around Rosa."

"I don't mind," she piped up.

I glanced down at her. She was watching the ground where she walked, almost skipping to keep pace with Pepper and I. Suddenly I felt absurdly proud of her. She believed her brother was dead. She believed a ghost shared the island with us. She'd spent a night on her own beneath a bed. And here she was telling me she didn't mind if someone cussed around her? She was made of something tougher than the rest of us put together.

"Can I ask you something, Rosa?" I asked her.

She bobbed her head. "If you want."

"How long was Miguel seeing Lucinda for?"

"Hmmm. Maybe two months? Maybe more?"

"Did they ever fight?"

"No, not really. Why?"

"Well, I've been thinking," I said, "and maybe Lucinda got angry at Miguel yesterday and did something to him. It might not have been on purpose, not completely. It might have been an accident, sort of."

"An accident?"

"Maybe she wanted to hurt him a bit, but she ended up hurting him a lot. Maybe that's why he screamed..."

Rosa seemed to think about this, then she shook her head. "I don't think Lucinda would even want to hurt Miguel a bit. She was really nice."

"But why would a ghost want to hurt him?"

"Because this is *her* island. She doesn't want us here."

"That's what Miguel told you?"

Rosa nodded gravely.

"Hey, Rosa," Pepper said. "Do you want to be on TV?"

"She's not going in your documentary, Pepper!" I said.

"Why not? She'd be great."

"Why can't I be on TV?" she asked me.

"Because," I said.

"Because what?"

"Just because...your mother wouldn't like it," I added.

Rosa frowned at this. "You're probably right. She doesn't like me doing anything fun."

"She let you come to this island though...?"

"No, she didn't."

"She doesn't know you're here?"

Rosa shook her head. "My sister—my oldest one—is getting married soon. She and my mom went to a special party all weekend. Miguel was babysitting me."

"And he brought you all the way here?"

Rosa nodded. "Because he couldn't leave me alone."

"What about your father?" Pepper asked. "Couldn't he look after you?"

"He's living in France right now."

"He works there?"

She nodded again. "He's an *embajador*. I don't know the English."

"A diplomat?"

"I think that's it."

"What school do you go to?" Nitro asked.

"Greengates."

"The British international school?" Pepper said. "That's where Jesus and Pita went!"

"They went to my school?"

Pepper nodded. "Their dad was rich like yours. But that was a long time ago."

"How long?"

"More than ten years."

"Wow, I didn't know they were so old."

"Don't tell Pita that," I said.

"She's like as old as my mom—"

Nitro called out abruptly, cutting Rosa off.

Twenty feet ahead was the canoe.

3

The canoe was pulled up onto the bank so it wouldn't float away. Scuffs and dents marred the aluminum hull. Two wooden paddles lay within it, propped against the yoke.

"This is the one you came in?" I asked Rosa, using my hand to shield my eyes against the rain, which had become a steady drizzle. The once mirror-smooth canal was now a simmering boil. Waves crashed against the bank, the penumbra of their spray dissolving into fine droplets.

She nodded. "That means the campground isn't far. It's just that way, past a big pond." She pointed to the trees.

I hesitated. "Maybe it would be better if you stayed here—say, with Pepper—while Nitro and I checked it out. What do you think?"

"Why?"

I didn't want to splinter the group further, but I hadn't been thinking clearly before when I'd suggested Rosa lead us to the campground. Exposing her to whatever might have happened to her brother had not been one of my better ideas. "Pepper's a big scaredy cat," I told her by way of explanation. "He doesn't want to go to the campground. He needs someone to look after him."

Rosa studied Pepper. "He doesn't look like a scaredy cat. He looks like the Purple People Eater."

"I should tell you, young miss," Pepper said, indicating his clothing, "this is a very fashionable ensemble."

"Well, I guess I can look after him."

I said to Pepper, "You don't mind staying back?"

"As long as you two don't dawdle."

"You should find some shelter."

He pointed to a nearby magnolia, the branches of which seemed to be bending beneath the weight of its wet blooms and foliage. "We'll wait under that."

"Okay," I said. "And remember, we'll be within hearing distance. So if you see anybody, yell."

Pepper tried a smile. "That's reassuring, Jack. Thanks."

4

The canopy and understory blocked out some of the rain and the wind. However, there was no path like the one I'd followed across the island earlier. Instead Nitro and I were forced to circumvent the tall trees and duck low-sprouting branches. A tangle of broadleaf shrubs and palms and woody plants obscured much of the ground, so we didn't really know where we were putting our feet down. Vipers could be found across Mexico, and their bite was dangerous to humans. I hoped if there were any on this island they abided by the old adage that they should be more scared of me than I was of them.

To take my mind off snakes, I turned my attention to what might await us at the campground. I wanted to believe that Rosa was wrong, that her brother hadn't been attacked, that it was an uncanny misunderstanding. But how could this be the case? She had heard him screaming. He had told her to run. So something had happened, something bad.

Which brought me back to the million-dollar question: Who would attack him? Rosa said Lucinda was nice, and she and Miguel didn't fight, but who knew what went on between them in private? Besides, there was no rule to say nice people didn't do bad things, especially in the heat of the moment.

Then again, if Lucinda suddenly lost the plot, why would Miguel tell Rosa to run? Wouldn't he instead implore her to help him? Telling her to run implied he thought she was in danger too. Yet why would he think she would be in danger from Lucinda if Lucinda's beef was with him?

And then there was the whole problem with the canoe. Why hadn't Lucinda taken it back to the docks? Why had she remained on the island?

To search for Rosa?

To silence the only witness?

"Nitro," I said, his name coming off my tongue awkwardly. I don't think I'd ever addressed him as anything but Muscles. "Any theories on what might have happened you're not sharing?"

"Why do you care what I think, chavo?" he said without looking back.

It was a good question. I suppose because while the others would have been content to play ostrich until the boatman returned to take us back to the docks, Nitro had been all action, gung-ho to discover answers, and that was something I respected.

I couldn't bring myself to tell him this, of course, and I was about to tell him to forget it, when he said, "Money."

"You think Miguel owed Lucinda money?"

"Think big, chavo. Her father's an ambassador. That means big bucks in Mexico."

"You mean a kidnapping?" Kidnappings were serious business in Mexico, a daily occurrence, the reason people like Jesus often had a bodyguard or two with him in public. Even I was a target simply because I was a foreigner, which was the reason I never took gypsy cabs. There were, I'd been told, roughly two thousand kidnappings a year. This was a conservative figure, as many were never reported because the police weren't trusted not to be involved. "You think someone would follow him all the way here just to kidnap him?"

Nitro shrugged. "A few hours work for a potential big payoff, why not?"

"What about Lucinda then?"

"What about her?"

"If they took Miguel," I said, pushing a branch out of my

way, "what happened to her?"

"Who's to say she wasn't the target? She might come from a wealthier family than Miguel. Unfortunately for him, wrong place, wrong time. Or maybe they took her too. Or maybe they offed her. No witnesses—"

Nitro came to an abrupt halt. I looked past him and saw the pond ahead and to the left.

Nitro put his finger to his lips, and we continued forward in silence. Twenty yards on he mumbled something and began moving more quickly. I stuck behind him, searching for what he'd seen.

I saw the body a moment later.

5

We entered the glade where Miguel and Lucinda had made camp. A dozen dolls, maybe two dozen, swayed from branches in the wind and rain, their glass eyes and evocative smiles all too lifelike. Two backpacks, one green and one orange, and two sleeping bags, both rolled up, sat on the grassy ground at the base of a cedar. Next to these items were a scattering of clothing: shorts, a T-shirt, boxers, a dress, a lacy bra, silk panties.

In the middle of the clearing lay Miguel—at least I assumed it was Miguel. He was facedown, naked, his back shredded with what appeared to be stab wounds. Red-brown blood covered his bare skin, from the nape of his neck to his buttocks.

My pulse quickened at the ghastly sight. My legs turned rubbery, as if they no longer wanted to support my weight. I opened my mouth to say something, but I didn't know what was appropriate.

He was dead, Miguel was dead, nothing now but offal and decay.

Nitro knelt next to the body, which was thick with flies. I hadn't noticed their maddening buzzing until right then, though now it seemed to fill the air, loud and angry. Same with the smell. I hadn't detected it before. But it hit me like a truck, a maggoty stench.

"Eleven," Nitro said, examining the cuts. "Someone stabbed him eleven times. Looks like they used a serrated knife."

Nitro rolled the body onto its back.

"Fuck me," I said softly. I wanted to look away, but I couldn't. The morbidity, the wrongness, transfixed me.

The man's eyes were missing.

In the next instant a startled centipede, sinuous and black with bright yellow legs and a flattened head bearing probing antennae, scurried out of the left bloodied orbit, down the once handsome face to the ground, and wiggled beneath the leaf litter.

Nitro glanced back at me, scowling. "I think we might have stumbled into some deep shit, chavo."

1955

1

Patricia Diaz entered through the front doors of María's school, trying to ignore the apprehension that had been churning in her gut ever since the phone call from the principal the day before. She had been summoned to the school on several previous occasions to discuss her daughter's academic development or bullying or other sensitive topics. However, these meetings had always been with María's teachers, never with the resident psychologist.

In the front office a secretary told her the directions to the psychologist's office, and a few minutes later Patricia was knocking on a door with a bronze plate attached to it that read: Dr. Lola Cavazos.

The door opened and a woman wearing a champagne-colored dress smiled at her. "Mrs. Diaz?" She had an urchin haircut and a friendly demeanor. She stuck out her hand. "I'm Dr. Cavazos."

"Good afternoon," she said, shaking.

"Please come in. I'm so happy you were able to come this morning. May I get you a cup of tea?"

"No, I'm fine, thank you."

"Have a seat." She gestured to a seat on one side of a desk, while she settled into the seat on the other side. "How are you today?"

"A little nervous to be here."

"Understandably. So let me get to the point. I'd like to talk to you about your daughter, María. Specifically, how she is coping in grade four. First, however, let me begin by saying I've had the pleasure of spending some time with her over the last week, and she is a very well-mannered child."

Patricia smiled. "Yes, she is."

"She is also sweet and helpful."

"She always has been."

"Mrs. Diaz, from what I understand, you've had several meetings with her teachers in the past. What have they told you about her academic performance?"

"That she's a little behind some of her classmates. Her last teacher, Mrs. Ramirez, said she was having difficulty concentrating and was easily distracted."

"And her general behavior?"

"She hasn't made many friends. She...keeps to herself, I guess you would say."

"Would you say, generally speaking, her behavior resembles the behavior of other eight year olds?"

Patricia wanted to say yes, but she wasn't here to deceive anybody. She was here to get María help. "No, I suppose not."

"If you were to name an age you believe her to be functioning at...?"

"Perhaps a seven year old." She hesitated. "Perhaps even a six year old."

Dr. Cavazos nodded. "From the assessments I have done, I would say she has the overall skillset of a five year old, so we are both pretty close—"

"Five?" Patricia's stomach sank.

"The point, Mrs. Diaz, is that we are in agreement that she is progressing at a much slower rate than her classmates not just academically but in all areas. Would you agree with this statement?"

"Well, yes. But *five*... Are you sure? I know she's a little shy around other students—"

"Yes, I've noticed that. Nevertheless, I don't think it's a case of mere shyness. I don't believe she can carry a two-way conversation with her peers. Also, she seems to have a difficult time remembering things. For example, she struggles to retain simple math facts that should come very easy to someone of her age. She also can't recall details of a book that she has read only minutes before."

"I've tried to help her with her math and reading at home. Her father works late. But I usually spend an hour with her each evening."

"And how has this been working out?"

"I think it's helping. I know she's a bit forgetful. But she's still very young."

"You are aware that she has temper tantrums?"

"Don't all children?" she said with a bit too much asperity. She was beginning to feel as though the psychologist was attacking María.

"They do, certainly," Dr. Cavazos said calmly. "Such outbursts arise because young children have difficulties expressing themselves, especially complex emotions. Having said that, by grade four they have usually grown beyond this stage. María, it seems, hasn't. She still can't fully express herself, what she wants to say, what she's feeling. Which, I believe, is why she isolates herself from other children. And why she has her temper tantrums. She's frustrated." Dr. Cavazos paused. "Mrs. Diaz, have you heard of intelligence quotient tests—or IQ tests?"

"I believe so. They measure a person's intelligence."

Dr. Cavazos nodded. "You can't study for them. They test how individuals solve brand new problems, both verbal and visual. Does the word 'idiot' or 'imbecile' or 'moron' mean anything to you?"

"I don't think so, no."

"In the psychiatric community, those with an IQ between zero and twenty-five are referred to as idiots. They can't respond to stimuli or communicate with any level of competency. Those with an IQ between twenty-six and fifty are termed imbeciles. They are stalled mentally at about six years of age. And those with an IQ between fifty-one and seventy are termed morons. Morons can communicate with others and learn common tasks, though they often need specific instruction or guidance." Dr. Cavazos retrieved a chart from the shelf behind her and placed it on the desk, facing Patricia. It was divided into several different sections, the bottom one labeled idiot, the top, genius. "Here is a representation of where most students score." She pointed to the range between ninety and one hundred ten. "On both visual and verbal problem-solving, however, María scored here." She pointed to seventy. "For example, when I asked her how a banana, apple, and orange are alike, she said, 'Pear.' That's not quite...it's related to what I said...but it misses the point that they are all fruit."

Patricia didn't know how much more of this she wanted to hear, and she said, "Please just say what you have to say, Dr. Cavazos."

"Well, the good news is that María isn't functioning at the level of an idiot or imbecile."

"But she's not normal either. She's...what did you say? A moron?"

Dr. Cavazos nodded. "She can take care of herself. She doesn't have any physical challenges. She has some typical life skills. But, yes, she does fall into the moron range."

Patricia swallowed the tightness in her throat. "Well, how long is this...this phase...going to last? How long until she grows out of it?"

The psychologist hesitated. "In my experience, Mrs. Diaz, it isn't a phase, and one doesn't grow out of it."

Patricia stared blankly. What was this woman telling her? María wasn't just developing slowly. She was in fact...what was the word people used...feebleminded? "I'll spend more time with her at home," she said softly, quickly. "I'll help her —"

"I'm sorry, Mrs. Diaz," Dr. Cavazos said. "What afflicts María is not something you can 'fix.' Now, don't get me wrong," she added. "María can and will continue to learn and add to her skillset. She can love and be loved—"

"But if she continues to fall further behind her classmates, how is she going to graduate? How will she cope in high school? How will she ever get a job?"

The psychologist leaned forward. "I don't think you understand fully what I am saying, Mrs. Diaz. María will never graduate. She will never attend high school, or college for that matter. And she will almost certainly never hold a job. She is going to need special care."

"For the rest of her life?"

"That's correct. But thankfully there are special schools where she can get the help she needs, and where she will be among others like her, where she will no longer be singled out and bullied."

Patricia felt all of a sudden hot and woozy at the same time. Then she began to cry. "It's my fault. Her birth, it went on for far too long. I wasn't pushing right. She was distressed. The doctor had to perform a caesarian section..."

"No, Mrs. Diaz. María's ailment is not the result of something you did or didn't do, so don't blame yourself."

"Oh dear me...my María...my poor María..."

"I know how hard all this must be for you to take in, Mrs. Diaz. I know how hard it was for me to tell you—"

Patricia stood decisively. "Where is María right now?"

"She should be in class, I imagine."

"Would you please fetch her for me? Tell her I'll be waiting out front the school. I'd like to spend some time with her."

2

María burst out the front doors, her book bag slung over her shoulder, Angela gripped in one hand.

That doll, Patricia thought with vitriol. *I never should have let her keep that doll. Maybe if I'd put my foot down years ago, maybe she wouldn't be...*

"Mamma!" María said, her face lighting up. "Why are you at school?"

Patricia knelt on the pavement and opened her arms wide. María crashed into her, hugging her tightly—and in that moment Patricia realized her daughter was the same daughter she had always known, and she would continue to love her, she had a duty to love her, feebleminded or not. "I thought you would like some ice cream," she said, brushing fresh tears from her eyes. "Would you like some ice cream?"

"Yes, please! Can I have chocolate? Can I have chocolate? Can I?"

"You can have anything you want, sweetheart."

"What about after? Do I have to go back to school after?"

Patricia stood and took her child's hand. "That's something we're going to talk about."

ELIZAVETA

1

Not long after Jack and the others left, a mild wind picked up, and the slate-gray sky began to spit. Then, maybe twenty minutes after that, the sky let loose, unleashing torrents of driving rain, which now plinked against the hut's corrugated iron roof, sounding like a carnival Wheel of Fortune at the height of its spin. Elizaveta sat cross-legged on the floor, her back against a support post. Jesus and Pita were seated across from her. Dolls covered almost every inch of wall behind them, their eyes glinting in the murky half-light, shadows carving hard edges into their round child-like faces.

The first peal of thunder rolled across the sky. Elizaveta glanced out the hut's door. Through the swaying trees she could see a section of the canal. It looked to be all foam and spray. No way the boatman was coming back any time soon, she thought. Which meant they would be spending the night on the island, cold and wet. She wondered whether the others had found Rosa's campground. And if so, had Miguel and Lucinda been there? Were they okay? Or were they injured, dead, or missing altogether?

Elizaveta couldn't believe their newfound circumstances. How had they gotten tied up in a possible murder mystery? This was supposed to be an easy day out. A relaxing cruise down the canals, sun and Mexican food, a lighthearted adventure, that was it.

They should have listened to the boatman, she knew. They should have shelved the documentary and returned to Cuemanco with him. If they had, she would have been back in the casita, or guesthouse, on the estate in San Angel where she worked as a governess. It was currently home for her. And home was the place you wanted to be during one of Mexico's summer tropical storms because they could be absolutely vicious. Last month she'd been in Acapulco with Jesus when a tropical storm struck hundreds of miles off Mexico's Pacific Coast. While the resort they were staying at continued to operate normally, most of the outlying neighborhoods lost access to power and water. Streets turned into gushing rivers while landslides shut down highways. On the low-income periphery of the city, steep hills funneled rainwater into neighborhoods of cinderblock homes, washing many away. During the drive to the airport, which had also flooded, Elizaveta had seen people with picks and shovels digging in mounds of mud and rubble, perhaps for buried friends and relatives.

That was one thing Mexico and Russia had in common, she thought: endemic poverty. The difference was that the poor in Mexico took it in stride and were for the most part content and upbeat, while the poor in Russia were angry, bitter, always grumbling about how bad things were.

Elizaveta had been born on Vasilyevsky Island in Saint Petersburg. Her parents were both journalists, critical of the Cold War and the oppressive authoritarian regime in power at the time. Consequently, the KGB kept them under constant watch. Elizaveta remembered a small Russian-made Lada would follow their car around the city, and a man in a dark suit would always seem to be wherever they went, keeping tabs on them. Her father told her their phones were tapped, their apartment bugged, their mail opened. He also believed their government-provided housekeeper filed frequent reports on them. Then one day when Elizaveta was ten years old she came home from grade school to find the man in the dark suit waiting for her. He told her that her parents had been taken away and she would not see them again, and she never did. The next day she was installed in a state-sponsored orphanage that was like a mini gulag for children. Many infants had fetal alcohol disorders, and it wasn't uncommon to see them sitting by themselves, staring blankly at nothing, or knocking their heads against the walls. The older children such as herself were frequently mistreated, abused, even "rented out" to local farmers to work on their farms. Needless to say, many of Elizaveta's Dickensian housemates became psychologically scarred. One girl she got to know well picked up the unhealthy habit of rocking herself to sleep each night, while another rubbed the same part of her head so frequently she went bald there over time.

Elizaveta left the orphanage at the age of fifteen, in accordance with Soviet guidelines. She moved into a room in a state-subsidized Kommunalka, or communal apartment, in which none of the floors, walls, and pipes seemed to line up right. She shared the kitchen, two toilet closets, and a single bath with six other families. Although the building was warm during winter, it was not uncommon for the heat, or hot water, to shut off without warning—which had happened to her on several minus-thirty-degree days, and which was why she kept a giant jug of water handy so she could flush the toilet or wash dishes if needed.

The Soviet Union collapsed when Elizaveta was eighteen. Retail stores were routinely empty, and you had to wait in long queues for food supplies. You never threw out a vodka bottle because you could get small change for it at a recycling point. People with PhDs drove taxis, while neighbors banded together to chase off looters.

For the next four years Elizaveta pursued a university degree in education, focusing on English, French, and Spanish. She had grown sick of her homeland—sick of the daily indignities, the endless prostitution of everybody and everything —and her plan was to move to Western Europe or the United States. Upon graduating, however, she discovered there were few legal channels for low-paid employment abroad such as teaching. Elizaveta considered simply getting on a plane to the West with the intention of never returning—the Russian Federation was not the USSR; you were no longer persecuted or imprisoned if you applied for a visa—yet she hesitated. If she violated her visa regulations, she would not have any legal status in her new country, which was why most Russian women who attempted such an escape ended up trafficked as sex workers.

In the end Elizaveta accepted a job in an elementary school in Saint Petersburg, where she taught for several years. Life in the new Russia improved slightly, but a pair of sneakers were still something you showed off, and a VCR was still a luxury far out of her reach. Then, in 1997, when she was twenty-five years old, her close friend, Olga, who worked as a nanny for a wealthy family, told her the family was moving to Mexico— and interviewing for a governess of Russian nationality who could speak Spanish.

2

Elizaveta folded her arms more tightly across her chest, to ward off the damp chill in the hut. She told herself to be positive. She shouldn't be thinking about being back in San Angel. They'd made their decision not to return with the boatman to Cuemanco, they couldn't change that, so they had to deal with the situation the best they could. Besides, who would have thought the weather would have deteriorated so implacably and quickly?

Pita examined Jesus's ankle, pressing her fingers to it gently. The ankle had turned a virulent purple and had swollen to the size of a melon.

"Stop it," Jesus told her. "That's not helping any."

"We need to reduce the swelling," she replied.

"Got a spare bag of frozen peas?" he remarked.

"Hopefully it will be better in the morning."

"Fucking Jack," Jesus grumbled.

"He didn't mean it," Elizaveta said. Her Spanish accent wasn't native, it never would be, but her Spanish was about as fluent as her English.

"Didn't mean it?" Jesus said to her. He'd pushed his Aviators up onto his forehead and was looking at her with incredulity. "Did you see how hard he shoved me?"

"Pepper said Nitro started it."

Jesus waved dismissively. "Pepper doesn't know anything."

"I saw you and Nitro double-teaming him."

"You're taking Jack's side?" Pita asked. Her long-lashed eyes were dark and disapproving. She shot a Camel from her pack and lit up.

"I'm not taking any sides," Elizaveta said. "I'm saying Jack didn't mean to make you sprain your ankle, Jesus. He was going after Nitro. You were in way."

"He caught me by surprise, that's all," Jesus said. "I wouldn't have fallen otherwise."

"And Jack has a bad temper, Eliza," Pita said. "He has to learn to keep it under control."

"Nitro's a bully," Elizaveta said.

Jesus chuckled. "What grade are we in?"

"To tell you truth, Jesus, I don't like him. I don't know why you like him. You two are so different."

"Nitro isn't a bully," Pita said, blowing smoke out the corner of her mouth. "He's actually a very nice guy when you get to know him."

Elizaveta didn't say anything. She knew why Pita was defending Nitro. She was fooling around with him behind Jack's back.

They'd all been at a beach house party two months or so ago. Jesus and Elizaveta picked up Pita on the way there, though Jack stayed behind. There was some important American football game on the television he wanted to watch. The beach house was packed with people when they arrived. Jesus and Pita went into mingle mode, working the room. Elizaveta poured herself a glass of wine from the bottle she'd brought, left the rest in the kitchen, and went to the deck for a cigarette. She much preferred going to bars or clubs than these private parties. There was a great community of ex-pats living in Mexico City, and she knew many of them: Russians, French, Canadians, Australians, a few New Zealanders, a lot of Americans and British. They were all intelligent and friendly, and she always had a good time with them. The people around her that evening, on the other hand, fell mainly into two groups: young Mexican socialites who didn't work and lived off their parents' credit cards, and older businessmen who drank whiskey and smoked cigars. The bratty socialites looked down on Elizaveta because she was a "salary worker," while the businessmen often treated her like a prostitute until she firmly put them in their place.

Around midnight Elizaveta asked Jesus if he was ready to leave. He wasn't. He was surrounded by admirers hanging on to his every word, most holding one of his brewery's beers in their hands. Tired of talking to strangers, she decided to walk along the beach. The night was cool and dry. The ocean droned on endlessly while waves lapped gently at her bare feet. She walked for close to thirty minutes, and she was on her way back to the beach house when she ran into Pita and Nitro. She didn't know it was them at first. They were little more than amorphous shapes on the sand beneath a palm tree. Then she heard Pita speaking in that throaty voice of hers, and Nitro replying in that gruff way of his. Elizaveta froze, dumbstruck. She was contemplating whether to make her presence known, to ask them what they were doing out here, when she realized they weren't merely talking; they were making out. She hurried back to the party, told Jesus she wasn't feeling well, and took a taxi home.

She'd seen Pita and Nitro at parties together three times since, but Jack had been present at each one. She'd been tempted to confront Pita, or even tell Jack what she'd witnessed. She didn't, because she'd been hoping it had been a one-time thing, a drunken fling. For a while it seemed this might be the case until last night at Jack's place. Jack had been inside refilling his drink, and Pita had been trying to convince Jesus to invite Nitro to the Island of the Dolls the next day. Jesus didn't want to, given the animosity between Nitro and Jack. Pita, however, was persistent, arguing that Jack was so drunk he likely wouldn't even get up in the morning. So Jesus rang Nitro, who confirmed he would come on the spot.

Again, Elizaveta didn't confront Pita. It wasn't her business to intervene. Besides, these types of things, romantic affairs, never remained secret for long. Jack would discover Pita's infidelity on his own. It was simply a matter of time.

At least, that's what she told herself. But there was another reason she remained silent: Pita was vindictive. Elizaveta didn't want to get into her bad books for fear Pita might turn Jesus against Elizaveta herself. Pita wielded a surprising amount of control over her brother, and if push came to shove, Elizaveta didn't know with whom Jesus's loyalty would lie. If he dumped Elizaveta, what would become of her then? The twin girls she was tutoring turned fourteen this year; they would enter boarding school in autumn. Consequently, she would be out of a job, and her visa expired early next year. She would have no choice but to return to Russia...to poverty. And she couldn't do that. She'd worked too hard to get to where she was in society now. She couldn't go back to waiting an hour in line for a loaf of bread, or to teaching fifty-hour weeks for a couple of thousand Rubles—the equivalent to what she currently earned in one morning.

"What's taking them so long?" Jesus said, tugging Elizaveta

107

from her reflections. He was staring out the door at the slanted rain and the swaying trees.

"They've only been gone thirty minutes," Pita said.

"How long do you think it takes to walk the circumference of the island?"

She stubbed her cigarette on the floorboards. "Longer than thirty minutes."

"You know," Jesus said, "we're going to be stuck here overnight now. We're going to be stuck here with whoever killed Rosa's brother."

"We don't know he's dead," Elizaveta said. "All we know is he screamed."

"Eliza's right," Pita said. "He might just be injured."

Jesus shook his head. "Like Jack said, if he was simply injured, he would have gone looking for Rosa. He would have been calling her name. We would have heard him."

"What about Lucinda?" Elizaveta asked. "Do you think she was attacked too?"

"Of course," Jesus said. "Otherwise we would have come across her already."

"Unless she took canoe back to docks."

Jesus shook his head again. "If she did that, she would have gotten help. She would have returned with the police."

"So who attacked them?"

"Thugs," Jesus said.

"Thugs?" Elizaveta repeated skeptically. "Why would thugs be out here, in middle of nowhere?"

"We are."

"Well—why would thugs attack them?"

Jesus shrugged. "Rosa said her brother sent her away so he could be alone with Lucinda, right? So they were getting it on, these guys saw them, they got a hard on, they wanted a ride."

"You think they killed Miguel so they could rape and kill Lucinda?"

"There's a motive behind every murder," Jesus said. "And when the victim or victims are strangers, the motives are usually sex or money."

"What about a ghost?" Pita asked. "What are a ghost's motives?"

"We're not talking about ghosts," Jesus said.

"Why not? That's what Rosa thinks. She thinks a—"

"Rosa's a child, Pita. And that story about that little girl who drowned, that's all it is, a story, a legend—"

"Legends don't just materialize out of thin air," Pita said defiantly. "People don't just make them up."

"That's exactly what they do. And they tell other people, and other people tell other people. There's no such thing as ghosts, Pita. Okay?"

Pita glared at him. "What about Susana?"

Jesus opened his mouth, closed it, shook his head.

Elizaveta frowned. Susana—as in Pita's and Jesus's deceased younger sister? "What about Susana?" she asked.

Pita said, "She was our younger sister."

"I know. Jesus told me what happened."

"Did he tell you I saw her ghost when I was a kid?"

Elizaveta shook her head.

"Well, I did," Pita said. "It wasn't long after she drowned. I woke up in the middle of the night. She was at the bedroom window."

"Did she speak to you?"

"Yes—sort of. Not with her mouth. I don't know how to explain it. It was like I could feel her thoughts. They were inside me. She told me she was okay. She told me not to worry about her."

"Did you see her again?"

"No. Only that one time."

"Huh..." Elizaveta said, not sure what else to say.

"You were a kid," Jesus said.

"I didn't make it up!" she snapped.

"Fine. Say you did see Susana. That's one thing. But the ghost of a girl who died fifty years ago, haunting an island filled with dolls, killing two strangers who trespassed on it...?"

"All I'm saying," Pita said, "is that we need to keep an open mind. We don't know what happened, and we need to keep an open mind. Right, Eliza?"

"Yes, we should keep open mind," she said diplomatically. "We should also wait until the others return, hear what they've learned, before we jump to conclusions."

3

They returned some twenty minutes later. Pepper came first, his head ducked against the cauls of rain. Jack and Rosa followed, and finally Nitro, who carried a medium-sized canoe on his back. They were all drenched, their hair sticking to their heads, their clothes to their bodies. Elizaveta and Pita leapt to their feet and went to the hut's door, though they remained inside, out of the downpour.

"Jack!" Pita said. "Did you find the campsite? Did you find Miguel and Lucinda? What happened to them?"

Jack wiped water from his face and pointed to a different hut maybe thirty meters away. "I'm going to take Rosa there so you guys can talk. Pepper or Nitro can tell you everything."

He led Rosa away. They didn't run; the rain didn't seem to bother them as they were already as wet as they could get. Nitro dumped the canoe on the ground, then he and Pepper entered the hut. Their shoes squeaked, trailing mud. Nitro removed the elastic band from around his ponytail and shook his hair out like a dog. Pepper found a spot against the wall and sat down with a tired sigh. His complexion appeared ashen in the dying light. A grimness etched his usual merry features.

"Well?" Jesus demanded. "What happened, man?"

Pepper looked at Nitro, who was running his fingers through his hair in an effeminate manner. Nitro said, "It's not good, buddy."

"What do you mean?" Pita asked. "What happened? Are

they dead?"

"Miguel's dead. Stabbed eleven times."

"Eleven times!" Pita said.

Jesus swallowed. "What about Lucinda?"

Nitro shook his head. "No sign of her—except for her clothes."

"Her clothes?" Elizaveta said.

"Her clothes were on the ground, discarded. Same with Miguel's."

"She ran away naked?"

"They took her," Jesus mumbled.

Nitro frowned. "Who took her?"

"Thugs. They killed Miguel, raped Lucinda, and took her with them."

"I don't think thugs killed Miguel," Nitro said, tying his hair into a ponytail once more. He hesitated. "His eyes were missing. Cut out, or even plucked out, it was tough to tell."

4

Elizaveta folded her arms across her chest to ward off the chill that suddenly reached all the way to her bones, and stared big-eyed at the others, waiting for someone to explain what this might mean. Jesus seemed equally bewildered. Pita was pacing back and forth, her head down, brooding anxiously. Pepper wouldn't look at anybody. Only Nitro seemed calm.

"Why would someone take his eyes?" Elizaveta asked.

"He's sick, obviously," Nitro said.

"You think it's just one person?" Jesus said.

"Doing something like this, cutting out the eyes, it fits the profile of someone who kills for the thrill of it."

"You mean a serial killer?" Elizaveta said.

"Yeah," Nitro said. "And serial killers act alone."

"Bloody hell!" Jesus said. "There's a serial killer loose on the island?"

Nitro held up his hands. "We don't know that. Miguel was killed yesterday. The killer might have already left the island. We only saw the one canoe—Miguel's and Lucinda's."

"Lucinda," Elizaveta said. "What about her?"

Nitro shrugged. "This guy could have chased her down and killed her somewhere else on the island. Or he could have taken her with him. Without a body, there's no way to know."

"Should we go looking for her?"

Nitro shook his head. "I said this guy *might* have left the island. But he might not have either. Best thing to do is bunker down here for the night and leave as soon as the storm dies down."

"It wasn't a serial killer," Pita said, stopping her pacing and facing them. Her voice was flat, her color drained. "It was the ghost. I know none of you believe ghosts are real, but they are. Jesus said so."

"I never—"

"Not you! The real Jesus. It's in the Bible—"

"The Bible's just a book—

"A little girl died here!" Pita exploded. "She *died* here, perhaps in a horrible, inconsolable way. Her spirit's not at rest. Solano knew this. Look around you! Look at all the dolls! They're offerings to her, to appease her spirit." She glared at each of them in turn. "But now he's dead, and she's alone, and she's angry. Isn't this obvious? She killed Miguel and stole his eyes. So isn't this pretty damn obvious?"

1956

1

María stood at a tall window, her nose pressed against the glass, watching as her parents drove away. Then hedges obscured them from view and they were gone.

She didn't understand why they had brought her here. Her mother had told her it was a special school. She would like it. She would meet new friends. That all sounded okay. But then she said María would have to sleep at the school too. That wasn't good. That was terrifying. She wanted to keep living in her house. She wanted her room, her bed, her dolls. She glanced at Angela, who she held by the arm. "I want to go home," she said.

"Maybe you'll go home soon?" Angela said.

"I want to go *now*."

"I don't think you can."

"Why're my mom and dad leaving me here? What did I do —?"

The door to the room opened and a nun entered. She had a strawberry pudding face framed by tufts of white hair visible beneath her funny hat. Mean eyes peered out from behind silver-rimmed spectacles. "My name is Sister Lupita," she announced.

"My name's María."

"No, it's not, you snottery pup," she snapped in a completely different demeanor than when she'd spoken to María's parents. "It's 46. From this point on, your name is the number 46. Do you understand that?"

She didn't. "My name's María."

Sister Lupita leaned toward her. María didn't know what was coming and simply stood there. The nun clapped her hands against the side of María's head simultaneously with the flats of her palms. Pain lanced through her ears, and she almost fell over.

"Ow!" she cried.

"What's your name?"

"46!"

"Remember that. Now give me that doll."

"She's mine!"

Whack. Harder this time.

"Ow!"

"Give me the doll."

María began to cry.

Whack.

"Ow!"

"There will be no crying in this school. Crying is a sign of weakness, and weakness is the work of the devil. Now give me the doll."

Biting her bottom lip to stop the tears, María thrust Angela at the woman.

Sister Lupita took her and said, "Well, well, you can learn. Maybe you're not as dumb as everyone says."

2

Sister Lupita led María to a nearby room that had a sewing machine on one desk and a typewriter and transistor radio on another. A number of framed photographs lined the windowsill above a magazine rack.

In the center of the room a short, frail nun stood next to an empty chair. She held a pair of metal scissors in her hand.

"Sit in the chair, 46," Sister Lupita instructed.

María went to the chair and sat. She liked haircuts. The hairdresser her mother took her to always gave her a lollipop when the cut was finished.

The short nun lifted a handful of María's long black hair and snipped it close to the roots.

María was horrorstruck. "My hair!" She tried to leap off the chair, but Sister Lupita seized her shoulders and pinned her in the seat. She twisted and thrashed.

The short nun produced a hairbrush from her pocket and rapped María on the head sharply with its wooden backside.

"Ow!" she cried, tears springing to her eyes.

"Sit still," Sister Lupita said.

Her skull throbbing, María obeyed, and the short nun went back to work.

Snip, snip, snip.

All around her, clumps of hair fell to the floor.

3

After the horrible haircut—her hair was now shorter than most of the boys' hair had been in her old school—Sister Lupita marched María down a hallway, stopping when they came to a staircase. There, she used a key on her keychain in an angled door built into the side of the stairs. She opened it to reveal a pitch-black space and said, "This is where little girls who don't know how to behave go to think about their sins and pray for forgiveness."

4

María didn't know how long she was in the cupboard, if that was indeed what it was. She guessed maybe she'd been there a day, maybe longer. She couldn't see her hands if she held them directly before her face, and there was a strong toilet smell. The long stretches of silence were occasionally punctuated by footsteps treading the steps above her head. She wanted to yell out, ask for help, but she didn't, fearing it might be Sister Lupita or another nun.

Mostly María closed her eyes and tried to banish her sadness and loneliness and fear with sleep, but she always ended up thinking about her mom and dad. Where were they right then? What were they doing? Why did they bring her to this awful place? Didn't they want her anymore? Didn't they love her? What had she done to make them hate her so much? And perhaps the most immediate question: Was she going to be living here forever, or would she be allowed to go home again at some point?

5

She was dreaming about her old school, walking into class with no hair while all her classmates pointed and laughed at her, when she heard the key in the cupboard lock. A moment later the angled door opened.

Squinting against light that seemed as bright as if she were staring at the sun, María nevertheless recognized the pudgy, blushed face of Sister Lupita peering in at her.

"Good morning, 46," she said.

Morning? So she really had been in the cupboard for nearly a full day.

"Good morning," she replied, trying to sound pleasant.

"Have you repented your sins?"

"Yes."

"Yes, *Sister.*"

"Yes, Sister."

"Then climb out of there. Hurry, I don't have all day."

María scrambled out of the cupboard and stood before Sister Lupita, avoiding eye contact.

"You didn't soil yourself?" the nun said, and it sounded as though she were surprised.

"No, Sister," María said, though now that the woman mentioned it, she realized she did have to go pee very badly.

"I suppose it's off to breakfast for you then. This way."

Sister Lupita led her through a series of echoing hallways to a large dining hall. There were a dozen tables in neat rows of fours. Six or seven children sat on long benches at each, eating in silence. Two nuns patrolled the room.

"Go on," Sister Lupita said, ushering her forward. "Go get your food."

María went to a small window that opened to the kitchen. A grubby-looking man smoking a cigarette scowled through it at her before dumping a bowl of beans and a crusty piece of bread onto a tray and pushing it toward her. As an afterthought he added a glass of milk.

María picked up the tray and turned to face the room. Sister Lupita was gone. The only sound was the clack of spoons on bowls.

María carried the tray to the nearest table and sat at the end of the bench. She looked at the beans before her. They were covered in a gunky sauce and didn't resemble the beans her mother made her. Ignoring them, she said to the girl next to her: "Hi."

The girl didn't reply.

"I said, 'Hi,'" she said again.

"You're not allowed to talk," a skinny girl hissed from across the table.

María frowned. Not allowed to talk? She returned her attention to her beans. Despite not eating since yesterday morning, she wasn't hungry. She was too upset, and she still needed to go pee. She glanced about for a bathroom and discovered one of the nuns looming behind her.

"What's your name, child?" the woman said. She was younger than Sister Lupita and had a mole on her chin.

"María," she said.

The nun rapped the handle of a feather duster across her head.

"Ow!" she cried

"What's your name?"

"Ma—" She remembered. "46!"

The nun lowered the feather duster. "What's wrong with your food, 46?" she asked.

"I'm not hungry."

"The Lord has provided you with nourishment, and you shun His generosity?"

"I'm not hungry."

The nun gripped María by the hair and jerked her head back. She scooped beans onto the spoon and tried to force-feed her as if she were a bird.

María pressed her lips together.

"Open your mouth, 46."

María kept her lips pressed together in a lipless line.

The nun released her hair and pinched her nose closed.

Pressure built in María's lungs until she had no choice but to open her mouth. The nun shoveled beans straight to the back of her mouth, forcing her to swallow them. She shoveled in another spoonful, then another, feeding María faster than she could swallow.

María gagged, then coughed, spitting beans at the skinny girl across the table. Then she lurched forward and vomited. Through teary eyes she watched in horror as the nun scooped up some of the sick with the spoon.

"Open up," she said.

ELIZAVETA

1

Elizaveta dashed through the rain and wind to the next hut. The interior was dark, shrouded in shadows, and inhabited with more ominous dolls, no two of which were alike. Jack sat next to Rosa on the floor, and it appeared they were playing an English nursery rhyme that involved clapping each other's hands.

"What are you playing?" she asked them, rubbing her wet arms to generate warmth.

"Jack's teaching me 'Pat-a-cake, pat-a-cake, baker's man!' Rosa said. "He promised to teach me 'Little Miss Muffet' next."

"Jack is a man of many talents," she said.

"They tell you everything?" he asked her.

Elizaveta nodded. "I can't believe—" She looked at Rosa, closed her mouth.

"Rosa," Jack said, "can you go play over there with one of those dolls for a bit? I need to talk to Elizaveta about some adult stuff."

"Which doll can I play with?"

"Whichever one you want."

"But they're all attached to the wall."

"Here." He took a Swiss Army knife from his pocket and popped the blade. "Choose one and cut the string. Be careful though."

"I will!"

She accepted the knife carefully and went to the dolls, where she began examining the ratty things with great deliberation.

"I can't believe someone...killed him like that," Elizaveta said softly, even though Rosa wouldn't be able to hear her over the rain and wind. "Nitro thinks it was a serial killer. Do you believe that too?"

Jack nodded. "Lucinda didn't take the eyes. Neither did kidnappers."

"Kidnappers?"

Jack explained Nitro's previous theory.

"You're right," she said. "There's no reason Lucinda or kidnappers would do something like that. Still, a *serial killer*...?"

"Think about all those movies and stuff when the serial killer pins pictures of victims to his wall, and they all have their eyes cut out."

"Those are movies, Jack."

"But they're probably based on fact," he said. "Besides, there's a name for it. Dehumanizing or something. The eyes are windows to the soul, right? Or to the personality or whatever. Serial killers cut them out to make their victims less human, to make them easier to kill."

Elizaveta considered that, then said, "You know what Pita thinks?"

"That the ghost did it?"

Elizaveta nodded. "She was...how you say...flipping out? She even quoted Jesus—of Nazareth. I knew she was religious, but I never knew so much."

"It's her upbringing. Her whole family is super religious. Jesus is named Jesus after all."

"But Jesus isn't religious."

"Apparently his mother's death changed him. You know

the details?"

"Of her death?" Elizaveta nodded again. "After Jesus's and Pita's younger sister died, their parents tried to have another child. There were complications with pregnancy. Their mother died along with unborn child."

"That's only half of it," Jack said. "Her death wasn't sudden or unexpected. She had pulmonary hypertension. Doctors told her if she had an abortion, she would live; if she didn't, she would die. Their father, Marco, forbade it. Abortion went against his beliefs. So, yeah, their mother died along with the unborn child. But it didn't have to happen. That's why Jesus changed his tune toward religion."

"Pita told you this?"

"Marco did," he said. "We were pretty close. He eventually came to regret his decision not to save his wife."

"But Pita, she never changed?"

"Nope," Jack said. "She's still as zealous as they come. The way she talks about God sometimes, and faith, it's like she thinks He lives in the attic or something." He shrugged. "Look, I might not be religious, but I don't really have a problem with it. In fact, I think in moderation it might be a good thing. It teaches you values and all. My problem is when it's taken to extremes, when it makes you choose between knowledge and myth. You know, Pita still takes everything in the Bible as the literal word of God. She doesn't believe in evolution. She doesn't believe in the Big Bang. The first time she mentioned the world was made in seven days, I thought she was joking. She was dead serious. I couldn't get my head around it, and she couldn't get her head around the fact I didn't believe this too. We argued, but you can't get through to her. Even when the proof is right in front of her she refuses to see it. I mean, if humans and other living things existed in their present state since the beginning of time, how do you explain the variety of dogs and horses and other animals we've created through selective breeding?" He shrugged. "The neurons that fire together wire together."

"What do you mean?"

"The more you believe in something, the more that something becomes your reality. It's probably why Pita's so into ghosts. Part of it stems from her spirituality. But more, I think, stems from seeing her sister's ghost, or thinking she did, at such a young age. She's believed this for so long, that ghosts exist, she can't change her beliefs. When her Yorkshire terrier died, she buried it in a pet cemetery in Vegas and packed its coffin with all sorts of things that it could use in its afterlife. I felt like we were back two thousand years in Ancient Egypt. And when her father died, she lit one of those candles for him at the bedroom window for a couple of months, every night."

"That's not so strange," Elizaveta said. "Many people do that. Pay respect to dead."

"Yeah, but Pita would actually sit there in front of it some nights. She said she was praying, but I'm pretty sure she was waiting for her father's spirit to appear, like her sister's supposedly did. Anyway, just a heads up. Don't get sucked into a debate about the supernatural with her. You won't win. You can't."

"I guess that's why Jesus agreed so easy."

Jack frowned. "Agreed to what?"

"We're having séance, Jack."

2

They returned to the hut with the shrine to find everyone in a sober mood. Jesus and Pepper and Pita sat on the floor. Jesus's face was impassive while Pita appeared both quietly angry and terrified. Pepper seemed to be dozing. Nitro stood by himself in a far corner, his back to everyone.

Pita looked at Elizaveta. "Did you tell him?"

She nodded.

"Well?" Pita said to Jack, and it was almost a challenge.

"We have all night and nothing to do." He shrugged. "You want to hold a séance, let's hold one. The question is, do you know how to?"

"Pepper does. He performed one before on his show. He'll be the medium."

Elizaveta had seen the episode of *Mexico's Scariest Places* to which Pita was referring. It had focused on a haunted vicarage in Todo Santos, a small coastal town at the foothills of the Sierra de la Laguna Mountains. According to the locals Pepper interviewed, supernatural events had been documented there since the nineteen twenties when the chaplain, who kept a journal of the goings-on, claimed an unseen force would tear his laundry off the line and toss him out of his favorite chair. In the following decades several different priests claimed to have seen the apparition of an old woman dressed in gray. In the eighties, the vicarage was turned into a café, which included a guesthouse. One guest that Pepper tracked down said she had been staying in the guestroom in 1987 and was awoken in the middle of the night to find three old women staring at her. She turned on the light and could still see them for a few moments, though they were blurry, before they disappeared.

Pepper and his crew held a séance in the guesthouse, which resulted in strange noises, automatic writing, and the table levitating. The Travel Network received close to one hundred complaints, mostly from religious groups that took offence to the show's pagan subject matter.

"Pepper?" Pita said. "Hey—are you sleeping? Wake up. You need to tell us what to do."

Pepper opened his eyes. Yes, he really didn't look well, Elizaveta thought. His complexion remained grim, and his bouncy energy was gone. In fact, he seemed downright lethargic. She wondered whether he was drained from the ordeal of discovering Miguel's body, or whether he had come down with something.

Pepper cleared his throat and said, "First we need to decide who's participating in the séance. The number must be divisible by three."

Pita counted everyone present. "Good, we have six!"

"No," Pepper said, shaking his head. "Rosa can't participate. Children can't participate."

"I'll sit it out with her," Jack said.

Pita frowned. "That leaves us with four."

"Count me out too," Nitro said.

"So it's just me, Pepper, and Jesus?" Pita shook her head. "No, the more participants the better. We can generate more psychic energy that way. Pepper, are you sure we can't let Rosa join?"

"Please?" Rosa said.

"Oh...well...okay," Pepper said, and he didn't seem to care one way or another. He was definitely not in top showmanship form. "Now," he went on, "spirits seek warmth and light. Candles would be best, but since we don't have any, we're going to have to improvise." Moving slowly, like an old man with aching joints, he opened his bag and withdrew an LED lamp that could either be mounted on his video camera or held via a handle. He turned it on and set it in the middle of the floor, so it shot a beam of white light to the ceiling, scattering the shadows nesting there.

Pita appeared dubious. "That doesn't look very séance-like."

"It going to have to do. Also, we need food."

"Food?" Jesus said.

"You don't have incense, do you?"

"No..."

"So we need food, something with a strong aroma."

"I didn't bring any food."

"I have vodka," Jack said.

Pita frowned at him. "Why do you have vodka?"

"I brought it."

"You can't go a day without alcohol?"

Jack ignored that. "Will vodka work, Peps?"

"Better than nothing."

Jack withdrew a bottle of vodka from his daypack, unscrewed the cap, and set the bottle next to the LED light.

"The ghost is only a little girl, Pepper," Pita said. "I don't think she drinks vodka."

"She's not going to drink it," he told her curtly. "But the smell can help attract her."

Next, Pepper instructed them to form a circle and hold hands. Elizaveta sat between Jack and Rosa, Jack's big hand in her left one, Rosa's little hand in her right one. Pita was to Jack's left, then Nitro, then Jesus, then Pepper.

"To summon a spirit..." Pepper began, then frowned, as if he'd just realized something. He cleared his throat. "There might be a problem, Pita. To summon a spirit, you need the spirit's name."

"But we don't know the girl's name," she said.

"We can't summon her without a name."

"Well, that was a quick séance," Jesus said, and started to stand.

"Sit down, Jesus!" Pita said. "We'll just make up a name. She's the only ghost on this island, right?"

Elizaveta was watching Pita, trying to figure out whether she was having a lark, or whether she truly believed they were about to summon the spirit of a little girl who died fifty years before.

What was it Jack had said?

The neurons that fire together wire together.

"Why don't we summon Solano instead?" Nitro offered as a solution to their dilemma. Elizaveta suspected he, like everyone else with the exception of Rosa, was playing along for Pita's benefit. "He died here too."

Pita seemed to contemplate that, then shook her head. "No, I want to summon the girl. We'll just call her...Candelaria. Is that okay, Pepper?"

"Sure, Pita, why not?" he said. "Candelaria's fine."

"You okay, Peps?" Jack asked him. "You're not looking all

that great."

"I'm just tired. I might lie down after this. Okay—we're ready?"

"Ready," Pita said.

"Ready!" Rosa said earnestly.

Pepper offered a short prayer and a request for protection, told them to repeat after him, and said in a theatrical voice: "Spirit of the past, move among us."

They repeated: "Spirit of the past, move among us."

"Be guided by the light of this world and visit upon us."

"You couldn't miss that light," Jesus mumbled.

"Quiet, Jesus!" Pita said.

"People!" Pepper said. "Negative energy will dissuade the spirit. And try sounding a bit more respectful, like you're inviting someone into your home." He started from the beginning again: "Spirit of the past, move among us."

"Spirit of the past, move among us."

"Be guided by the light of this world and visit upon us."

"Be guided by the light of this world and visit upon us."

"Beloved Candelaria, be guided by the light of this world and visit upon us."

"Beloved Candelaria, be guided by the light of this world and visit upon us."

"Now close your eyes," Pepper instructed them softly. "And wait."

Elizaveta closed her eyes. She half expected someone to scream, to try to scare them, but no one did. One minute stretched into two, then three.

Finally she opened her eyes to peek at the others. Jesus and Nitro both had their eyes open as well. Jesus was screwing up his face, trying to make Nitro laugh.

"Did you feel that?" Pepper said suddenly.

"What? Pita breathed.

"I felt a presence."

"I think I did too!"

Elizaveta hadn't felt anything. She closed her eyes again.

"I think Candelaria's spirit is with us," Pepper said. He adopted the theatrical voice: "Our beloved Candelaria, thank you for joining us on this cold and wet evening. We are honored by your presence. We seek answers from the world you inhabit beyond the grave, and if you so choose to reply, please use one rap for 'yes' and two raps for 'no.'" He whispered: "Okay, Pita. Ask your questions, but keep them simple."

"What should I ask?" She sounded unsure of herself.

"How about next week's lottery numbers?"

"Jack!"

"People!" Pepper said.

"Our beloved Candelaria," Pita said loudly, mimicking Pepper's mannered intonation, "did you drown on this island fifty years ago?"

There was no response.

"Ask again," Pepper said.

Pita repeated the question.

They waited in silence until Pepper whispered, "Did you hear that?"

"Yes!" Pita said.

Elizaveta did too. A knock on the exterior of the hut. A chill iced her spine, but she quickly chided herself. It was nothing but a doll blowing in the wind, a limb striking the wall. She didn't know whether the dolls had been making these noises all along, though she suspected they had been; she simply hadn't been listening for them. Yet Pepper would have been. It was likely why he suggested this method for communication.

"Ask her another question," Pepper said. "She might not remain for long."

"Our beloved Candelaria, is your spirit trapped on this island?"

There was no response.

"Ask again," Pepper said.

"Beloved Candelaria, is your spirit—"

Knock.

Pita gasped.

Elizaveta opened her eyes. Everyone else had theirs closed now. Rosa's were not merely closed but squeezed shut, as if she was terrified. Jack appeared bored, while Nitro and Jesus seemed to be biting back smiles.

Pita's face was a mask of concentration.

Elizaveta closed her eyes.

"Beloved Candelaria," Pita went on, "are you responsible for the murder that occurred on this island?"

More knocks.

"Was that three?" Pita breathed.

"It was two," Elizaveta said.

"It was three!" Rosa said.

"Ask again," Pepper said.

"Beloved Candelaria, are you responsible for the murder that occurred on this island?"

Two raps on the wall.

"Beloved Candelaria, is the killer still on this island?"

Silence.

"Beloved Candelaria, is—"

A clap of thunder, the loudest yet, exploded above them.

At the same time a doll began to cackle.

3

Everyone, Jesus with his sprained ankle included, sprang to their feet. Although dusk had descended while they'd participated in the séance, claiming the last of the daylight, Pepper's LED lamp continued to illuminate the hut. Elizaveta was able to zero in on the laughing doll. "It's that one!" she said, pointing a finger at a doll clad in a blue dress with white polka dots. Its lips seemed to be smeared with red lipstick.

"Don't touch it!" Pita said, her voice jumping to a soprano level. She backed toward the hut's door. "It's possessed! She's in it! The girl's in it! Don't touch it!"

Ignoring her hysterics, Nitro went to the doll.

Jack grabbed Pita's wrist as she passed him. "Calm down!" he said.

"Don't touch it!" she wailed.

Nitro lifted the doll away from the wall and turned it over. He cried out and stepped back.

Everyone started shouting, asking what happened.

It was instant chaos.

Pita tore loose from Jack and disappeared outside.

Nitro was flapping his hands madly.

"What happened?" Jack demanded.

"It's covered with spiders!" he said.

Not understanding Nitro's Spanish, Jack reached for the doll.

"Jack, don't!" Elizaveta said, hurrying toward him. "There are spiders!"

He tugged his hand back. Together, they bent close to examine the doll. Dozens and dozens of tiny black spiders were scrambling out from beneath the dress.

The doll continued to laugh.

"Shut the fucking thing off!" Jesus said.

Jack produced his Swiss Army knife and lifted the doll's dress with the tip of the blade, revealing a cobweb that was as thick as cotton candy and crawling with more spiders.

"Move back," he told Elizaveta even as he cut the string from which the doll depended. It dropped to the floor. The impact sent spiders flying off it. Jack raised his foot and crushed the plastic torso where the electronics and battery would be located.

The laughing stopped.

4

In the stunned silence that followed Pepper blurted, "What

the hell just happened?"

"It was the thunder," Jack said.

"What are you talking about?"

"The thunder set off the doll."

Spiders continued to pour out from beneath the doll's dress, searching for refuge between the floorboards. Elizaveta kicked the ghastly doll into the far corner.

"Thunder?" Jesus said. His back was pressed to the opposite wall, by a window. "It started laughing right after Eliza asked if the killer was still on the island!"

"At the same time as the thunder," Jack said.

"Thunder doesn't make—"

A scream cut him off.

5

Nitro burst out the door of the hut first, Elizaveta right behind him. Pita stood rooted to the ground, staring into the rain-thrashed jungle, still screaming.

Elizaveta saw the woman immediately. She was twenty meters away, leaning against a large tree, supporting herself with one arm. She was naked, her pale skin standing out in stark contrast to the gathered darkness.

All Elizaveta could think was: *It's the ghost, ghosts are real, I'm seeing the ghost, we summoned the ghost, oh my God ghosts are real!*

Then, from behind her, Rosa cried, "Lucinda!"

Lucinda! Elizaveta sagged with relief. *Of course it was, of course—*

Nitro rushed past Pita to help the woman. Elizaveta forced her legs to move and went to Pita. "It's okay," she told her, slipping her arm around her friend's waist and turning her back toward the hut. "It's Lucinda, the friend of Rosa's brother. It's okay."

Pita stopped screaming and started to mumble gibberish.

Elizaveta led her to the hut and eased her to the floor where she had previously been seated. Nitro came in a few moments later, carrying Lucinda, telling everyone to get out of the way. He set her down on the floor. Her head lolled to one side, limp. Long black hair, wet and tangled, spread away from it like a bed of snakes. Her face was ashen and muddied. Elizaveta's eyes flicked over the woman's body, almost guiltily: slender shoulders and large breasts with light brown nipples, the left one pierced; an hourglass waist and wide hips; a pierced belly-button above her pubic hair; long, toned legs; fingernails and toenails painted plum.

Everyone was crowding around her. Rosa, clutching Jack's legs, said, "What's wrong with her?"

"She's hurt," Nitro said, and rolled her gently onto her chest.

An angry cut split open her right shoulder. It was filled with blood the color of puce that turned a brighter red where it leaked down her back. Elizaveta thought the wound resembled a slightly parted mouth smeared with raspberry jam.

Pita was saying something in a frantic, frightened voice. Rosa began crying. Jack scooped her into his arms and carried her away.

"Was she stabbed?" Jesus asked. "Was she stabbed too?"

Nitro nodded. "Looks similar to Miguel's wounds."

"What should we do?" Pepper asked. "She needs help. What should we do?"

Elizaveta grabbed Jack's bottle of vodka, knelt next to Lucinda, and dosed the gash.

Lucinda moaned softly.

Nitro asked the woman what happened, who did this to her. She didn't respond. Her eyes remained shut. He peeled off his tank top. Bare-chested, he folded it into a compress and pressed it against the wound.

Elizaveta felt the woman's forehead. "She has fever."

Pepper draped his purple blazer over her, covering her

nakedness.

"She needs something warmer than that," Jesus said.

"Got anything handy, bro?" Nitro said.

"We should take her to Solano's cabin," Jack said. He stood separate from them in the corner, holding Rosa in his arms.

"There are clothes there?" Nitro asked.

"I didn't check. But there were two bedrooms, two dressers. At the very least there were sheets on the beds."

"How far is it?"

"Ten minutes."

Elizaveta glanced out the hut's door, at the dark and rain.

"I'm not going out there," Pita said. "No way. She's out there, she'll get us—"

"Enough, Pita," Jesus said severely.

"She's out there—"

"Enough!"

She bit her bottom lip and glared at him.

"We'll vote," Nitro said. "Everyone in favor of moving to the cabin, raise your hand."

Everyone except for Pita raised their hand.

6

The icy rain pelleted Elizaveta's skin. The wind threw her hair in front of her face and threatened to knock her over. She planted her legs apart and held onto a tree for support. Everyone was struggling against the storm, especially little Rosa, who was holding onto Jack's leg with all her might.

Pita went down with a yelp. She lay on her back, unable to get back up. It was as though she were wrestling an invisible opponent who had close-lined her and now was sitting on her chest. Her wavy black hair seemed electrified, whipping this way and that. Pepper removed his arm from around Jesus's waist and helped Pita back to her feet.

"The storm's gotten too strong!" Jesus shouted, balancing on his good foot. Like Elizaveta, he held onto a tree for support.

Nitro, who was in the lead, turned to face them. He carried Lucinda in his arms. His biceps flexed powerfully. Raindrops pinged off his bare shoulders. "Don't stop!" he shouted as he continued on.

Heads down, blinking away rainwater, they followed. Progress was exhausting. They'd been in the storm for all of five minutes and already Elizaveta felt waterlogged, each step an effort.

She focused on the ground, where she stepped. In the dark everything was layered in shades of gray, browns, and blacks, and it was hard to see hazards such as fallen branches. The rain churned the dirt, making it thick and slippery.

She almost bumped into the back of Jack when he stopped to hike Rosa into his arms. The girl's face poked over his shoulder, her skin glistening wetly, her black eyes wide and haunted. Nevertheless, she smiled at Elizaveta. Elizaveta wanted to reach out, touch her, reassure her. The poor thing had just lost her brother. She'd been adopted by a band of strangers, and now she was slogging through what felt like the end of the world.

Elizaveta raised her hand, but Jack was moving again. Rosa squeezed her eyes shut and buried her face against his neck.

The odd couple. That's what came to Elizaveta's mind. Jack didn't like children. He often said as much, and when Elizaveta saw him around kids, he was stiff and awkward, and he usually did his best to ignore them altogether. So why had Rosa taken such a liking to him? Because he was the first person she had contact with after Miguel's death? Because he reminded her of her brother in some way?

A peal of thunder rumbled across the turbulent sky, drawing near. A particularly nasty gust of wind whooshed through the trees, icing her blood.

A loud crack sounded.

Elizaveta snapped her head up and saw a large branch strike the ground next to Nitro. He spun toward it, cursing. The branch was massive, the length of a car and sporting several smaller boughs sprouting spiraling needles. It hadn't missed him by much.

They all looked up. The branch had fallen ten or fifteen meters; Elizaveta could see the where it had broken away from the trunk. If it had struck Nitro, it likely would have killed him.

"We have to go back!" Pita shouted above the weather.

"How much farther is the cabin, chavo?" Nitro asked Jack, shielding his eyes from the lashing rain with his hand.

Jack bumped Rosa higher up his chest. "It's not far!"

"You better not be lost!"

"I'm not lost!"

"We have to go back!" Pita repeated. She was scanning the blowing canopy, as if expecting another branch to fall.

"Maybe we should..." Elizaveta said before the wind drowned out the rest of her words.

"It's not far!" Jack insisted, and marched on.

7

They reached Solano's cabin five long minutes later. It sat to the right of the path, little more than a tenebrous mass huddled amongst the trees, unwelcoming. It featured a crude open porch sheltering a drunkenly leaning door. No windows adorned the exterior, only dolls, all banging about animatedly in the wind.

Jack, still carrying Rosa, started toward it.

"Wait," Nitro hissed. He set Lucinda on a grassy patch of ground, gestured everyone closer so he didn't have to shout to be heard, and said, "We need to check it out first. Make sure it's all clear. I'll go."

"I'll come," Jack said.

"No, stay here and keep watch."

Without another word, Nitro approached the cabin. He stopped in front of the closed door, pressed his ear to it. He waited, a motionless silhouette. Then he pushed open the door and disappeared inside.

"I don't like this," Pita said.

"It'll be dry inside," Jesus said.

"It feels like a trap."

"What feels like a trap, Pita? It's just a—"

"Shhh!" Elizaveta said. Because she thought maybe Pita was right. The cabin appeared not only sinister but...wrong? This was a feeling, nothing more. Still, the sight of the ramshackle place gave her the creeps.

Thunder boomed overhead, though no one took their eyes from the gaping door and the blackness beyond it.

The seconds dragged. Elizaveta blinked water from her eyes and wondered what was taking Nitro so long. The cabin wasn't that big. He only had to poke his head in the different rooms. Had the killer been waiting inside for him then? Had he ambushed him, taken him out silently? Was he waiting for the rest of them to investigate?

Elizaveta looked at the others. Only Jack looked back at her. He seemed uneasy as well.

"I'll check," he said quietly. He set Rosa down.

"No," she said. "We should go together—"

Nitro shouted a curse.

8

Something small and black darted out the cabin's door and past Jack's legs. It brushed Elizaveta's right ankle before vanishing into nearby vegetation.

A cat, Elizaveta thought, her heart pounding. *Just a cat.*

"What the fuck?" Jack said. He had already stepped inside the cabin and was presumably speaking to Nitro.

Jesus and Pepper and Pita piled in behind him. Elizaveta glanced at Lucinda's inert body lying on the ground in the rain. But she couldn't move the woman by herself. Nitro or Jack would have to get her. She took Rosa's hand and entered the cabin as well.

It was nearly pitch black—nearly, because Elizaveta could make out what Jack was pointing at.

Nitro held a semiautomatic pistol in his hand.

He slipped off his backpack and dumped the weapon inside the main pocket.

"Why do you have a fucking gun?" Jack said.

"Why do you think?" he said. "For protection."

"Protection from what? Solano's nephew? Because he's the only other person we had any reason to believe might have been here—unless you knew something we didn't?"

"Fuck off, Jack Goff. You're pissing me off more than usual."

Jack said to Pita, "Did you know he carried a gun around?"

Pita seemed stunned. She shook her head.

"I didn't know either," Jesus said, frowning.

Nitro scowled. "What's the big deal?"

"What are you, a fucking gangster?" Jack said.

"I bought it legally."

Pita said, "I thought you could only have a gun for home protection?"

"That's what it's for," Nitro told her.

"So you don't have a permit to carry?" Jesus asked.

"A permit? Fuck, no."

"Bro, if you're caught with that gun, you're looking at up to thirty years in prison."

"There might be a fucking killer on this island! You should all be happy I have a gun—"

"Okay, okay," Elizaveta said. "Calm down. Maybe it's a good thing he has—"

"It's fucking weird," Jack said.

"Don't ask me to save your ass when you're getting your eyes ripped out—"

"Enough!" Elizaveta said. "Let's just..." Her gaze fell on a table behind Jesus and Pita. "Look, candles."

She went to the table, took her lighter from her pocket, and lit two red candles set in glass jars. The scent of burning wax fumes and the sight of the tiny flames buoyed her tremendously. The dark became a little less threatening.

"Light!" Pita said. "Thank God."

"There're more candles over there," Jesus said, pointing to what appeared to be a big pirate chest. "And there..."

Elizaveta went around the room, lighting six candles in total. The candlepower was modest, but at least they could now see each other clearly.

While she did this, Nitro collected Lucinda from outside and carried her to one of the two bedrooms.

"I don't trust that guy," Jack said under his breath to nobody in particular.

"Cool it, Jack," Jesus said.

Pepper cleared his throat. "Would anyone object if I lay down in the spare bed?" He stood a few feet away from everyone, his arms folded across his chest, huddled into himself. His cherub face drooped miserably. He appeared ten years older.

"Shit, Peps," Jack said, frowning. "You look... What's wrong?"

"Just tired. I know it's not fair I take the bed, but just for a bit..."

"Come on," Jack said, leading Pepper toward the vacant bedroom. Rosa followed dutifully.

Knowing they would need water at some point, Elizaveta went to an old enamelware bucket bristling with paintbrushes in one corner. She dumped the brushes onto the floor and looked inside it. Clean enough. She went to the door.

"What are you doing?" Pita asked, alarmed.

"Getting water. I'm not going far."

Outside Elizaveta set the bucket on the ground a meter

from the cabin, then retreated to the rickety porch. She crossed her arms and studied the storming night. There was a feeling of foreboding and desolation to it, nothing moving yet everything moving.

There's a murderer out there somewhere.

The thought came easily, opening a pit in her stomach. She clenched her jaw and told herself she didn't know there was a murderer out there for sure, and even if there was, it didn't matter. There was only one of him and eight of them. And Nitro had a gun. That was protection enough for any threat. So, no, they didn't have anything to worry about, not really. Night would come and go. The storm would end. In the morning the boatman would arrive. If not, someone could take the canoe and get help. Either way, they would be dry and safe by noon at the latest.

A flash of lightning shocked the sky, turning patches of black a deep-sea blue. Rainwater began spilling over the lip of the bucket.

Elizaveta snatched it up and returned inside.

1957

1

The days at Saint Agatha's School for Lost Children were long and busy, and there was never any time for rest or play because, according to Sister Lupita, these were Satan's darling hours to tempt children to all manner of wickedness.

Each morning at five o'clock one of the nuns would enter the dormitory clapping her hands or banging a wooden spoon on the bottom of a metal pot. Once all sixty or so girls were up, the nun would supervise them getting changed. There was always a scramble to be the first to line up before the communal wardrobe. María sort of understood the others did this to select the best pieces of clothing for themselves. But then she sort of didn't understand either; she didn't understand why clothes needed to look good, which was why she often ended up in ill-fitting and mismatched outfits.

After everyone was dressed, the nun marched them in single file to the dining hall for breakfast. There, she would choose a girl to sing a hymn as well as say grace. María had been selected once before, and because she couldn't sing the hymn right, or remember the words to grace, she was made to sweep the hallways with a toothbrush.

For the rest of the morning the girls went to "work." Depending on what you were assigned each week, you might be sewing, knitting, peeling sacks of potatoes in the kitchen, cleaning, fetching water, or cutting wood. A lot of the girls complained in private about the jobs they were made to do, but this was María's favorite part of the day. It was all pretty straightforward, and she could do what was asked of her as well as anyone else without getting in trouble.

The same couldn't be said for school, which began after lunch. They had different nuns for each subject. María liked arithmetic the best, not because she was good at it but because Sister Francesca who taught it never punished her for getting the answers wrong. The other nuns were not so forgiving, especially Sister Vallín who taught scripture. She must have hit María on the head with her cane three or four times a class, and on the rare occasion she wasn't in a hitting mood, she would make María copy out pages from the Bible until her hand didn't work anymore.

Dinner was at six o'clock, followed by church at seven, during which the school's only priest, Father Pardavé, used his sermons to remind the girls they were unwanted and unloved, castaways, forgotten by the world, lower than a snake's belly, and they would never amount to anything. Some of the older girls called him Father Finger behind his back because of special examinations he did to them when they reached puberty. And sometimes at nighttime he would select one of them to accompany him to his cottage for "special lessons," though no one ever told María what these special lessons were about.

Finally at eight o'clock a nun supervised everyone as they changed into their nightgowns and knelt at their bedsides to pray for a half hour. María always prayed for her parents to come and take her away from the terrible school, and when she didn't find them downstairs waiting for her in the morning, she would pray a little harder and a little louder the next night, so God would hear her above all the other girls likely praying for the same thing.

Then it was lights out, and regardless of whether you were tired or not, you had to go to sleep. If you didn't, the nuns said the Sandman would come for you. He'd pluck out your eyes, put them in a bag, and carry them to his nest on the moon, where he would feed them to his beaked children, who loved nothing more than the eyeballs of naughty human children.

2

One Saturday morning María woke before dawn and found Laura sleeping next to her, sucking her thumb. She must have climbed into María's bed at some point during the night.

Laura was six years old, one of the youngest girls in the ward. As there were more girls assigned to the dormitory than there were beds, the younger ones often shared beds with the older ones. Laura, however, usually ended up sleeping on a pillow on the floor by herself because she was a bed-wetter and nobody allowed her in their bed—nobody except María.

María was about to go back to sleep when she realized her nightgown was wet. She peeled back the quilt, sat up, and swept her legs to the floor. There was a damp patch in the center of the mattress.

She shook Laura awake. The little girl looked at her tiredly.

"You wet the bed," María whispered.

Laura sat up slowly, rubbing her eyes.

María pointed to the damp patch.

"I didn't mean to!" Laura's chin began to tremble.

At that moment the door to the dormitory opened and Sister Vallín entered, rapping her cane against the wall loudly. She was a sturdy woman with beady eyes and a permanent scowl.

Almost immediately all the girls roused themselves, yawning and stretching and taking their places next to their beds.

María and Laura did the same.

Sister Vallín moved down the line of beds, examining each mattress. She stopped at the foot of María's. Bright malice lit her beady eyes.

"Bed-wetter!" she crowed triumphantly.

An excited rustle passed through the other girls: anticipation at the entertainment in store for them.

Sister Vallín smirked at Laura. "You just can't help yourself, can you, 53? This is, what, your third bed-wetting so far this month? You are a filthy little girl, a filthy, disgusting little girl —"

"It was me," María said, not really knowing what she was doing. "I couldn't hold it in."

"You?" Sister Vallín said, surprised.

"I'm sorry."

Sister Vallín glared at her, and María was convinced the nun knew she was lying, could read her thoughts. But all she said was: "Bring me the sheet."

María peeled the sheet from the bed and handed it to her.

"Take your places, children," Sister Vallín instructed. "You know how we discipline bed-wetters."

The girls formed a big circle, each of them swallowing the smiles wanting to worm their way onto their faces. Sister Vallín draped the sheet over María's head. The smell of pee was strong. All she could see was white.

Then a sharp pain tore across her backside as Sister Vallín struck her with her cane. María yelped. She heard laughter erupt from the other girls. The nun struck her again and again, parading her around the circle, calling her everything from "child of the devil" and "enemy of God" to "unclean animal." This went on until María's behind hurt so badly she began to limp. Eventually she could no longer remain on her feet and collapsed to the floor, where she curled in a ball, sobbing in humiliation and pain.

Distantly she heard Sister Vallín speaking to the girls, heard them lining up before the wardrobe, heard them changing into their day clothes. Then they filtered out of the room, heading downstairs to the dining hall for breakfast.

A long time passed, and just as María was beginning to forget what she was doing on the floor, she heard the door to the dormitory open. Footsteps approached. The sheet was torn away.

Scowling down at her, Sister Vallín said, "The one thing God despises more than a filthy little girl is a filthy little liar." She raised her cane.

"Don't—"

The cane struck María on the side of her head. Stars exploded across her vision, and she was already spinning into unconsciousness as the nun struck her again and again and again.

3

María came around in a bed in a room she didn't recognize. Vivid light shone through the tall, arched windows, making her squint. Vaguely, she made out Sister Vallín and Father Pardavé. They were standing by some metal filing cabinets, speaking to each other. They seemed somehow very far away, and she could only catch snippets of their conversation:

"...becoming difficult...deceitful..."

"...mentally deficient..."

"...fits...dazed, unresponsive..."

"...God's mistake..."

"...no friends...Laura..."

"...equally unfortunate..."

"...her disobedience...aggression..."

"...American doctor...operation...very successful..."

María could no longer keep her eyelids open, they fluttered and shut, and then there was nothing but darkness once again.

ELIZAVETA

1

Lucinda's bedroom was furnished with a small, plain dresser and an iron-framed twin bed. A candle sat on the dresser, the stout yellow flame staving off the encroaching darkness. Nitro had hung Pepper's purple blazer from a hook on the wall to dry. Lucinda lay on the bed on her side, a ratty red sheet pulled to her chin.

"How is she doing?" Elizaveta asked, moving next to Nitro, who remained bare-chested, not an ounce of fat on him. She studied Lucinda. The woman's eyes were closed, her face gaunt and insipid. Her breathing had developed a burr, a phlegmy rasp, as though she had been a two-packs-a-day smoker for twenty years.

Nitro shrugged. "We need to keep her warm. But there're no covers, nothing, only these sheets."

Elizaveta looked at the dresser.

"Empty," he said, "except some socks and underwear."

"Where are Solano's clothes?"

"He was a hermit. He probably only had one outfit."

"What about the wound in her back?"

"Bleeding's stopped. Not much more we can do."

She raised the bucket. "Can she drink water?"

"Not while she's unconscious."

Elizaveta frowned, frustrated. She wanted to help, but there was nothing for her to do. She looked around the room for something warm, for something Nitro might have missed. Her eyes fell on his backpack. He'd taken it off and set it on the floor against the wall.

She recalled the way he had acted when Jack caught him with the pistol in his hand: surprised, guilty. How he'd quickly stuffed it away.

Why hadn't he told them he had it earlier? What was the big secret? It wasn't like they'd turn him in.

She felt Nitro watching her and said, "Will you stay here?"

"For a while," he replied. "Need to keep an eye on her. Make sure she doesn't stop breathing or go into shock."

"Shock?"

"From loss of blood."

"Oh..." Elizaveta hesitated, still wanting to help. "Is there anything I can do?"

He shook his head. "Go get some rest."

2

Jesus and Pita were seated in the two rattan chairs at the table, speaking softly to one another, Pita smoking a cigarette and appearing agitated. Elizaveta let them be and went to the far side of the room, where she found a spot against the wall to settle down. Her clothes and undergarments clung wetly and miserably to her skin. A hearth would have been wonderful right then, the heat of the fire and the musky smell of burning wood divine.

At least there were candles, she thought. It would have been horrible to have to sit there in midnight blackness, the only sound the violent wind and rain, not knowing where the others were, not knowing whether someone had slipped into the cabin with them.

Elizaveta cleared her throat and reigned in her imagination. She lit a Camel, noting she only had four left in the pack. She took a drag, held the smoke in her lungs, almost as if this action would warm her up, then exhaled slowly, reluctantly.

Unlike the Spartan bedroom, the main room was filled with Solano's personal belongings. Alongside the countless dolls, there were primitive-looking farming tools, miscellaneous items of the variety you might find in a homeless man's shopping cart, an incongruous car seat, and wood carvings of, unsurprisingly, miniature dolls. These were colorfully painted and reminded her of *matryoshka* dolls, a popular toy of Russian children for much of the last century.

Elizaveta hated *matryoshka* dolls. They reminded her of the orphanage and of a man named Yevgeny Popov. Yevgeny had been part of the staff at the orphanage. At first Elizaveta liked him. The other care-workers were indifferent and cruel to her. They were trained to be like this, products of a cold-hearted system, for orphans were as stigmatized as the disabled and the elderly and femininity in the Soviet Union: a problem to be dealt with in the shadows far from the public eye. Yevgeny, however, always smiled and waved at her. Sometimes he would sneak her a piece of chocolate when no one was looking. He also told her lots of haunted stories concerning the orphanage, strange things that had happened to him, such as lights mysteriously turning on in certain rooms and footsteps sounding behind him, even though when he turned around nobody was there. These tales gave her nightmares, but she eagerly awaited the next one. Life then was bleak and routine, and they relieved the doldrums.

One day Elizaveta had been in the girl's dormitory rec room. It had a vaulted ceiling with twelve windowed eves and had once served as the chapel before it moved to the administrative building. She was alone, cleaning; all the children had daily chores that rotated on a weekly basis. Yevgeny arrived, crouched before her, and told her he had a surprise for her. Smiling, showing his crooked and yellow cigarette-stained teeth, he presented her with a *matryoshka* doll. He told her it was her birthday present, even though her birthday wasn't for another month. Regardless, she had been thrilled. She had not had a toy of her own since her parents vanished and she was taken from her home.

Yevgeny told her to go ahead, play with the doll. Elizaveta sat on the floor and studied the outer layer. It depicted a woman dressed in a *sarafan*. She separated the top and bottom of the doll to reveal a smaller figure of the same sort inside. There were three more in total, each hidden inside the previous, the smallest being a baby turned from a single piece of wood and non-opening.

While she played with the dolls, Yevgeny began massaging her shoulders with his strong hands. She didn't like this, though she didn't know why. It simply made her feel uncomfortable. Even so, she didn't say anything; she didn't want to hurt his feelings. He was her friend, one of her only friends in the orphanage, so she let him knead her shoulders all the while wishing for him to stop. Then his hands moved down the front of her chest. She was twelve then and had started to develop breasts. His hands moved around the small mounds, then over them, rubbing. She told him to stop. He didn't, saying he wasn't doing anything, they were just playing. His fingers pinched her nipples. Jumping to her feet, leaving the *matryoshka* doll behind, she hurried from the rec room. She thought Yevgeny would follow her, but he didn't. She went downstairs to the inner courtyard to be with the other children. She didn't tell anyone what Yevgeny did. She didn't think anyone would believe her. Plus, she still wasn't sure what actually happened, or if it was wrong. She just knew she didn't like the feeling of Yevgeny's hands on her.

After that day she hoped Yevgeny would go back to being the old Yevgeny. He didn't. He stopped smiling and waving at her...even though he rarely took his eyes off her. She became afraid of him, and afraid of being alone in the orphanage, yet sometimes the latter couldn't be helped. Twice, Yevgeny caught her on her own, exiting the bathroom. The first time she managed to dash past him to safety, but the second time he blocked her escape. He tried to give her the *matryoshka* doll again. She refused to accept it. He slapped her across the cheek, knocking her over. He slid his hand up her dress, between her legs. She screamed, which scared him off—but not before he threatened to kill her if she told anyone what happened.

Elizaveta didn't tell anyone. She believed his threat. Nevertheless, a few days later the headmistress, Irina Igorevna, summoned Elizaveta to her office and asked her why she hadn't been eating anything at mealtimes. Elizaveta broke down and confessed what occurred outside the bathroom. Irina Igorevna listened stoically, asked a few specific questions, then told Elizaveta a story she would never forget. It was about an Auschwitz survivor, a young Jewish woman who Elizaveta would many years later come to suspect had been Irina Igorevna herself. Although imprisoned under inhuman conditions, the young woman was the only one in her ward to wash her stockings each day, as she had done each day before the war. The other inmates shrugged their shoulders at her routine, having abandoned any attempt at hygiene to conserve energy. Yet when a typhoid epidemic struck the camp, the young woman was the only person to survive and to eventually find freedom at the hands of American soldiers.

"The world you enter after your time at the orphanage will be a very challenging place, Elizaveta," the headmistress concluded. "You will encounter others like Yevgeny Popov, men who would take advantage of you or worse. You can bow to their superior strength and hope they grow tired of you and leave you alone, or you can stand up for your core dignities, remain true to yourself, even if this means making difficult choices. You stood up for yourself today by confiding in me what happened, and it will be up to you whether you continue to stand up for yourself in the future, whether you choose to merely survive, or refuse to survive and live."

The next morning at breakfast the children learned that Yevgeny died in his sleep. No explanation was given, though over the following days rumors swirled he had taken his own life.

Elizaveta didn't believe this, but she never spoke of her suspicions to anyone.

3

Jack emerged from Pepper's bedroom, closing the door behind him. Despite the crazy stuff happening on this island, he stood tall and strong and confident. It might be selfish, but Elizaveta was very glad he was stuck here with her. She no longer trusted Nitro, not completely, Pita was a mess, and Jesus…well, he might control a boardroom, or a meeting with millionaire investors, but he was out of his element here. She knew him too well, could see past the brave front he put on. There was a sharpness to his eyes, a jerkiness to his movements, an uncharacteristic air of indecisiveness.

Elizaveta ashed out her cigarette, then went to Jack. "Where's Rosa?" she asked.

"I put her in bed next to Pepper," he said.

"She really likes you."

"Because I'm so handsome."

"Yes, you are handsome man." This came off sounding sincerer than she'd intended, and he gave her an inquiring look. She cleared her throat. "I joke, Jack. Please."

"Pepper says he's cold," he said…and was he trying not to smile? "He needs something warm, but there's nothing in the dresser."

"There was poncho in dresser there." Elizaveta indicated Lucinda's bedroom. "But Lucinda needs it."

"That was all?" Jack said. "One poncho?"

"And some socks and underwear."

"Where the hell are all Solano's clothes?"

"Nitro says hermits probably only own one outfit."

Jack grunted. "He has an answer for everything, doesn't he?"

Elizaveta wasn't sure whether he was being sarcastic, or whether he was implying something.

He lowered his voice. "What do you think...?"

She assumed he was asking what she thought about the fact Nitro had a pistol in his possession. "I don't know, but—"

"What are you guys whispering about?" Pita asked, standing up. She glared at them suspiciously.

"Pepper's cold," Jack said. "He needs something warm."

Jesus said, "What about the rug you're standing on? It's dry."

Jack and Elizaveta glanced at the rug beneath their feet. It was green with a beige pattern, natty, sullied. But Jesus was right. It was dry.

"Better than nothing," Jack told him. "Eliza, give me a hand."

They moved off the rug, took a corner each, and folded it back.

Elizaveta blinked in surprise. "*Yo-moyo!*" she said. "What is this?"

4

Jack and Elizaveta set the rug aside and knelt next to the trapdoor they'd uncovered. Jesus and Pita hurried over, Jesus limping because of his injured ankle, both of them clamoring loudly at the discovery. A moment later Nitro emerged from Lucinda's room, asking what all the fuss was about.

Elizaveta wasn't paying attention to them. She was focused on the trapdoor. It wasn't much larger than a manhole, square, and flush with the floor. A cord of rope nailed to the hatch opposite the hinges served as the handle.

Jack reached for it.

"Whoa, chavo," Nitro said. "Maybe you don't want to open that."

"Why?" Jack said, cocking an eye at him suspiciously. "You know what's down there?"

Nitro turned to Jesus. "What do you think?"

Jesus shrugged. "We should check it out."

Jack tugged the rope. The hatch had torqued a bit, and he had to tug a second time with both hands. This time the hatch lifted, revealing a dark hole and a crudely hewed wooden ladder. Cool, stale air wafted up.

Elizaveta couldn't see the bottom. She fetched a nearby candle, returned, and lowered the candle into the hole, careful not to move too quickly and extinguish the flame. "It's not so deep," she said, the bottom visible now. "Two meters maybe."

"And then what?" Jesus asked. He, Nitro, and Pita were looming over her. Jack held onto her shoulder so she didn't fall down the hole.

"I don't know," she said. "It's dark, but I think...maybe there is...how do you say...?"

"Crawlspace?" Jack said.

"Yes, crawlspace." She maneuvered herself back to her knees and set the candle next to her.

"Crawlspace?" Nitro said. "This shithole doesn't have pipes or nothing. Why would Solano need a crawlspace?"

"Maybe it's a tunnel?" Pita suggested.

Jesus said, "Why would he dig a tunnel?"

"An escape route?"

"Escape from who?"

"Could be a hurricane shelter," Jack said. "This house isn't too sturdy."

Pita said, "It's holding up to this storm."

"Fuck this dicking around," Nitro said. "I'll go down and

have a look."

Elizaveta glanced at him. Was Jack right? Did he know what was down there? Would he do a perfunctory search and tell them there was nothing but dirt—all the while concealing... what?

Apparently Jack was thinking along the same lines and said, "I'm going to go."

"You?" Nitro said. "Why you?"

"Because I want to see what's down there."

"You're too big, chavo. You'll get stuck."

"I'll take my chances." Jack began positioning himself to climb down the ladder.

"We'll both go," Nitro said.

"I think you should stay here, Nitro," Elizaveta told him, not wanting Jack to be alone and out of sight with him. By way of explanation she added, "You have gun. Keep us safe." He was, she'd noticed, wearing his backpack again.

"That's why I should be the one to see what's down there," he said. "I can protect myself. All Jack Goff can do is scream like a girl."

"You want to put your shirt on again, Muscles?" Jack said. "You're giving my eyes a headache."

"I don't think you should go down by yourself, Jack," Pita said.

"There's nobody down there, Pita," he said.

"You don't know—"

"If someone went down there," he told her, "how could they pull the rug back over the trap door again?"

Pita folded her arms across her chest. "I was going to say, you don't know it's a some*body*."

Shaking his head, Jack attached himself to the ladder. Elizaveta, however, couldn't rid herself of the image that had popped into her mind: a handful of dolls huddled underground in the tomb-like blackness, knives or other deadly weapons clutched in their small hands, waiting.

"Maybe you shouldn't go," she told Jack, hating herself for

letting Pita's superstitious hoopla get to her.

"We need to know what's down there."

"Why?"

"Pita was right when she said it could be a tunnel. Which means it's not just a way out, but a way in as well."

A drawn-out silence ensued.

"Fuck it," Nitro said. "Let Jack Goff go. Maybe he'll get stuck after all and we'll have some peace and quiet tonight."

Jack collected the candle and started down the ladder. After a moment's hesitation, Elizaveta latched on to the ladder as well.

Jesus seized her shoulder and said, "What do you think you're doing, cariño?"

"Jack shouldn't go by himself—"

"You're not—"

"I am, Jesus," she said, shrugging free.

5

The wood ladder leaned against the wall of the hole at a steep angle. The risers felt rough beneath Elizaveta's hands, and she hoped she didn't incur any slivers. Below her, Jack had stepped off the last rung and was now on his knees and elbows, bent sideways, as if he were peering beneath a sofa. "What do you see?" she asked him.

"You were right," he said. "Some sort of crawlspace. Dark."

"Be careful!" Pita called from above.

Jack army-crawled forward until his upper body disappeared, then his legs. Elizaveta continued down the ladder to the bottom of the hole. The ground was hard-packed earth. The crawlspace was barely half a meter in height and extended away from her in every direction; she couldn't be certain how far it went because everything was black. She started the way Jack had gone, the dirt cool beneath her hands and knees, the low ceiling scraping her back.

"Hey!" Jack said suddenly.

Elizaveta's heart leapt. "What?" she whispered. The claustrophobic space deadened her voice.

"There's a basket or something ahead."

Elizaveta scuttled to catch up. Jack pointed. The candlelight's reach didn't extend far, and she had to squint. At first she thought she was seeing a cardboard box, but it resolved into a wicker basket of the sort you might find on an apple orchard.

"Wonder what's in it?" he said, army-crawling forward again, pulling himself with his elbows.

Elizaveta reached the basket first. She tipped it to see inside, flinching in anticipation of the unexpected. She relaxed. "Potatoes!" she said.

Jack stuck his arm in the basket and retrieved a spud. He turned it over in his hand. The skin was yellowish-brown and covered with small sprouts.

"This is nothing but Solano's root cellar," he said, sticking the potato in the pocket of his shorts.

"You will eat that?" she said, surprised.

"Why not? Potatoes don't go bad."

"Everything goes bad."

"It's still firm. That means it still has its nutrients."

"You are some potato expert?"

"Are you?"

"Russians know potatoes."

"I'm hungry, I'm keeping it. And look, I think that's another basket over there."

They crawled through the deeper darkness and discovered two baskets placed side by side, one containing carrots, the other turnips.

"Nice," Jack said. "I love carrots." He grabbed three. They had lost their rigidity and flopped. The tip of one had turned black. Still, he tucked them in his pockets, adding a turnip as well. He had to roll to his side to do this, and when he rolled back his shoulder pressed against hers. It seemed accidental. In fact, he didn't even seem to notice.

"You're like chipmunk," she said, and blew out her cheeks to demonstrate what she meant.

"Some are for Rosa," he said.

She pointed. "There's another basket over there."

"This is like Easter," he said.

"What do you mean?"

"Don't you have Easter in Russia?"

"Of course," she said. "Easter is very important holiday." Some of Elizaveta's fondest memories of her pre-orphanage childhood were of saving yellow onion peels a month or two leading up to Easter day, which was always the first Sunday after the spring full moon. She and her mother would boil the peels with a half dozen eggs to turn the eggs a rich red.

Jack said, "What about the Easter bunny?"

She frowned. "What bunny?"

"The Easter bunny! On Easter morning it leaves a trail of chocolates all throughout your house, leading to a hidden Easter basket filled with a chocolate Easter bunny and chocolate eggs."

"Are you making this up?"

"Maybe it's an American thing..."

"It is definitely not a Russian thing." Elizaveta thought about the monthly stipend she'd received from the state to attend college. It was supposed to be enough to cover all her living expenses, yet it was barely enough to purchase two large chocolate bars. And Americans sprinkled their floors with chocolates and ate chocolate bunnies and eggs?

"You're supposed to follow your own trail so you can find your basket," Jack went on. "But my sister and I always picked up the chocolates as quickly as we could, erasing the trail, so sometimes it took hours to find where our baskets were hidden."

Elizaveta snorted. "What other stupid holiday traditions do you have?"

"Halloween was my favorite."

"Yes, I know Halloween. You dress up like ghost or witch."

"And go trick-or-treating."

"What's that?"

"You go around the neighborhood with a bag—I usually used a pillowcase—and knock on doors. Everyone gives you a chocolate bar or some other kind of candy. One year I think I filled up three pillowcases."

"Three pillowcases full of candy? And strangers, they just give you this?"

"If they have a jack-o-lantern on the front porch, yeah. If they don't, it means they probably don't want you knocking."

"You Americans are like cartoon character. You live in cartoon world."

"What are you talking about?"

Elizaveta was about to tell him if he walked down a street in Russia—the Russia she knew before she left four years before —with a pillowcase full of candy he wouldn't make it to the corner before he was robbed, if not killed. Instead she simply shook her head.

They continued their "Easter bunny hunt," moving in a general clockwise direction, discovering several more baskets filled with more vegetables.

The crawlspace turned out to be quite vast, and Elizaveta suspected it mirrored the floorplan of the cabin above. She wondered how long it had taken Solano to dig out. Even with a shovel and pickaxe it would have been long and laborious work. But what else did you do when you lived on an island by yourself with little to no human contact?

Elizaveta contemplated this. What *did* Solano do with all his time? He didn't have company, aside from the occasional local who swapped him dolls for produce. He didn't have electricity, which meant he couldn't watch TV or listen to the radio, even if he found either in a trash heap on one of his jaunts to Mexico City. Then again, people had managed without such modern conveniences for the vast majority of human history. They were hardly necessities for happiness. Solano had his freedom, his heath, a tropical climate, food and shelter. Maybe this was enough. Moreover, he created, didn't he? He built all the huts, and the cabin. He cleared the paths and constructed the bridges they had seen. And he hung up all the dolls, of course—and that was creating too, that was art.

Elizaveta recalled life in Saint Petersburg in the early- to mid-nineties. The brutal winters, the jostling for food and other basic supplies, the overcrowded buses, the cynicism and aggression, the robberies and racketeering, the misfortune and disdain etched on everyone's faces. Despite all this, her compatriots certainly had more than Solano—yet were their lives any better than his? Were they more fulfilled?

"There's another basket," Jack said.

"My knees and back hurt," she said.

"Okay, last one."

They adjusted their course slightly and stopped before the basket. Jack raised the candle to see inside it. "Whoa. Check this out," he said excitedly. He set the candle aside and withdrew from the basket a small, unadorned wooden box.

"What is that?" she asked.

"Beats me."

"Can you open it?"

"No, it's locked. Look, a keyhole."

"Can you break it?"

"Not down here." He glanced past her into the surrounding darkness. "Where the hell was the ladder?"

6

When they found the ladder, Elizaveta climbed it first. Nitro and Jesus and Pita were all bent over the trapdoor, looking down, talking to her, talking heads. She emerged from the hole into the candlelit room, which seemed bright in comparison to the dungeon-like crawlspace, then helped Jack out. His shorts bulged with vegetables, impossible not to notice.

"It's just a root cellar," he said in response to the barrage of questions. He emptied his pockets, setting the vegetables on the floor. "Help yourselves."

"They're dirty," Pita said.

"They're food," he said. "And we haven't eaten since mid-day." He took a crunchy bite of a carrot.

Nitro chomped into a turnip and shrugged.

"I'll pass," Jesus said.

"Ugh," Pita said.

"Oh," Elizaveta said, lifting her T-shirt, revealing the mystery box she'd stuffed down the front of her shorts. "We found this also."

"Let me see that." Nitro reached for it.

Elizaveta batted his hand away and unhoused the box from her shorts herself. "It's locked," she said, going to the wall on which hung the farming equipment. There was no shortage of tools to choose from. Large spanners, fencing pliers, an old fashioned saw. She selected a hammer, returned to the others, and set the box on the floor so the lock was facing upward. She gave it a solid whack with the hammer. Wood splintered but the lock held. She whacked it again. This time the lid flipped open. A battered leather wallet tumbled out, along with several sepia-toned photographs.

"That's all there is?" Jesus said, unimpressed.

"Solano's wallet?" Nitro said.

"Who are those photos of?" Pita asked.

Jack picked them up. There were four in total: a handsome woman, two young girls, and a group shot.

"Solano's family?" he said, passing them to Elizaveta. She studied them before passing them to Pita.

"Open the wallet," Nitro said.

Elizaveta did. There was a single identity card printed on green paper issued to Don Javier Solano. In the money sleeve was an old article cut from a newspaper. Elizaveta unfolded it.

"What does it say?" Pita asked.

She read the Spanish out loud:

MEXICO CITY - At least 25 people were killed and 17 others severely injured when a firecracker factory exploded Sunday in a blast of flames and black smoke.

The factory was located on the ground floor of a 28-family apartment building. Officials searching the smoldering ruins said most of the victims sustained severe burns. Dozens of people were still unaccounted for, raising fears that the death toll could rise.

Police said the explosion took place at about 11:30 p.m. and could have been triggered by burning heating oil from an overturned stove in an adjoining apartment. They were not ruling out other potential causes, including the improper mixing of the raw materials used in firecrackers.

Dolores Elias, a twenty-year-old retail clerk who lived in the neighborhood, said the explosion sounded like the end of the world, and she saw people flying through the air "like flies."

Firecrackers are often produced in small, home-based factories that are unregulated and lack proper safety equipment. They are usually used in rural areas to celebrate weddings, circumcisions, and other festivities.

Last month, a spark set off boxes of fireworks in a market in Celaya, killing 55 people, injuring hundreds, and levelling parts of the downtown area. Most of those killed or injured were buying firecrackers for the celebration of the Day of the Virgin of Guadalupe.

While Jesus, Pita, and Nitro debated with alacrity why Solano would care enough about a firecracker explosion to keep a newspaper clipping in his wallet, Elizaveta summarized the story for Jack in English.

"Maybe Solano caused it?" Jack said.

Elizaveta frowned. "Set off explosion?"

"Could be why he ended up on this island. He was wanted by the cops and needed a place to hide out."

"For fifty years?"

Pita was listening to them and said, "What about the photographs?"

"What about them?" Elizaveta said.

"They're probably of his family. You think he'd just leave his family behind?"

"Maybe they died in explosion."

"But if he caused it," Jesus said, chiming in, "you really think he would stick around to search the rubble for family photos?"

"The photos are all the same size, wallet size," Jack said. "Good chance he always had them in his wallet. Anyway, whatever," he added. "It doesn't matter what happened. The question is: why would he hide the wallet and pictures in a basket in a root cellar?"

Jesus shrugged. "Painful memories?"

Pita nodded. "He wanted to forget them, forget his old life."

"Why bother even keeping the wallet and photos then? Why not—" Jack cut himself off, and when he spoke again his voice was low and edged with caution: "Eliza, don't move."

7

Elizaveta froze, her muscles in lockbolt, every nerve ending tingling with sudden alarm. "What?"

"There's something on your back," Jack said.

Pita and Jesus were crouched before her, while Jack and Nitro were to either side of her. They both had a view of her back.

"Oh, fuck," Nitro said, seeing whatever Jack had seen.

"What is it?" she blurted.

Pita and Jesus both scrambled around behind her so they had a view too. They gasped.

"*What is it?*" She couldn't feel anything on her back. Nevertheless, she wanted to tear off her top and toss it across the room. She didn't do this though. Whatever was freaking everyone out might bite her.

Jack was up and moving, looking for something.

"*What is it?*" Elizaveta said.

"Stay still," Nitro told her. Then to Jack: "Get the saw."

Saw? *Saw?* Did they need to cut it off? *What was it?*

She was going to ask what was on her again, but she didn't. She realized she didn't want to know until it was off her.

Jack returned with the saw. It was old, the hard-toothed blade rusted.

"Careful," Nitro told him. "Just slip it beneath it."

Elizaveta felt the saw blade press against her back, near her left shoulder.

"Slip it under."

"I'm trying!"

"Ow!" A white hot pain seared her back.

"It stung her!" Pita exclaimed.

"Get it!" Jesus said.

In a blind panic now, Elizaveta leapt to her feet, tearing her shirt off her back, tossing it away, so she stood there in nothing but her bra. Pita was yelling, but so was she.

"Is it off?" she cried. "Is it off?"

"Yeah, yeah," Jack said.

Jesus and Nitro hurried to her shirt. Nitro toed it, trying to startle whatever was hiding within it into the open.

"What is it?" Elizaveta said. "It bit me!"

"It didn't bite you," Jack said.

"I felt—"

"It stung you."

Stung her? Was it a wasp?

"There it is!" Jesus cried.

"Kill it!" Pita shrieked.

Elizaveta felt sick. On the floor, scurrying away from her shirt, was a great fat scorpion. It was black, its segmented tail carried over its body. Its pincers alone must have been a couple of inches long.

And it had been on her back.

It had stung her.

Nitro tried stomping it beneath his flip-flop, but it escaped under the table.

"Fuck!" he said.

"Get it!" Pita said.

Jack, still holding the saw, went to the table. He ducked down and swung the saw, using the flat of the blade to squash the awful thing.

"Did you get it?" Jesus asked.

"It's still moving."

Jack swung the saw again, then again. He stood a moment later, holding the saw before him. The scorpion rested on the blade, its pugnacious body twisted and broken.

"It's dead," he said.

8

"It stung me," Elizaveta said, folding her arms across her breasts. She didn't care she was half naked; she wasn't being modest. She was shaking with fright, her flesh covered in goosebumps. "Scorpions are venomous, and *it stung me.*"

"Most are harmless," Nitro said.

"Most? What about that?" She pointed to the big fat horror

that still rested on the saw blade, which Jack had set down on the table.

"Turn around," Jesus said. "Let me see the sting."

Elizaveta turned.

"It's red," he said. "But it doesn't look too bad. How do you feel?"

"Are you a doctor? Have you been stung by scorpion before?" She was acting a bit hysterical, but she had every right to. Most scorpions might be harmless to humans, but some had venom that could be fatal. And that one—God, it was so *big*.

"How do you feel?" Jesus repeated.

"It hurts. Like bee sting."

"But you can still breathe fine, talk? That's good."

"Nitro's right, Eliza," Jack said. "Most scorpion stings are harmless. You usually only have to go to the hospital if you're a kid or elderly."

"In Las Vegas maybe, Jack," Pita said. "Not in Mexico. The scorpions here—"

"They're not that different," he said brusquely, silencing her with a look.

Elizaveta didn't miss this, and she knew he was trying to reassure her...which made her all the more alarmed.

Was she going to die?

"I can breathe now," she said. "But what of future? Maybe I will get worse. And there is no help here, no hospital, no antivenom."

"Someone should suck it out," Pita offered.

"What?" Jesus said.

"Someone should suck out the venom. I saw it on TV once. A person was bit by a snake, and this man sucked the venom from the wound with his mouth."

"That doesn't work, Pita."

"You don't know, Jesus. We should at least try. Nitro—you do it."

He shook his head. "I'm not sucking out venom with my

163

fucking mouth."

"I'll do it," Jack said.

"Nobody will suck my back!" Elizaveta snapped. "This is serious!"

"Look, Eliza," Jesus said reasonably. "You said you feel okay. If the scorpion was really poisonous, you would know by now. We're overreacting."

"You are just saying that—"

"No, I'm not, cariño," he said. "I promise, okay? You'll be fine."

9

Elizaveta retrieved her damp shirt and pulled it on, shivering as the cold material slid over her bare skin. Jack took the green and beige rug to Pepper's bedroom, to drape over Pepper, while Jesus and Pita and Nitro stood near the dead scorpion, speaking quietly to each other. Elizaveta began to pace back and forth. She couldn't relax. She couldn't stop thinking about the sting in her back. Originally she'd felt a sharp pain, followed by a burning sensation. Now, however, all she felt was a strange tingling. Still, she didn't believe Jesus when he said she would be fine. She had seen people stung by scorpions in movies. They always ended up foaming at the mouth, having heart attacks, and dying.

Jack returned from Pepper's bedroom. She went to him.

"How is Pepper?" she asked.

"Sleeping," he said.

"What can we do?"

"Nothing. He just needs rest. You do too."

"I'm not tired."

"Still, you should rest, relax."

"How can I relax? I have venom inside me. It's spreading—"

"Right, Eliza," he said, touching her arm. "And the more

worked up you get, the faster your heartbeat, the faster the venom gets absorbed."

She considered this, nodded.

"Take a deep breath," he said.

She did.

"Another."

"I am not in labor, Jack."

He smiled. She did too.

"Thank you," she said softly.

"Why don't you go to Pepper's room, lie down?"

"What will you do?"

"Keep watch."

She blinked. "Watch? Oh, you mean..." She'd gotten so caught up with the discovery of the trapdoor and the subsequent scorpion sting she'd completely forgotten about the potential killer on the island. "You need partner," she added. "I will keep watch with you."

Jack shook his head. "Pita will."

Elizaveta frowned. "Why her?" she said, feeling a bump of irrational jealousy.

"Because if we let her go to sleep, she won't want to wake up again for a subsequent shift."

Elizaveta glanced at Pita. She stood by the table with Jesus and Nitro, the three of them still talking softly in Spanish. She couldn't hear what they were saying—and she sensed that was the point.

"I'll keep second watch then," she said.

Jack shook his head again. "I don't want you alone with Nitro."

"So I keep watch with Jesus."

"That leaves Nitro and me on the last watch, and I know he won't be cool with that."

"So who keeps second watch?"

"Nitro and Jesus. Then, if you're feeling up to it, you can join me on the last one. Two hours each. That should get us to dawn. Hopefully the storm will have died down, and we can

165

head to the pier to wait for the boatman."

"And hopefully," she said solemnly, "I will not die a painful, poisonous death."

10

They went over to the others and explained to them the watch schedule.

"Does anyone have any problems with this?" Jack concluded.

"Do we get the gun?" Pita asked.

Everyone looked at Nitro.

"Fuck no," he said.

"But whoever's on watch should have the gun."

"She has a point, Muscles," Jack said.

"You'd just end up blowing your own balls off, chavo."

"I've fired a gun before," he said.

"There's no way in hell anyone's touching my piece, and that's that."

"If I'm sitting out there on the porch," Pita said, "I want a weapon."

"Help yourself," Nitro said, gesturing to the wall of farm equipment.

Resigned to the fact Nitro wasn't giving up his pistol, they scrounged through Solano's wall of farming instruments for something to defend themselves with. Pita selected a sickle, Jesus a hatchet with a broken half and rusty patina, Elizaveta a long-handled garden claw scabrous with corrosion. Jack considered an antique post-hole digger but apparently deemed it too unwieldly and instead settled on an eleven-inch iron hay hook.

Standing there examining their weapons of choice, they resembled a motley band of peasants about to march on Doctor Frankenstein's castle. Nevertheless, they were armed.

Jack opened the cabin's front door for Pita. Wet air blew inside, accompanied by a blast of angry wind.

"Scream if you see someone, Jack Goff," Nitro said.

Ignoring him, Jack followed Pita into the voracious night.

1957

1

The lobotomy was originally developed in 1936 by a Portuguese physician who would go on to win the Nobel Prize in Medicine. The procedure involved drilling two holes in either side of the patient's forehead to sever some of the nerve fibers in the frontal lobes of the brain. The hope was to treat intractable mental disorders by reducing the strength of certain emotional signals.

A few years later the procedure gained traction in the United States in a different incarnation called a trans-orbital lobotomy. It was not a precise surgery and simply involved hammering an icepick through the thin layer of skull in the corner of each eye socket and wiggling it about to scramble the white and gray matter located there. It took less than ten minutes to complete, and oftentimes no anesthesia was required (though patients were usually given electroshock treatment first so they were unaware of what was happening).

Around this time a neurologist and Harvard graduate named Dr. Jerome Asper was working as head of laboratories in a sprawling Boston mental institution that housed thousands of patients in abject Victorian conditions. Wanting to make a name for himself as a medical pioneer, he began performing hundreds of these trans-orbital lobotomies at the hospital. Despite his critics decrying that he was doing nothing more than turning his unwitting patients into vegetables, he had his share of successes, published his work in respected journals, and built a reputation for himself as one of the foremost experts in psychiatric science.

For much of the nineteen fifties, he became an evangelist for trans-orbital lobotomies, touring hospitals and asylums across the country, performing the procedure on thousands of individuals to treat a range of illnesses from schizophrenia to depression to compulsion disorders. It became so routine he started prescribing it for symptoms as mild as a headache, and he sometimes brazenly ice-picked both eye sockets simultaneously, one with each hand, to impress the media that usually gathered to cover his "miracle cures."

Nevertheless, by the end of the decade Asper's fortunes made an abrupt reversal due to two unforeseen developments. The first was the rise of antipsychotic drugs, which yielded the same pacifying results in the mentally ill as the lobotomy without the invasiveness of an icepick to the brain. The second was the widespread rumor that Joseph Stalin and the Chinese were using lobotomies to control their political enemies, fueling the Red Scare that vilified any activity related to Communism.

Consequently, Asper quickly fell out of favor with the mainstream medical establishment, and it wasn't long until no state hospital would touch him—not in the US at any rate. So in 1957 he relocated his sideshow to Mexico where he enjoyed revived success.

He had been performing the operation throughout Mexico City for several months when he received the call from Saint Agatha's School for Lost Children regarding a particularly troublesome ward.

Asper had never performed a lobotomy on someone so young before, but as one of the great men of medicine of the twentieth century, he was always up for a new challenge.

2

Dressed in a worsted suit and bowtie, Dr. Jerome Asper stood next to the school's resident priest, Father Pardavé, in a classroom turned makeshift operating theatre. His patient, a twelve-year-old girl named María Diaz, lay supine on the teacher's desk before them.

According to the priest, the girl had the IQ of a moron, participated in disruptive behavior, and was capable of violent outbursts. Moreover, she suffered several fits a week, during which time he believed the devil took control of her body and mind. Nonsense, of course. Religious gobbledygook. These fits would be the physical manifestation of the illness epilepsy, not some occult affliction. Even so, in his opinion the surgery was necessary. It would not only calm her down but also make her happier.

Looking up at him with frightened yet trustful eyes, the girl asked him a question.

Asper had learned enough Spanish in his short time in Mexico to know she was inquiring whether the procedure was going to make her more like her housemates.

"*Sí*," he said, smiling as he slipped a mouth guard in her mouth and placed two paddles on her forehead. He gave Father Pardavé a brief nod. The priest held the girl down tightly by her shoulders. Asper adjusted the timer on the small ECT machine on the desk and flicked the main switch. The electrodes delivered an electrical stimulus of several hundred watts that caused the girl's body to convulse powerfully, her jaw to clamp shut, and the tendons in her neck to stand out. The current flowed for five seconds before shutting off. Her muscles immediately relaxed.

Now that she was suitably dazed, Asper selected his

icepick and hammer from his medical case and went to work.

JACK

1

The storm had attained Armageddon proportions, yet it showed no signs of relenting. The rain fell in diagonal curtains with amazing force, chewing the ground and flooding shallow depressions. The wind, vicious and cold, threatened to strip leaves from their branches and uproot the smaller vegetation. Yellow bursts of lightning tortured the sky and lit the frenetic faces of the dozens of dolls dangling from nearby trees. Thunder boomed and crackled.

Pita and I sat side by side, our backs to the cabin's façade, sheltered by the porch roof. We both had pulled our knees to our chests, wrapping our arms around them, in an attempt to retain our body heat. I remained alert, my eyes scanning the devastated jungle, the shadows dancing beneath the wind-frenzied trees. Yet as the minutes ticked away, and there was no sign of anybody lurking in the night, my mind began to drift, and I found myself reflecting on the racing accident that had ended my career. I didn't like going there. It filled me with sadness and resentment and regret. Nevertheless, sometimes I couldn't avoid it.

It was the third race of the 2000 NASCAR Winston Cup

Series, the Daytona 500 at Daytona International Speedway in Florida. I won the Pole, and with the help of my teammate I ended up leading the field for the first ninety laps. But a miscue from my pit crew and a couple of other mishaps saw me fall back as far as twelfth at one point. However, I made a late charge, and with two laps to go I was running second to Ed Melvin in the No. 93 car. On the inside of Turn 1 I attempted to pass him. We made light contact, both cars veering up to the wall, my Chevy leaning on his. As soon as I cleared him I pulled off a bump 'n' run to take the lead. By Turn 4 Melvin caught up and we were at a virtual dead heat. At the white flag he pulled a car length ahead. I stuck directly behind him through Turns 1 and 2. I tried an overtake during Turn 3 but couldn't get around him. My chance came in the final turn. I'd entered it low and Melvin high. I cut to the bottom groove, straddling the double yellow out of bounds line, and drew even with him as we exited the turn for the front stretch. As we sped for the checkered flag at two hundred miles an hour, we were so close our side panels traded paint, and then somehow his car caught mine in such a way air got under me. The next thing I knew I was looking at my roof for a long time—and then waking in the ICU with the immediate and uncanny memories of floating above my body while I'd been dead.

I mentioned what happened to the surgeon who'd operated on me, more in passing than anything else. He didn't agree with my neurons dying theory, as the observations occurred while the EEG was recording a flat line, and he wanted to bring in a specialist to see me. I declined. I wasn't going on record as a near-death-experience survivor and an out-of-body nutter.

Instead, I put all my energy into my physiotherapy, hoping to jump back into the Winston Cup Series in March...not knowing then that my racing days were gone and over.

2

"What are you thinking about?" It was Pita. She was staring into the storm.

I blinked, coming back to the present, the cold and the rain and the wind. I considered making up something to tell her, because whenever the accident came up, we fought. Nevertheless, deceiving her seemed like too much effort, and I said, "Florida."

She didn't say anything, and I thought that was the end of the conversation, when she added belatedly, "It happened, Jack. You can't change it. Get over it."

Get over it?

Thunder rumbled. It sounded distant, as if the storm might be retreating. This illusion was shattered a second later by another blast directly above us.

Still, I barely registered it.

Get over it.

"I'm sorry," Pita said quietly, knowing she'd struck a nerve. "I didn't mean that…I'm…I'm just scared…"

The antagonism building inside me evaporated. I reached out my hand, squeezed her knee, and said, "Me too."

She looked at me. "I didn't think you got scared."

I chuffed and released her knee. "Why did you think that?"

"Because I've never seen you scared before."

"I used to get scared before every race."

"I don't mean like that. I mean… I don't know." She seemed to be reflecting. "Those were fun times."

"The races?"

She nodded, then laughed to herself.

"What?" I asked.

"Remember when we got locked out of our room in Kansas City?"

I nodded. I'd finished first at the Kansas Speedway that day, and we'd been out all evening celebrating.

She said, "We were staying at that old hotel that didn't have twenty-four-hour reception. We ended up in the laundry room."

I smiled. At some point I'd lost the keycard to the room. We searched the hotel for a game room or library or somewhere we could crash until morning. The only place that offered privacy was a launderette with six coin-operated washers and dryers. We ended up fooling around instead of sleeping—which we did a lot back then—and when things heated up Pita told me she wanted to have sex on top of one of the machines. She even made me put money in it so it would vibrate.

She said, "Who the heck does their laundry at one in the morning?" She was referring to the woman who entered the launderette with a basket of clothes just as Pita was climaxing and biting my neck to suppress a cry.

I said, "She had a good look at my bare ass."

"She probably loved it."

"Probably scarred her for life."

"Fun times..." Pita said this with a healthy dose of nostalgia, and although likely unintentional, her tone communicated more than her words did: they weren't fun times anymore.

"I'm sorry," I told her quietly enough I wasn't sure she heard me over the storm.

But she did, because she said, "For what?"

"I've changed."

"We've both changed, Jack. Everyone changes."

"I'm not the same person I was."

"Because you can't race." It sounded less like a statement and more like an accusation.

I didn't answer.

"Dammit, Jack," she said. "I know. Okay? I get it. Racing was a big part of your life. You can't do it anymore. Okay. But... stop looking back. You had a good career—"

"Four years."

"And you did more in those four years than most professional racers do in ten."

"I could have been great."

"You *were* great!"

"I mean the records—"

"Screw the records, Jack! You're lucky you didn't die."

"I actually did."

"Well, you didn't stay dead. That's a pretty impressive accomplishment. So you should be thankful for that, for being alive. Why can't you just accept what happened and move on?"

"You don't understand..."

"No, I don't!"

"Didn't you hear what I told you, Pita? *I'm not the same fucking person.* If I'm not a race car driver, who am I? What do you propose I do with the rest of my life?"

"The rest of your life? You only had another five years of racing anyway."

"Ten, minimum. More like fifteen, even twenty."

"Why don't you at least consider broadcasting? Your agent —"

"I'm not going to sit in a booth and watch other people race."

"It's better than doing nothing, Jack. And that's what you're doing now. Nothing. You're miserable, and that's made me miserable. Don't you see that?"

"Yeah, I do."

"So do something about it other than drinking yourself silly every night."

"Fuck off."

"You don't think you have a problem?"

"I've never said that."

"You're an alcoholic, Jack."

I stiffened. I didn't like that word. It brought to mind images of bums sitting on the street, begging for change. But I suppose I was an alcoholic—just one with money.

"What?" Pita said when I didn't respond. "You're going to ignore me now? You know, lately, if I didn't start a conversation, we would never talk."

"You want to talk about why I drink?" I snapped.

"I know why you drink," she said.

I shook my head. "It's not just that I can't race..." I hesitated, wondering if I should tell her what was on the tip of my tongue, and decided why the hell not. "It's...being here," I finished.

Pita frowned. "Being here? This island? We just came today —"

"Mexico," I told her.

Silence.

"We were supposed to come here for a month or two," I added, "to get away from the media. We've been here for almost a year now."

"We spent four years in the US," she said defensively.

"That's different. You liked it there. I'm bored out of my fucking mind here."

"So why don't you go back to the Las Vegas, Jack?" she said coldly. "Nobody's forcing you to stay here in this terrible country. Go. Then you can sit around your house all day there and drink."

I clenched my jaw but didn't take the bait.

A sky-wide burst of lightning shattered the night. Ancillary thunder followed.

Rain fell. Wind gusted.

More lightning, more thunder.

"Are we...okay?" Pita asked me eventually.

"Okay?" I said, though I knew what she meant.

"Us. Are we okay?"

I was going to tell her yes, we were fine, we were just going through a rough patch. But what was the point? We both knew the truth.

"No," I said. "I don't think we are."

We didn't say anything more after that.

3

I didn't want to think about racing, or Pita, or the fact we had just broken up—which I was pretty sure was what just happened—so I spent the next hour or so considering Miguel's murder, the mystery killer, the theories we'd come up with thus far. The more I dwelled on this, the more I felt as though we were missing something, overlooking some vital piece of the puzzle.

Miguel's eyes were not taken by someone doing something stupid in the heat of the moment. Whoever mutilated him—hopefully after he was already dead—was sick and twisted. So the serial killer premise I could buy. What bothered me was the fact the murder occurred here, on this island. Because a murderous sociopath was more often than not the guy next door who had a nine-to-five job, was on a first-name basis with the staff at the local Starbucks, paid taxes, had a mortgage, and waved to you from his car while you walked your kids to school. I'd never heard of Ted Bundy or Jeffrey Dahmer living as recluses in the wilderness. Jason Voorhees maybe, but we weren't dealing with an undead dude in a hockey mask. Despite what Pita may believe, there was nothing metaphysical going on. Whoever killed Miguel and injured Lucinda was flesh and blood. They put their pants on one fucking leg at a time.

So what were they doing on this goddamn island?

This line of thinking ultimately brought me back to Solano. He lived out here on his own. He was a crazy bastard. He would have been the obvious suspect, except for the fact he was dead...

I frowned. Sat a bit straighter.

What if he wasn't dead?

I mean, how did we know he was dead? All I knew was what Pepper told me. All Pepper knew was what someone told him. And what had that been? That Solano was found drowned in the same spot where the girl supposedly drowned fifty years before? Well, the first glaring problem with this was the fact nobody would have known where Solano found the girl's body except Solano himself—if there had ever been a girl to begin with. Moreover, Pepper had said the police hadn't been able to determine Solano's cause of death because he had been in the water, undiscovered, for too long, eaten by salamanders and fish. Well, if he was this badly gone, perhaps little more than a clothed skeleton, it went to reason they couldn't positively identify him either.

So the body might not have been his. It could have belonged to anyone.

But who?

Someone like Miguel who had trespassed on his island?

Holy shit! Was Solano the killer then? And if so, he surely knew of our presence on his island. Of course he knew. We were camping out in his fucking house!

I turned to Pita, to share this discovery.

Her eyes were closed, her lips parted slightly. She was asleep.

I stared ahead again, into the night, the rain.

Was Solano out there somewhere? Watching us? Plotting?

4

I was dozing off, my chin touching my chest, when a sound caused me to start. I jerked my head up, snapped open my eyes. But it was only Jesus and Nitro, coming outside to relieve us.

It was 2 a.m.

5

Inside the cabin the candles burned warmly, beacons in the tempest, though two had extinguished themselves. Elizaveta sat at the table by herself. She smiled diffidently at us. "You survived," she said.

"It's crazy out there," I said.

"I know, Jack. I can hear. The thunder, it's like earthquake."

I checked in on Lucinda. She lay on her back, the red sheet pulled to her chin. Her attractive face was hoary, sunken, almost cadaverous. I peeled back the sheet, then Solano's poncho, which made me think of Clint Eastwood in his Spaghetti Westerns. Trying not to look at Lucinda's bare breasts, I eased her onto her side. Her skin was hot and clammy. Nitro's tank top/compress was stiff with blood. However, it seemed to have worked, as the laceration had ceased bleeding. I eased Lucinda onto her back and once more covered her with the poncho and sheet. The pulse in her neck was difficult to palpate, but it was there, faint and slow. Her breathing sounded raspy.

"Lucinda?" I said softly, not expecting an answer.

I didn't get one.

I left the room and checked on Pepper next. He lay with Rosa beneath the green and beige rug, only their heads poking out. Two peas in a pod, I thought. But although Rosa seemed snug, perspiration sheened Pepper's face, and he appeared to be shivering.

I felt his forehead with the back of my fingers. He was burning up.

"Peps," I said quietly. "You awake?"

He opened his eyes, saw me, closed them.

"You got a bit of a chill in the rain, buddy."

He didn't say anything.

Best thing for him, I figured, would be a hot drink. We had rainwater, but Solano didn't have a stove or microwave to heat up the water, and I didn't think it would be wise to start an indoor fire.

Second best thing for him would be to get him up and moving.

"Hey, Peps," I said. "Can you sit up?"

He shook his head imperceptibly.

"Just for a bit. Get your circulation moving."

"Can't," he said.

"Can you try?"

He struggled to his elbows with great effort, then flopped back down. He shook his head.

"Okay," I said. "Just rest. Do you want some water?"

"No..."

"I'll be back."

I turned to leave and found Pita directly behind me.

"Trying to give me a heart attack?" I said.

"I'm going to sleep in here for a bit," she said.

"I don't think there's any more room in the bed."

"On the floor."

"Be my guest."

She moved past me and settled on the floor at the foot of the bed. Then she lay on her side and curled herself into a ball, using one arm as a pillow.

I waited for her to say something, maybe goodnight. She didn't. I exited the room and closed the door behind me.

I went to the table and sat next to Elizaveta. Tired of carrying the hay hook around, I set it on the tabletop.

"Lucinda seems stable," I said.

"She's lost much blood."

"Hopefully she can hang on until morning."

"And Pepper too."

"He's not that bad."

"I think he has...how do you say?" She shook herself and said, "*Brrrr...*"

"Hypothermia?" That had crossed my mind. "Maybe," I said. "But he has a fever. I'm pretty sure if you have hypothermia your skin would be cool to the touch, not hot."

"He is shivering."

"I think he just has a nasty bug."

Elizaveta seemed alarmed. "Bug?"

"No, not like that. Speaking of which, how's your sting?"

"It hurts."

"That's all?"

"I was a bit dizzy for a while."

I frowned in concern.

"It's okay," she said. "I'm okay now. I feel better."

"I hope so."

"I don't trick you, Jack. So what is this bug you say?"

"It's an expression for a really bad cold," I told her. "I had something similar once. I was a teenager. A bunch of friends and I went to Mardi Gras in New Orleans for a weekend. No one had a car, so we took a Greyhound—a bus. It was air-conditioned. A vent was right above my seat. I didn't know how to shut it off, and I fell asleep with freezing cold air blowing on me. When we got to New Orleans in the morning—it was an overnight bus—I had all Pepper's symptoms. Fever, shivering, no strength. When we got to the hotel, I dropped into bed and couldn't get out of it for twelve hours. I couldn't eat. Couldn't do anything."

"And then what?"

"It just went away. Literally within an hour I went from feeling dead to almost normal."

"So you think Pepper will magically get better too?" she asked.

I nodded. "I think he just needs rest."

On that note Elizaveta yawned. I did too.

"So what did I miss in here?" I asked.

"Miss?" she said.

"What did you guys do while Pita and I were outside?"

"Nothing amazing." She shrugged. "Jesus and Nitro had arm wrestle."

"Who won?"

"Take guess, Jack."

"Did they talk shit about me?"

"Shit? No. They said some bad things. But never shit."

"It's an expression."

She smiled. "I know."

"So?" I pressed.

"What?"

"What did they say?"

"Why do you care?"

"I don't... So what did they say?"

"I cannot tell you."

"Why not?"

"Because Jesus will be your brother-in-law. I don't want to make trouble."

"He's not going to be my brother-in-law."

"Yes, when you marry Pita, he will—"

I lowered my voice. "Pita and I broke up."

Elizaveta blinked in surprise. "When?"

"When you guys were inside here arm wrestling apparently."

She was reticent. She fiddled with the garden claw on the table before her, turning it over in her hands. "I'm sorry, Jack," she said finally. "Do you want to talk?"

"No."

She looked at me. I looked at her. She seemed as though she wanted to say something, but she didn't. Still, her eyes didn't leave mine.

"You'll be okay, Jack."

I nodded.

"You know what you need do?"

I waited.

"Move to Russia."

"Russia?"

"You are rich American man. Handsome American man. You can have every girl in Russia you want."

This comment surprised me, because although she wasn't in Russia, I couldn't help but feel she was speaking about herself too.

So was she hitting on me—all of five minutes after I'd broken up with Pita?

I glanced at the door to Pepper's room, glad I'd closed it. But was Pita on the other side, with her ear against it, listening?

No. We weren't speaking very loudly, and the rain drumming against the roof would make it difficult, if not impossible, for her to hear our voices.

Even so, I wanted to change the topic, though for some reason my mind was drawing blanks.

"Please, Jack," Elizaveta said, cupping my hand with hers. "I joke."

But was she joking? There was mischief in her eyes—because she was joking, or flirting?

This was bizarre, the turn of the conversation, bizarre. And what made it even more bizarre was the fact I was attracted to Elizaveta, I'd been attracted to her ever since Jesus introduced us, and I was hoping she *wasn't* joking.

I cleared my throat. She removed her hand from mine.

Thunder crashed above us, petering to a growl.

"This storm," Elizaveta said. "Oh my God."

The storm, the sanguinary killer out there—right. "I was thinking about everything that's happened on the island," I said, relieved to find the knot in my tongue had unraveled. "Do you want to hear a new theory about who might have killed Miguel?"

"Yes, of course," she said. "Tell me."

I explained.

"Solano murdered Miguel?" Elizaveta said, and I thought she was going to laugh, tell me this was outlandish. But what she added was: "I think you might be right, Jack. It all fits. Everything."

"It does, right?" I said. "He lives out here. He's a crazy hermit. He doesn't want people trespassing on his island."

"So he kills them."

"And dumps them in the canals. Pepper told me it was filled with skeletons anyway, from the revolution."

"I didn't know that."

"The army supposedly dumped thousands of bodies in them."

"But Solano didn't dump Miguel."

"No, but that's because he probably didn't have time. He would have wanted to find Lucinda and Rosa first. Make sure no one could leave and give up his secret."

"But why take his eyes?"

"Maybe that's just his thing. Serial killers do all sorts of weird shit like that."

"Look, Jack, I have goosebumps." She showed me her arms. "You have solved this mystery!"

"It doesn't mean we're safe," I said. "He's still out there."

"Yes, you are right. But I feel safer because Solano is not some Rambo. He is just old man."

"Which is probably why he hasn't tried anything."

"You mean attack us?"

I nodded. "He has to know we're here. We're staying in his house. But like you said. He's an old man. He might be able to sneak up on someone like Miguel and stab him in the back, but there's nothing he can do against so many of us."

"Oh, Jack I'm so relieved!" She leaned forward across the table and kissed me on the mouth. Her lips stayed pressed against mine for way too long to be a simple celebratory peck.

But I didn't mind. In fact, I felt electrified, like one of those bolts of lightning in the sky had just zapped me on the head.

Then her lips parted. Mine did too. Our tongues touched—

I pulled back, frazzled, guilt-ridden.

What the hell was going on?

Elizaveta was looking at me with her sparkling green eyes. Her face was slightly flushed. She clearly had no problem with that kiss.

And I realized I had to stop whatever had started. What we were doing wasn't right. It didn't feel right. People were going to get hurt. Pita would, Jesus would. I didn't care about Jesus actually. But I cared about Pita. And this was wrong. It was way too soon. Elizaveta was her friend.

"What are you thinking about, Jack?" Elizaveta asked.

It was the same question Pita had asked me two hours before, while we'd been sitting out on the porch together.

I felt worse than ever.

"We can't—" The rest of the words caught in my throat.

"What's wrong?" Elizaveta asked. She looked where I was looking, at the table. She stood quickly. "Another scorpion? *Where?*"

I shook my head, standing too. I pointed at the table. "Did you move the doll that was there?"

"What doll?"

I remembered it clearly. Black hair that smelled like citrus, painted lips, heavy eyeshadow, the dress that may or may not have been concealing a hole between its legs.

I said, "There was a doll on this table earlier."

"So what?"

"Where is it?"

Elizaveta looked around the room. "There are dolls everywhere, Jack."

"There was a doll right there. It was special."

"Why special?"

"It just was. It was all dressed up. Solano put makeup on it."

"What?"

I moved to the end of the table, opened the shoebox, and slid it to Elizaveta. "Makeup."

"I don't remember any doll on table, Jack."

"When I came here before, when I found Rosa, it was still daytime. It was the first thing I saw. A doll. Right there." I pointed again. "Did someone move it? Did Jesus or Nitro move it?"

"No," Elizaveta said. "Nobody did. There was no doll, Jack. I remember. I lit that candle when we first arrived." She indicated the half-melted candle on the table. "There was no doll."

"What doll?" It was Pita. She stood at the threshold to Pepper's bedroom. We'd raised our voices, woken her—if she'd ever been sleeping and not eavesdropping on us.

"Do you remember seeing a doll on the table?" I asked her.

"No..." She shook her head more decisively. "No."

"There was one there earlier, and now it's gone—

The front door to the cabin burst open, and Nitro staggered inside, spraying blood everywhere.

6

I'd never witnessed anything like the spectacle that unfolded before us, and I found myself rooted to the spot in horror.

Nitro's eyes blazed with blustery panic. His mouth was cranked open in a silent scream. His hands clamped his throat, trying to stem the freshet of blood gushing from it.

He came straight toward me, and for a moment I thought he was going to attack me.

He released his throat and seized my tank top with blood-soaked hands, pulling me forward. Powerful jets of blood shot from his jugular veins straight into my face, into my eyes, my mouth. I tasted it on my tongue, coppery, salty, sweet.

Nitro slumped to his knees, tugging me down with him. He was like a drowning person, flailing, dangerous.

I tried to pry his hands from my top, but he wouldn't let go.

Pita and Elizaveta were screaming. I wanted to tell them to shut up, but my mouth was full of blood.

Nitro was surely screaming too, though he could no longer make any sound. His throat had been slit from ear to ear, his vocal cords severed at the same time as the rest of his plumbing. I could see straight into his gaping windpipe.

Dismayed, disgusted, I shoved him away from me, hard. He released my top and fell onto his back, his arms and legs flopping akimbo. He suffered a paroxysm of agony, as if he were being kicked by an invisible boot. Then his body relaxed, went still. The fountain of blood spurting from his throat shut off.

His heart had stopped beating.

He was dead.

7

My paralysis broke. I dropped to my knees next to Nitro and attempted CPR. Nevertheless, I knew this was futile. His head was only half attached to his neck.

Someone was behind me, talking to me, pulling me away. It was Jesus. He'd returned inside. I stared at him blankly, watching his lips move, wondering what he was saying. Elizaveta and Pita were nearby, hugging each other and crying. I couldn't hear them either. I couldn't hear anything except for a plaintive drone in my ears.

I lumbered to my feet and went to a corner, away from them. My balance was skewed. I leaned against the wall, spitting blood from my mouth, waiting to be sick.

What the hell happened?

Nitro was dead...

Solano!

I whirled toward the cabin's front door, seeing Solano charging inside, bloody knife swinging, slashing.

He wasn't there.

It was my imagination.

I returned to Nitro's body. I rolled it over, which proved oddly difficult, for it was slick with blood and had become a dead weight. I cringed at the feel of the warm flesh beneath my hands.

Pita was asking me what I was doing in a semi-hysterical voice.

I unzipped Nitro's backpack and searched the pocket for the pistol.

It was missing.

I panicked before seeing the outline of the gun's handle poking out the top of his board shorts. I retrieved it and stood, leaving him facedown.

Better that way. Nobody wanted to look at his sightless eyes or smiling throat.

I checked the pistol's magazine. Still several cartridges locked and loaded.

Flicking off the safety, I went outside.

8

I scanned the night, searching for movement—but everything was moving in the near hurricane winds: trees, branches, shrubs, dolls, grass.

Pistol held close to my chest, muzzle pointed skyward, I followed the trail of blood. It went right along the porch, all the way to the bannister.

What had Nitro being doing down here? Pita and I had remained huddled near the door our entire watch. Had he heard a noise and come to investigate?

Then what? When his back was turned, Solano emerged from the night and slit his throat?

I poked my head over the bannister, looked down the length of the cabin.

Nobody there. No footprints. Nothing.

Whoever had killed Nitro, it seemed, had vanished into thin air.

1957

1

Patricia Diaz was putting Salma, her six-month-old new-born, to bed in her crib when there was a knock at the front door. She tucked Salma's blanket beneath her chubby chin, then left the bedroom. In the foyer she opened the front door and was surprised to find a policeman standing on the little stoop. He had a moon face and a large belly testing the buttons of his uniform. He was holding the hand of a feral looking girl dressed in a ratty nightgown, her hair chopped short—

"María!" she exclaimed.

"Mommy?"

"Baby? Oh my God...*Oh my God!*" She enfolded her daughter in a great hug. "Oh baby! What's happened to you?"

"Officer Rodriguez, ma'am," the policeman said. "I picked her up earlier not far from here. She was loitering in the park. Actually, she appeared to be living there."

"Living?" Patricia released her daughter and frowned at her. "Why were you in the park, sweetheart? Why weren't you at Saint Agatha's?"

"I didn't like it," she said simply.

"The school?"

"I just left."

"You left?"

"I just left," she repeated. And she sounded angry. Her voice was shrill, her eyes hard.

"Why don't you go inside, honey. You can lie down in my bed. Okay? I'd like to speak with the policeman in private for a moment."

When María disappeared inside the house, Patricia looked at the policeman and swallowed tightly. "This is very strange," she said, feeling suddenly nervous even though she had done nothing wrong. "You see, María has a certain condition. She doesn't learn well like others her age. Two years ago her school psychologist recommended she enroll in a special boarding school."

"Saint Agatha's?" the policeman said.

"Saint Agatha's School for Lost Children. Some of the children, their parents have died, or they're alcoholics, or...there are many reasons why they are placed there. But some are like María. They are mentally deficient in some way."

"How long has your daughter been at this school?"

"Eighteen months or thereabouts."

"When was the last time you saw her?"

"Well, when we placed here there." She added quickly, "We tried to visit her early on, but the nuns wouldn't let us see her. There was always some excuse or another. But they assured us she was doing fine. And then, well, I became pregnant, and that sort of took over my life, and then Salma was born..." Patricia took a deep breath, realizing the hot poker inside her wasn't nervousness; it was guilt. "Anyway, my husband and I decided if María was happy, perhaps it would be best if we kept our distance. It would be easier for her this way." She glanced over her shoulder the way María had gone, then returned her attention to the policeman. "What have they done to her? She seemed so..." The word that came to mind was "cold," but she only shook her head. "How did you know where to bring her,

Officer? I didn't think she knew her address. She could never remember information like that."

"She didn't," the policeman said. "When I asked her where she lived, she said the park. It took a while until I got her to tell me the name of her school—her old elementary school. I took her there. The principal recognized her. He had your address on file." He shrugged. "But if she belongs in this school—Saint Agatha's—I'll take her back there."

"No," Patricia said. "I mean, no thank you. Not until I know why she left. Something must have happened to her for her to just leave like that, for her to prefer to live in a park, for God's sake. And surely the nuns would know she was missing. So why haven't they contacted me?" She shook her head. "I need to talk to María. I need to talk to my husband. But thank you, Officer Rodriguez, thank you for bringing my daughter home."

2

Patricia went to her bedroom, but María wasn't there, sleeping or otherwise.

"María?" she called.

No response.

Patricia ducked her head into the kitchen, then the dining room. She was on her way to the back door, to check the backyard, when she passed the playroom-turned-nursery. María stood next to the crib, holding Salma in her arms, rocking her gently.

"María?" Patricia said, alarmed. "What are you doing?"

"I found Angela."

"That's not Angela, sweetheart. Her name's Salma. You have to be very, very careful with her." She started forward, holding out her arms. "Please give her to me."

"No."

Patricia froze. "What do you mean no?"

"She's mine."

"She's your baby sister, yes, but—"

"She's mine!"

"María, pass me your sister." She steeled her voice. "Right now."

María glowered at her, and for a terrifying moment Patricia feared she might throw Salma across the room. But then she held the infant out at arm's length, gripping her by the wrist as if she were nothing but a doll.

Salma woke and began to cry.

Patricia snatched the baby quickly and cradled her tightly against her chest, staring over her head at María with frightened eyes.

3

Patricia didn't know what those nuns did to María, but the eight-year-old girl who had been living in her home for the last three days was not her daughter—or at least not the daughter she had once been. She was a stranger. A violent, angry stranger. Patricia felt she was walking on eggshells whenever she was in the same room with her, worried about saying something or doing something that would set her off. María had already had several temper tantrums. The worst occurred earlier that morning when Patricia found her in the kitchen, carving up a heel of cheese. Afterward she placed the dirty knife back in the knife block. Patricia explained she had to wash the knife otherwise someone could get sick. María responded by throwing the knife block against the floor and going around the house shouting and slamming doors. Patricia had been so terrified—for both herself and Salma—she quickly collected the baby and went down the street to her girlfriends', remaining there until her husband Diego returned from work. By then María had calmed down and was curled up in her bed (they had left her bedroom untouched in her absence), staring at the wall.

Presently Patricia sat in the living room, rocking Salma in her arms. Diego sat in a chair across from her, still in his construction clothes, a beer in his hand.

"Saint Agatha's was supposed to help her," she said softly.

"It didn't help her," Diego grumbled. He sipped his beer and wiped foam from his mustache with the back of his hand.

"At least before she would listen. Now...now nothing gets through to her."

"She doesn't listen," he agreed.

"When she threw the knives, all I could think was..."

"What if Salma was in the kitchen, playing on the floor?"

Patricia nodded. "I'm scared, Diego," she admitted. "When María was younger, when she had her temper tantrums, they were almost cute. But they're not cute anymore. And what of when she's older? When she's fifteen, or twenty, or thirty? Will she still be having temper tantrums? What will people think? They won't understand."

"That's a long way away, dear."

"But it's inevitable. She's not going to get better. She's not. I know that now. Not even a little bit." Patricia adjusted Salma and wiped a tear from her eye. "She's never going to fall in love. Never get married. Never have children of her own. Never..." More tears leaked from her eyes. "And I should be there for her. I'm her mother. I should be there for her. But I don't think I can be, Diego. I don't think I can. I'm...I'm scared of her. I'm scared of my own daughter."

He hushed her, getting off his chair, kneeling beside her, stroking her back.

"We never should have given her away," she went on. "She was our daughter. We should have loved her. We should have taken care of her. Now look what's happened to her. Look what's happened to our daughter."

"We'll take her back. I'll take her back. Tomorrow—"

"To Saint Agatha's?" she said, shocked. "Look what's happened to her there!"

"We'll be better this time. We'll visit her. We'll make sure they treat her right."

"No, Diego." She was shaking her head. "She can't go back there."

His face hardened. "She can't stay here, dear. Not with Salma. I won't allow it."

"No, she can't stay here," she agreed.

"I'll start looking for another school then—"

"Who's to say another school will be any more kind to her? And what of when she's too old for school? She will have to go to one of those institutions. Do you know what those places are like? And she's pretty, Diego. She's still so pretty. That's the worst part. She will be a victim, taken advantage of. I don't think I could live with myself knowing she was locked away in one of those places, getting beaten and raped and—" She took a deep breath and held her husband's eyes. "I know this is a terrible thing to say. I pray for my soul. God, I pray for my soul. But this world wasn't meant for her. There is nothing in it for her except suffering and pain."

"What are you getting at, dear?"

"I'm saying..." But she found she couldn't form the words. She couldn't bear to hear them coming from her lips. Yet in the end it didn't matter. She didn't have to say anything.

Diego understood.

JACK

1

I returned inside the cabin. Pita and Elizaveta still embraced, their heads buried in each other's shoulders. Jesus hovered next to them, speaking softly. And...aw shit. Rosa stood at the threshold to the bedroom, her eyes sullen, her hands clamped over her mouth. She seemed to be staring at everything and nothing.

Sticking the pistol into the waistband of my shorts against the small of my back, I went to her, knelt so we were the same height. She tried to hug me. I held her at bay; I was covered with blood. In fact, my face must have been painted red.

"It's okay, Rosa," I said absurdly, the empty reassurance something only a child would find comforting. "It's okay."

Tears shimmered in her eyes, yet she didn't say anything.

"Go back in the bedroom. You'll be safe there."

She opened her mouth but no sound came out.

I stood, turning her around, nudging her into the room. She went obediently.

Pepper was propped on his elbows, staring at us with dusty eyes.

"Hop back in bed," I told her.

Instead of climbing back into the bed, however, she crawled beneath it, her hiding spot where I'd found her earlier.

"What happened...?" Pepper asked me. He couldn't see out the door from his position, but he certainly heard all the shouting.

"Nitro was attacked."

"Who...?"

"Solano."

"Solano?"

I explained my theory to him.

"We need to leave," he said, lying back down.

"We will. In the morning."

"Keep watch..." He closed his eyes.

He didn't say anything more, and I figured he'd sunk back into sleep. I left the room, closing the door behind me.

I confronted Jesus. "What the hell happened?" I was tingling everywhere—arms, thighs, balls, the nape of my neck—but I kept my voice controlled.

"I—I don't know." He shook his head.

"Don't know? You were out there with him, man!"

"I was sleeping."

"Fuck, Jesus..."

"He *said* I could sleep. He said he would keep watch. All I saw, when I woke up, all I saw was him pushing open the door and disappearing inside. I didn't even know he was injured—until you guys started screaming." He almost seemed like he might cry. "*What the hell's happening, Jack?*"

So I was right. Solano must have made a noise, lured Nitro to the end of the porch. Then when his back was turned...

I hadn't given the old hermit enough credit. It seemed he wasn't deterred by our superiority of numbers after all.

"You have to get rid of him," Pita said, looking at me over Elizaveta's shoulder. Her cheeks were streaked with tears and mascara. Her nose leaked snot. She wiped at it with the back of her hand.

She meant Nitro. And she was right. We couldn't leave him

in the middle of the room, pretending he wasn't there, ignoring him.

"Jesus, help me," I said.

"Where are we going to move him?"

"The porch."

I pushed open the cabin's front door, then went to Nitro's legs. Jesus went to his arms. On the count of three we lifted Nitro and carried his heavy weight outside, stepping through the small lake of blood that had pooled around his body. We set him on the floorboards a few feet to the left. I folded his hands atop his bare chest in an attempt at dignity, but I couldn't bring myself to slide closed his eyelids. I recalled attempting that with the Pepper-doll earlier in the day—or yesterday now, for that matter—and the eyelids springing open again. If this happened with Nitro...I don't know, but I already had my fill of ghastly images from this island, and I didn't need another.

Back inside, I closed the cabin's door, then dragged the table in front of it. The rudimentary barricade would not stop a persistent assault. That was not the intent. It was meant to prevent Solano from sneaking up on anybody again.

"That's not going to stop her," Pita said.

"Not now, Pita," I said.

"Not now? *Not now?*"

"I don't want to hear anything about ghosts."

"Why are you so blind?"

"There's no ghost on this island."

"We contacted her—"

"It was a hoax—"

"I felt her—"

"Ghosts don't fucking exist!"

"Jack..." Elizaveta said.

"Solano snuck up on Nitro. That's it."

"Solano?" Pita said. "Solano's *dead*."

"Solano?" Jesus said, frowning.

I explained my theory again. Jesus seemed thoughtful. Pita,

of course, wouldn't have any of it.

"I *felt* her, Jack," Pita repeated. "She's here and she's angry and—"

"It's okay," Elizaveta said. "We are safe."

"Safe?" Pita said. "*Safe?* Look what happened to Nitro!"

To Jesus I said, "Can you calm her down?"

He went to her, speaking reassuringly. She lashed back. Their argument escalated until she threw up her hands and went to Pepper's bedroom, slamming the door behind her.

I could hear her crying from the other side of it.

2

Later. I wasn't sure how much later. I'd fallen asleep and had just woken up.

It was quiet—too quiet—and I realized the storm had stopped.

No wind, no rain.

Silence.

The cabin was dark. A few candles still burned.

I was alone.

Elizaveta and Jesus must have gone to the bedrooms.

I should probably get up, stick my head outside, make sure the storm was indeed over, but I found I didn't want to move.

The table was no longer in front of the door.

Where was it?

Who'd moved it?

Jesus?

Probably. He'd probably gone outside just as I'd planned to go outside.

Too quiet.

Was I alone? *Alone* alone? Had Jesus and Pita and Elizaveta left me? Were they down at the pier, waiting for the boatman?

That's what it felt like, that the cabin wasn't empty, that it was deserted.

A noise—from Lucinda's room, like the shuffle of cards.

"Hello?" I said.

The door swung inward. The hinges protested, issuing a prolonged *weeeeeeek*. I squinted, trying to see into the room. I couldn't make out anything but darkness.

"Hello?"

A giggle.

I stiffened.

Rosa? I wanted to believe it was Rosa. But it wasn't her. The giggle was more a cackle, malevolent, threatening.

Lucinda? Had she recovered? Was she sitting on the bed, naked and giggling in the dark?

Time to get the hell out of there, I thought.

I stood—but didn't leave. The person was cackling in the bedroom again. I knew I should ignore whoever it was, leave the cabin, run, but instead I found myself moving toward the witchy sound.

I stopped inside the door. I still couldn't see anything in the room. It was cauldron black.

"Hello?"

"Jack…"

The voice was female, young, raspy.

Something moved very quickly. I heard the frantic patter of small footsteps. Then a snick, a whoosh. A tiny flame appeared to my right.

A doll stood on its tiptoes, a burning match in its hand. It was attempting to light the candle on the dresser. The wick caught and light bloomed. The doll extinguished the match with a quick flick of its wrist.

Its head twisted ninety degrees, owl-like, to look at me.

"Jack…" it rasped.

"Who are you?"

"Jack… It's *me*…"

The doll was female. It had dark wavy hair that fell halfway down its back, thick-lashed brown eyes, a tiny nose, playful lips—

"Pita?" I said.

"Jack..." Her lips weren't moving, and I realized she was communicating to me how she claimed to have communicated with her sister Susana, telepathically.

"What happened to you?"

"Solano..."

"What about him?"

"He caught me..."

"Caught you? But what did he do? You're a doll, Pita."

"That's what he does... He catches people... He turns them into dolls... He hangs them up everywhere... But we're still alive... We're alive inside them..."

"Where's Eliza?" I asked, alarmed. "Where's Rosa?"

"Dolls..."

"No!"

She began to cackle once more.

3

I came awake with a start and found myself in candlelit darkness. It was late, the time when graveyards yawned and decent folks slept snugly in their beds. Not me though. I sat cross-legged on the hard floor in the middle of the cabin's main room, groggy and exhausted.

I raised my head from my chest, blinking. I remembered sitting there, closing my eyes, not to fall asleep, to think... and maybe to forget. Yes, I'd wanted to forget I was covered in Nitro's blood, forget his lifeless body was lying on the porch, his eyes staring at eternity, forget we were trapped on the island, stalked by a killer.

My stomach, I realized, felt bloated and bilious. At first I thought this was due to hunger. But it wasn't hunger. It was fear.

I glanced at the barricaded door, then at Elizaveta, who sat in front of me, hands held together on her lap, head bowed. She could have been meditating had her posture not been slumped. "Hey?" I said quietly.

Her eyes blinked open. "What happened?" she whispered.

"You were sleeping."

Her shoulders sagged. Her fingers massaged her face, making small circles.

"And you snore," I said.

"I do not."

"How would you know if you were sleeping?"

She grimaced. I glanced at my watch. It was 3:41 a.m.

I'd only been asleep for twenty minutes or so. Still, that was twenty minutes too long. Solano could have sneaked into the cabin during that time, slit my throat, slit all our throats...

Dismayed by my lack of vigilance, I sat straighter. "Where's Jesus?" I asked.

Elizaveta gestured to Pepper's bedroom. "He said smell bothered him."

I sniffed. The room reeked of blood, cloying and sickly sweet. It made me think of a cookie factory my parents had taken me to while we'd been RVing around the country, a visit that turned me off cookies for the rest of my life. The smell of molasses and dough and butter hadn't necessarily been bad; it had simply been too omnipresent, too overpowering. I'd ended up disgorging the contents of my stomach on the floor in front of everyone.

"I brought you this," Elizaveta said, indicating an enamelware bucket next to her which was filled with rainwater. She slid it to me.

I dunked my hands into the cold water and scrubbed them. The water turned red.

"Let me help." Elizaveta picked up a rag she'd fetched. She dampened it in the water and proceeded to clean my face. Her touch was delicate yet firm at the same time, maternal. "There," she said when she finished.

I looked around for my daypack. It was by the junk heap that included the car seat. I stood and stretched, retrieved the bottle of vodka from the pack, then sat back down. I twisted off the cap and offered the bottle to Elizaveta. She took an impressive sip and passed it back. I took an even bigger sip, swishing the vodka around inside my mouth to kill the lingering taste of blood. I didn't have anywhere to spit it out, so I swallowed.

Elizaveta produced her cigarettes, offered the pack to me.

"You only have four left," I said.

"I'm trying to cut down. You have one, you help me."

Shrugging, I accepted a cigarette. She held forth a lighter and pushed the button that ignited the flame. I lit up. She slid a cigarette between her lips and lit up too. I didn't smoke. Well, I did, but not regularly. I wasn't addicted. During one of my binge nights out, I could burn through a pack by myself just for the hell of it. But I wouldn't crave a cigarette the next day. In fact, I could go a week, or several weeks, until the fancy for one took me again.

Funny why that was, given I was addicted to almost every other vice.

I took a drag and turned my head to the left, so I didn't blow the smoke in Elizaveta's face. I couldn't help but see the blood-smeared floor, the crimson splatter leading to the front door. My mind hit me with an image of Nitro, the way he looked at me when he'd stumbled into the room, scared, pleading, expressions so alien to him.

"I didn't like him," Elizaveta said, as if reading my thoughts.

"Nitro?"

"I didn't like how he always teased you."

"He was a prick," I said. Then laughed. "But he was sort of funny."

"Funny?"

"If we weren't arch enemies I probably would have liked him."

"That makes no sense, Jack."

203

I took another drag. "You know what he told Pepper earlier, when we were looking for Rosa's canoe? He told him to switch weather channels because the weather girl on his channel had a major hot front."

"Yes, that was his humor. He was always telling Jesus sexist jokes except when—" She stopped abruptly.

"Except when what?"

Elizaveta shrugged, contemplated her cigarette. "Except when Pita was around."

"Pita?"

"Yes. But anyway…"

I frowned. Did Elizaveta know something I didn't?

Avoiding eye contact, she picked up the bottle of vodka and took a sip.

I said, "What's up, Eliza?"

"Nothing is up, Jack." She still wouldn't look at me.

"Were Nitro and Pita…" I didn't know how to articulate the question. "Was something going on between them?"

"I don't know, Jack. I don't know anything."

She was lying. That was clear as day…and that meant… what? What did she know? Had Nitro and Pita fooled around? Had they fucked? Had they been fucking on an ongoing basis?

The girl I'm pounding right now, she's vaginamite.

My heart sickened, and I felt suddenly nauseous, as if I'd inadvertently stepped on a baby bird. I was also angry—furious —though this almost immediately burned itself out. If Nitro were alive, I would have beat the living shit out of him. But he wasn't. He was dead, and no matter what he did, I couldn't be mad at a dead guy.

Pita though—she was a different story. I had half a mind to go wake her up, confront her. But what would that accomplish? She wasn't coping well. A confrontation like that might push her over the edge.

Are we okay? she'd asked me earlier on the porch.

Yeah, except for the fact you're fucking Nitro behind my back.

"Jack?" It was Elizaveta. She was looking at me with concern.

She'd known. Jesus had likely known too. How many other people had known?

"I'm sorry," she added.

"Whatever," I said. It wasn't her responsibility to tell me Pita was cheating on me. She was dating Jesus. Her loyalty was to him, to his family, not me—

Elizaveta rocked forward onto her knees. She stubbed out her cigarette on the floorboards, plucked mine from my fingers, and put it out as well. Then she placed her hands on my chest. For a moment I thought she was going to try to hug me, console me. She didn't. Instead she pressed me backward. I resisted. I didn't know what was going on.

"Lie back," she whispered, still pressing.

And then I was lying back. My baseball cap slipped off my head.

"Eliza..." I said.

She lifted her pink top, exposing her midriff, then her violet bra, lifting the top over her head. She moved forward so she straddled me, her groin against mine. She took my hands in hers and pressed them against her breasts.

This was reckless, I thought. Madness. Nitro's corpse was outside, no more than two dozen feet away. His blood stained the floor. Pita and Jesus were in the next room.

But a switch had flicked inside me, and none of that mattered.

My hands were working on their own, exploring the firmness of her breasts, the weight of them, the hardness of her nipples.

I undid the clasp of her bra. The spaghetti straps slipped down her arms. The cups released her breasts, which were perfect in the dim candlelight, full and round.

Setting the bra aside, she leaned forward, placing a hand to either side of my head. Her lips tickled my neck, my ear, her breath warm, erotic. She leaned farther forward, so her breasts brushed my face. I could smell her sweat pushing through her perfume, but it wasn't unpleasant.

My tongue probed, trying to catch her moving nipples. She moaned quietly. I fumbled open the button on her shorts, tugged the zipper down. But that was all I could manage with her straddling me. She understood this and eased back, then stood, gracefully, like a cat.

Her emerald eyes never left mine. They were intense, beautiful. She was beautiful.

She skimmed her shorts down her legs. They dropped around her ankles. She fit her fingers into the elastic waistband of her panties, which were violet like her bra, and skimpy. She pushed one side down, then the other, revealing a trimmed strip of pubic hair—then pulled them back up.

Teasing.

Finally she slid them down her thighs to her ankles. She stepped out of them, and her shorts. I kicked off my board shorts and boxers.

She settled on top of me, warm, tight, rocking, gripping, gliding.

Soundless.

4

Afterward, clothed again, we sat on the floor as we had before, almost as if nothing had happened. And I couldn't believe something had happened. It had been so unexpected, spontaneous, surreal.

I felt lightheaded, amazed not only at what we'd done, but that we'd gotten away with it.

I also felt like total shit.

Pita cheated on me, I told myself.

We broke up.

I've done nothing wrong.

Only it felt wrong. Very wrong.

But right too.

"Can I ask you a question, Jack?" Elizaveta said.

"What?" I said.

"Why did you stop racing?"

"Oh," I said, relieved. This wasn't my favorite topic of discussion, but it was better than talking about what just happened between us, what it meant. "You don't know?"

"I know about crash. Jesus told me. But that was one year ago. You are better, da? Why not race again?"

"Because I can't."

"But why?"

"I'm not better."

"You look better."

It was true. My body was fine and functioning. I'd bruised my ribs in the accident, fractured my wrist, and whacked my tailbone so hard I couldn't sit comfortably for days. Even so, I was back in my Chevrolet within two weeks...yet I wasn't the same. I was getting daily headaches that affected my racing, distracted me. At the CarsDirect.com 400 I hit an embankment with the driver's side of my car. Halfway through the Cracker Barrel Old Country Store 500 I smacked the wall in Turn 2 and spun out. Then, a few days before the next race at Darlington Raceway, I was scheduled to do a media tour. However, I bowed out halfway through the day due to the worst headache yet.

My sponsors became worried. My PR guy wanted me to stay off the track. I stubbornly refused. The next race was the Food City 500 at Bristol Motor Speedway. Around lap 340 I developed another headache, this one so severe my crew chief threw in the towel at the next pit stop.

I ended up seeing three different doctors. None could answer for certain what was wrong with me. They simply advised me to slow down, get some rest, I'd feel better soon.

"I get headaches," I told Elizaveta now. "Sometimes when they get bad, my vision gets blurry."

She frowned. "That is problem?"

"Maybe not so much if you're a banker. But if you're a race car driver, running at three thousand feet a second, yeah, it's a problem, a big problem."

"Can you take medicine?"

"Nothing that's worked." I shrugged. "Well, except this, sort of." I picked up the vodka and took a belt.

"I didn't know this."

"You never asked."

"So what do you do now? I know, I see you at parties sometimes. But you don't race, don't work. What do you do every day?"

"Drink."

"I'm serious."

"I am too."

"Well, what do you do when you drink then?"

"Do you really care?"

"I'm curious, Jack."

"I have a car I'm working on rebuilding."

"That sounds fun."

"It's more work than fun, but it fills in the time. I'm also working on a board game."

She frowned. "A bored game? Why?"

"Huh? No—board." I pantomimed a square. "Like Monopoly."

"I know Monopoly."

"Do you know IQ 2000?"

"IQ 2000?"

"It's a board game too."

"You forget where I come from, Jack. We did not have Coca Cola or Pepsi when I was child in Soviet Union. You think we had this IQ 2000?"

Sometimes I did forget Elizaveta grew up in the Soviet Union. It might have only collapsed a decade ago, but to me it seemed as relegated to the past as Nazi Germany. "Well, the game I'm working on is like IQ 2000, trivia. But the questions and categories relate to NASCAR."

"That sounds fantastic. I will buy it."

"It's never going to be published. It's just a hobby." I shrugged. "What about you?" I asked, wanting to switch topics. "What do you do every day?"

"I work," she said. "I am governess, you know."

"But what about your free time?"

"Ha. Free time? I have zero free time, Jack."

"You're that busy?"

"I am like mother to these twins. It is exhausting."

"But rewarding, I imagine."

"Maybe if the children were...normal."

"They're not?"

"Their father is a Russian oligarch, Jack. They get anything they want. At last birthday party, they had pony rides, wild pigs, piñata, a cake bigger than me. They are..." She pinned her nose up with her thumb.

"Piggish?"

"Yes, but not that word. Snotty? Yes, they are snotty monsters."

"Can't you quit?"

"And do what? Go back to Russia?"

"Is it still that bad?"

Elizaveta nodded. "We have a president who says he will help poor, but he won't. He only helps himself. He is corrupt. Everybody is corrupt there. Da, it is still bad."

"Do you like Mexico?"

"Better than Russia."

"Then just get another job. There are some good international schools around."

"You don't understand, Jack. You are American. You can work anywhere. Mexico, Europe, anywhere. Your government has agreements with other governments. Russian government has agreement with nobody. No country wants Russian worker. No country gives visa. I was very lucky. The family I work for is very powerful. Only they can get me visa. I can't quit."

I chewed on this because I'd never given it much thought before; I'd never had any reason to. I said, "When does your visa expire?"

"Next spring. So I still have time."

"Time for what?"

"To convince Jesus to marry me."

Her words slapped me. I felt hurt, bitter. However, I immediately swept these emotions aside. She and Jesus were still a couple. Of course they were. What happened between us, the sex, it was just that: sex. A diversion, an escape, albeit temporary, from Nitro's death, this island of horrors.

Still, I found myself asking: "You want to marry him?"

"I would be a permanent resident. I would not be forced back to Russia. I could quit job as governess." She offered a playful smile. "Then I could build cars and make board games too."

I wasn't amused; I was jealous. It was stupid. Nothing more was going to happen between Elizaveta and I.

Still...

"So you're just with him for the visa?" I asked.

Elizaveta's smiled vanished. "I like him, Jack."

"Because he has money? Because he can get you a permanent visa?"

Her eyes flared. "Do not judge me, Jack," she said dangerously. "Not everyone has easy life like you."

"I've had an easy life?" I said, genuinely surprised. "I worked like a dog to get to where I was—"

"But you *could* get there," she said. "How many Russian race car drivers do you know? Well?"

"None," I admitted.

"Because they cannot drive race car? Nyet. Most cannot buy shee-it car. You think they can buy *race* car? You take much for granted, Jack." Before I could say anything, she added: "Let me tell you, okay? I lived in building with six other families. I woke up before light every morning just to avoid line for bath. In winter my floor, the fourth, was always very cold, but the third floor was always very humid with steam. Go figure. My school was also always very cold. You needed jacket, hat, scarf. Sometimes the ink in pens would freeze. The children I taught—you know what they all wanted?"

I shrugged. "To become astronauts?"

"To move to United States." She shook her head, reflectively. "Life in the Soviet Union was not so bad. You did not have to think about having food, paying bills. You had zero concerns really—as long as you didn't...how do you say... stand out of crowd. And most people didn't. They didn't know better, what they were lacking. But after Gorbachev, everything changed, everything. For first time you could see beyond iron curtain. You could watch CNN or BBC. People realized how shee-it their lives were compared to Western countries, especially the US."

I stared at her, digesting what she was saying.

"Let me tell you about one day," she went on. She was getting worked up, and I didn't want to interrupt her. "I was walking back from the school where I taught. I was carrying bags. You know, I carried bags everywhere I went—everyone did. This was no fashion statement, Jack. We didn't know when basic commodities would be available. So better to be prepared, right? I passed a grocery store near my building. There was line, forty people maybe, waiting in cold. I didn't know what they were waiting for, but I didn't want to miss out on getting something—anything was better than nothing—so I joined line too. I waited maybe one hour. Snow started to fall. My fingers and toes were frozen. My face and lips and nose, frozen. I remember a car pulled over on the road. The driver took the windshield wipers from trunk and attached them to car. They go automatically, there is no off switch, so you have to take them off in dry weather or they fall apart. I watched him from the line, him and his old car, thinking he was very lucky, because he *had* car. I got angry. Because why did he have car? Why couldn't I have car too? Why did I have to stand in line? Standing in lines was for grandmothers. That was their purpose in life. They wait and wait and wait for whatever might be at the end. But I was no babushka. I was about to go to front of line...bud in...when another woman tried this first. A man yelled at her. She yelled back, saying she had kids to feed. The man, he seemed drunk, he punched her. She fell to the ground, bleeding in snow. No one helped her. They didn't want to lose spot in line."

I was shocked. "You didn't help her?"

"Of course I did. I couldn't let her lie there in snow. I let her go in front of me in line. Others were not happy. They yelled at me too."

"Did you ever reach the front of it?"

"Yes. All that was left was bread. Crumbs, more like it. The shop owner, Yury, sometimes had items from black market, but that day I had nothing to trade him."

"What did you usually trade him?"

"My rations of vodka usually. Sometimes US dollars."

"Where did you get US dollars?"

She shrugged. "From trading something with someone else. That was how it worked. Once, I found fur hat on street. It was like finding gold. I ate very well that month."

"Someone traded you their rations for a hat?"

"A *fur* hat."

"Yeah, but if they were starving...?"

"You don't understand, Jack. It was because people had nothing that they wanted something. How do I explain? It is not wealth that makes you happy. It is simply having more than your neighbor. If you are poor, but have more than your poor neighbor, you are rich. It makes you feel good. Human nature, I suppose.

"Anyway, my point, the system was broken. Nothing worked. Then the war in Chechnya happened and everything got worse. Violence everywhere. People planting explosives in apartment buildings. Murders, robberies. So, no, Jack, my students didn't want to become astronauts. They wanted what they saw on TV, what they saw in America. Because you work hard in America, you can do anything, right? American dream, right? They just want fair chance in life." She paused for a long moment. "So you ask me if I am with Jesus for money and visa? Da, maybe. Do I love him? Do you want truth, Jack? I don't know love. I don't know what this is. But I do know surviving, and I don't want to survive always, I want to live. Can you understand that now?"

"Yeah, Eliza," I said, believing her last statement to be an apt aphorism. "I think I can."

"I hope so."

"I can."

"Good."

5

We were quiet after that, during which time Elizaveta smoked her last two cigarettes and I finished off the vodka. Elizaveta's revelations had caught me off guard. I'd had no idea how tough she had it growing up in the Soviet Union and the subsequent Russia that emerged from its ashes. All I'd really known of that part of the world was what I'd seen in movies, and this was more *James Bond* than *Gorky Park*: frozen tundra, international spies, Machiavellian women, and cold-hearted assassins. And what was that bit about Elizaveta not knowing what love was? What about her family, her friends? She made it sound as though she'd grown up in an icy hell.

With these thoughts in my head, I got up to give Elizaveta some space and to check in on Lucinda. Her condition hadn't changed. She was alive but corpse-like, pallid, unresponsive, fading inward. Even her hair seemed flat, lifeless. Her rapid deterioration bothered me all the more because I was helpless to prevent it. I could not provide her the medicine or assistance she needed. I could do nothing but hope she pulled through until morning, or whenever the storm moved on. Frustrated, I was about to leave when her eyes fluttered open.

I knelt next to her. "Lucinda?" I said softly, quickly.

She stared at me.

"Lucinda?"

"...*muñeca*..."

"What?"

Her eyes closed.

"Lucinda?"

She didn't reply.

6

When I returned to the main room Elizaveta was exactly as she'd been, sitting cross-legged, staring at the floor. The candlelight cast a gentle chiaroscuro pattern across her features, making her appear statuesque, ageless. When I sat down, she came out of whatever trance she'd been under and looked at me.

"Lucinda opened her eyes," I said.

"*Yo-moyo!*" Elizaveta swiveled her head toward Lucinda's room. "And?"

"It was only for a couple of seconds. She's unconscious again."

"Did she speak?"

I nodded. "She said, 'Monica,' I think. Something like that. She mumbled it. But that's what it sounded like."

Elizaveta frowned. "Monica, like person?"

"I don't know. Maybe it was 'munica?'"

"Munica..." She sat straighter. "*Muñeca?*"

"Yeah, maybe," I said. "What does that mean?"

"Doll," she said.

7

"Are you shitting me?" I said.

Elizaveta shook her head. "*Muñeca* is Spanish for 'doll.' This island, it is called, *Isle de las Muñecas*."

"Ah, right," I said. I pondered this, examining the possibilities, the implications, then added, "I wonder if she thinks she's in a hospital or something. She wanted to tell us where she was attacked."

"Hmmm."

"What?"

"Maybe she thinks doll attacked her."

I chuffed. "Come on, Eliza."

"I said she *thinks*. She is injured. She is dying. Maybe she is... What is word? Sees make-believe? Del...?"

"Delirious?"

"Yes, that."

I nodded. "She might not have been fully conscious. Could have been speaking from a dream."

"Should we try to wake her again?"

"How?"

"Shake her. Or pour water on her."

"On her face? I don't think that's a good idea, Eliza."

"But she could tell us what happened."

"Or go into cardiac arrest."

Elizaveta frowned. Thunder resounded. "Earlier," she said, "before Nitro...before what happened to him...you mentioned a doll. It disappeared. Do you think Solano took it?"

I nodded. "I think he's been watching us ever since we arrived at the island. I had a feeling, after I had that fight with Nitro and left you guys, I had a feeling of being watched. I thought it was the dolls...having their eyes on me. But now I think it was probably Solano. It makes sense he would follow me, doesn't it? He didn't want me stumbling across Miguel's body, or Lucinda and Rosa."

"But you found Rosa."

"And he realized he could no longer just wait and hide and hope we left. We knew something happened, we would call the police. So he went in the cabin after Rosa and I left to get more weapons or whatever he needed. That's when he must have taken the doll. I don't know why he would. Maybe it was special to him. His favorite. Actually, I think it was—the way he put makeup on it, bathed it. Anyway, he's crazy. It doesn't matter why he took it. He just did."

"He never attacked us though. When we split up, it was just Jesus, Pita, and me. Why not attack us then?"

"That's still three against one, and he's an old man. Besides, he would have known by then the storm was coming. He would have known we were staying on the island overnight. Probably figured he'd try to knock us off one by one."

"He didn't attack you or Pita. You had first watch. Why not attack you? Why wait for Jesus and Nitro?"

"Maybe he hadn't worked up the nerve yet. Or maybe he was waiting for us to all go to sleep. But when Nitro and Jesus went out, he realized we were keeping watches, and he had to act."

Elizaveta considered this. "These are many 'maybes,' Jack."

"It's speculation, yeah," I said. "But, hey, if you got something better, something that doesn't involve ghosts or animated dolls, please tell me, I'm all ears."

1957

1

María sat in the front of the *trajinera*, watching the trees and colorful flowers float pass on the banks of the canal. Angela was seated next to her, watching the scenery too. She wasn't the real Angela that Sister Lupita stole. She was a new one that her father had purchased for her the day before.

"What's that, Angela?" she said. "You want to go swimming?"

"Can we?" she asked.

"Do you know how to swim?"

"Not really. But I can learn."

"I guess I can learn too."

María turned to look at her mother, and her father behind her, pushing the boat with a long pole. They returned her look, puzzled. They couldn't hear her speaking to Angela. María and Angela were using their special voices that only each of them could hear.

She said out loud: "I want to go swimming."

"We're going to have a picnic first," her mother replied.

"I said I want to go swimming!"

"After we eat, sweetheart. Then you can go swimming. Is that okay?"

María faced forward again. She heard her parents talking behind her, but she ignored them. She said to Angela, "We can go swimming after we eat."

"Okay."

2

A short time later María's father steered the *trajinera* through weedy water until it bumped against the bank of an island. He got out and held the gondola steady as María climbed onto land first, then her mother. They went a short way inland until they found a patch of soft ground beneath a big tree. María's mother set down a *serape* for them to sit on. It was woven in shades of gray and black and had fringes at the ends. Her mother owned all sorts of these blanket-like shawls, and she used them for everything: bedspreads, sofa covers, car seat covers. There was even one hanging on the wall in the living room, next to the picture of the Virgin Mary. Before María went to Saint Agatha's School for Lost Children, she had loved all of them. They made her feel safe and special when she was curled up in one. Now, however, the *serape* on the ground meant nothing to her. In fact, if anything, it angered her. Everything seemed to anger her recently.

Except Angela.

"You're my best friend, Angela," she said in her silent voice.

"You're my best friend too."

"I'm never going to let someone take you again."

María's father and mother began unpacking the picnic basket they'd brought, setting the food on the ground: watermelon slices, tortas, nachos with avocado salsa, pickled potatoes, white-powdered cookies, candied pecans, and a big bottle of lemonade. María was hungry and stuffed herself until her belly ached. Afterward her mother asked María if she could brush her hair. María always used to like when her mother brushed her hair—when it had been long and thick—so she said yes. While brushing it, her mother began to sing a lullaby under her breath. It was one she had often sung to María when she was younger.

María closed her eyes, enjoying the warm sun on her face and the brush's bristles tickling her scalp and her mother singing in her soft, beautiful voice, and although she wasn't aware of it, she was smiling for the first time in a long, long while.

3

The water felt cold on María's bare feet and ankles, even though it was summer. Nevertheless, she waded farther into the canal, gripping Angela in her hand. The water rose to her knees. The rocks beneath her feet turned smooth and slimy, and she had to be careful not to slip.

She wasn't wearing a bathing suit, because she wasn't really going swimming. She was just splashing around, and that was okay with her. The hem of her dress was already wet and clinging to her thighs. That was okay too. It would dry when she got out.

She kept her eyes fixed on the water. It was very clear. She could see all the way to the bottom and the small little fish darting away from her feet.

"This is fun," she told Angela.

"Don't go too deep."

"I know that."

"Don't slip."

"I know, Angela! I'm not a baby."

On the rippling surface of the canal, she saw her reflection grinning up at her. And then she saw her father's reflection looming next to hers. His shadow fell over her.

"Turn around," Angela said quickly.

María was already turning when the rock her father was swinging struck her in the side of the head and sent her crashing into the cold water.

JACK

1

C lose to an hour later, pushing four in the morning, the storm finally seemed to show signs of moving on. The rain still fell in relentless droves against the corrugated iron roof, but the wind and thunder had eased off, and it no longer felt as though the cabin might be torn from its foundation and tossed to Kansas.

Elizaveta and I sat in silence, trying not to fall asleep. I was lost in half-lucid thoughts of Nitro, of his blusterous personality, his machismo, how I despised yet respected him, respected not only his ability to remain cool under pressure, to lead rather than be led, but also his discipline, the work he obviously put into keeping fit, which, oddly, made his death even more tragic. In my half-lucidity I drew a comparison between a neglected yard shriveling up in a drought to a lovingly tended garden suffering the same fate. Because all those years spent lifting weights and watching what he ate...for what? He would never lift weights or eat anything again. All his hard work ceased to mean anything in the second or two it took a maniac to slit his throat open. It all seemed so senseless.

At some point I realized I didn't want to reflect on Nitro

anymore, on his meaningless death, I didn't want to be sad or feel despair, and I ended up thinking about my sister, Camille. She was a year younger than me and still living in Vegas, a dancer in a show playing in the Broadway Theater at the Stratosphere Hotel and Casino. I saw the show once. It was a matinee, filled with dancing, music, and comedy. The dancing was great, the comedy not so much, with most of it being raunchy. I remember the singer though. She was pretty and a capable performer. I met her backstage. I'd been chatting with Camille when the singer—I think her name was Joan—came down the corridor carrying a bouquet of flowers, presumably given to her by an adoring member of the audience. Camille introduced us, saying, "Joan, this is my brother, Jack. He's a NASCAR driver." It always embarrassed me when she introduced me with not only my name but profession. After all, you didn't say, "This is Steve, he's a waiter over at The Olive Garden," or, "This is Joe, he's a dentist." Anyway, Camille was proud of me, I guess, and I was proud of her (and come to think of it, I do believe I've introduced her, saying, "This is Camille, she's a performer in a Vegas show").

I missed Camille. The last we saw each other was in Florida. She and my parents flew there to visit me in the hospital after the accident. They remained for a few days, leaving only when I assured them I was one hundred percent okay.

In hindsight, I wish I'd made more effort to see them over the years.

I'll be seeing them all shortly, I told myself. Once I'm back in Polanco, I'll arrange movers to transport my stuff, pay off whatever remained on the house lease, pack what I need into the Porsche, and drive north for the border. It was about a thirty-hour drive from Mexico City to Vegas. I'd split it up over a few days. I liked long road trips. Pulling over whenever you pleased, wherever you pleased, checking into random motels, trying local food, starting out again first thing in the morning with a hot coffee and some tunes on the radio. All this reminded me of the first two or three years I'd been with

Pita, when we would cruise the interstates from race to race together, free as birds, our biggest concern the distance to the next rest stop when we were busting to use the toilet.

And then I saw Elizaveta in the car with me instead of Pita. The image caught me off guard, yet it excited me too. I imagined the two of us heading north through the desert, stopping at small towns for a day or a week, we had no schedule to keep, making love whenever the urge took us, only with a bed beneath us, perhaps some music, clean and showered, no fear of waking anyone else up...

Nevertheless, this was a fantasy, nothing more. Even if she wanted to run away with me, she didn't have an American visa. She wouldn't get across the border.

We could always stay in Mexico. Go south instead of north, go to Cancún. Live in tropical paradise—until her visa expired and she had to go home.

I could marry her.

Right. It wasn't that easy. It took time to get a greencard, there was a lot of paperwork involved, a lot of hassles.

Besides, why would I want to marry her? I barely knew her. Plus, she'd only be marrying me for the same reason she wanted to marry Jesus: money and a visa.

I glanced at Elizaveta now. She was looking at me, and I couldn't shake the feeling she knew somehow what I was thinking about.

"You look tired," she said.

"I'm okay."

"You can rest. I will keep watch—"

The door to Pepper's bedroom creaked open.

Rosa appeared. She looked guilty, as though she were up past her bedtime and knew it

I said, "What's wrong, Rosa?"

"I can't sleep," she said.

"Do you want to hang out with us?"

She nodded.

I got up and went to her, closing the door quietly behind

her and leading her back to where I'd been sitting. She settled between Elizaveta and I.

"What are you guys doing?" she asked.

"Waiting," I said.

"For what?"

"For morning."

"Then we'll leave?"

"That's right."

"Good. I don't like it here."

"I don't either."

She studied the floor, and I could guess her next question.

"What happened to Muscles?" she asked.

"He was...hurt."

"Is he dead like Miguel?"

I couldn't see how lying would help any. I nodded.

"Did the ghost get him too?"

Elizaveta said, "We don't know anything for sure."

Rosa looked at her. "Why do you talk funny?"

Elizaveta blinked. "I don't talk funny."

"Yeah, you do."

"How funny?"

"Like the bad guys in movies."

Elizaveta snorted. "*American* movies."

"She's from Russia," I said. "That's how Russians speak English."

"Are there Russian movies too?" Rosa asked.

"Of course," Elizaveta said.

"I haven't seen any."

"There are, don't you worry," Elizaveta said, somewhat indignant.

"There are," I agreed. "But they're so bad nobody outside of Russia watches them."

Elizaveta made a *pfft* sound.

We fell silent and listened to the machine gun patter of rain on the roof.

Rosa said, "You promised to teach me 'Little Miss Muffet,'

Jack. Can you still do that?"

"Sure," I told her. "It's really easy. It's only six lines."

"I'm ready."

I recited the nursery rhyme, explaining along the way to both Rosa and Elizaveta the words "tuffet" and "curds" and "whey."

"What a stupid song," Elizaveta said at the conclusion. "Girl sits on tuffet? Runs away from spider?"

"Have you ever heard the Russian version?"

"There is Russian version?"

I nodded and said, "Little Miss Beautymark, crawled in the dark, searching for carrots and potatoes; along came a scorpion, who made her scream like an orphan, and frightened Miss Beautymark away."

"Wait!" Rosa protested. "Eliza doesn't have a beauty mark."

"I needed something that rhymed."

"Well, 'potatoes' and 'away' don't rhyme."

"Sorry, Rosa. I was sort of making it up on the spot."

"You can be real jerk, Jack," Elizaveta said, and her eyes were daggers.

I looked at her, surprised. "It was just a joke, Eliza."

"You think being orphan is joke? You think it's funny?"

"It rhymed with scorpion, that's all."

"You didn't know I was an orphan?"

"What? No! You were an orphan?"

"Pita didn't tell you?"

"No. Eliza, I swear. Shit... If I knew..."

"You don't have any parents?" Rosa asked her.

"No," Elizaveta said, still glaring at me. But then the edge left her. She shook her head and said to Rosa softly, "They were taken away."

"Where did they go?"

"I don't know."

"Did they do something bad?"

"No. They were good people."

"So why were they taken away?"

"It is complicated," she said. "But very simply, when I was growing up, the leaders in my country had great power. They were like... Do you know puppet-master? They were like that. They controlled everything. Media, economy, political opponents, free speech. They were so afraid of losing power they used surveillance to watch everybody, and terror to keep everybody obedient. They were especially afraid of people like my parents, people who told truth. So one day they just took them away."

I was watching Elizaveta closely. I could see the pain these memories brought her.

What was it she'd told me earlier?

Not everyone has easy life like you.

I really did feel like a jackass now.

Rosa said, "I don't think I ever want too much power."

Elizaveta smiled sadly and rubbed the girl's hair.

"Why don't you try to get some sleep, Rosa?" I said.

"I'm still not tired."

"Morning will come faster if you're asleep."

"Can you sing me a lullaby?"

"Me?" I said. "No. I don't sing."

She looked at Elizaveta. "Can you?"

"I don't know lullaby."

"I can teach you one. But I only know the Spanish. Is that okay?"

"Yes, I can understand Spanish—if you don't think I will sound too funny?"

Rosa missed the sarcasm and said, "Great! It's called 'A la roro niño.' It begins like this: *A la roro niño, a lo roro ya, duérmete mi niño, duérmete mi amor.*" There were six verses in total. Rosa would sing one verse, Elizaveta would repeat it, then they would move on to the next. They were melodic, repetitive, and soothing, with long pauses and alternating harmonies. Rosa sang with a slightly higher pitch than Elizaveta, though both conveyed the emotions of love and affection.

When they finished I said, "You guys are awesome."

Rosa beamed. Elizaveta blushed.

"I know more," Rosa said. "Can we sing another? Please?"

So over the next ten or fifteen minutes Rosa and Elizaveta sang several more lullabies. Some were mournful and haunting, like a lament. Others were hypnotic and moving. All were therapeutic, lifting some of the heaviness that had settled over my heart.

While Rosa sang the latest verse, Elizaveta smiled over the girl's head at me. I smiled back. Then her eyes focused on something behind me. Uncertainty and confusion flickered in them a moment before her face drained of color.

2

When I was a kid, traveling the country with my parents in the RV, we'd spent much of one summer in a caravan park in Montana near the Little Belt Mountains. I'd really enjoyed it. There were the remains of railways and mines to explore, cold streams to splash in, rugged trails to follow, and a lot of neat wildlife. I made friends with a raccoon that loved toffee, a particularly brave chipmunk that would hop right onto my outstretched hand for a few nuts, and a girl from Canada named Sally who was into catching insects. Sally carried around her insect of the day in a Tic Tac container, which she liked to show off. Her prepubescent interest in entomology rubbed off on me, and soon I had my own collection of ants, beetles, butterflies, crickets, so forth. Every now and then we'd have a beetle death match. A cereal box with the back cut away served as the gladiatorial ring. Usually the chosen beetles would try to escape rather than fight each other, but they were still fun to watch and egg on. One evening, however, I left the gladiatorial ring outside during a light rainfall, and the cardboard became soggy and warped. The cereal boxes in my RV were still mostly full, so I couldn't make a new ring. I knew

Sally would blame me and maybe beat me up—she was two years older and a bit of a bully—so I went to the edge of the campground to search the line of garbage bins for a cereal box. I tipped the first bin over as quietly as I could and prodded through the trash. That's when I heard a deep chuff. I turned, scanning the dark, and spotted a huge black bear no more than ten feet from me. It stood on all fours, a plastic bag hanging from its snout, just standing there and watching me. In fact, it must have been standing there and watching me for a good minute.

This had always held the title of the scariest moment of my life—until now—when I turned around and saw the eye peering through a hole in the wall, watching us.

3

The hole was an excised knot in a plank of wood maybe three feet from the ground. It was the size of a golf ball. The iris of the eye peering through it appeared brownish-red, surrounded with white. It gleamed wetly in the candlelight.

Then it blinked.

Elizaveta and Rosa leapt to their feet but remained oddly silent, as if they'd lost their voices. I was on my feet too, my blood icy sludge in my veins. I snagged the pistol from the waistband of my shorts. I raised it toward the devilish eye and squeezed the trigger.

Click.

The safety!

I found it, flicked it off, aimed at the eye again.

It was gone.

Nevertheless, I squeezed off two shots. The rounds blew two new holes through the wall.

The reports were earsplitting and toneless. Blue smoked trailed up from the end of the barrel. Cordite filled my nostrils.

Jesus and Pita emerged from the bedroom, demanding to know what was going on.

"Solano's outside!" I said, shoving the table aside and throwing open the door. I expected an ambush, a blade to arc through the air.

Nothing.

I swung the pistol to the left, to the right.

Nobody on the porch.

I scanned the dark forest.

Nobody fleeing.

Nobody anywhere.

From behind me Jesus swore softly.

4

He was looking at Nitro's body. It was exactly where we'd left it. I was about to ask him what was wrong when I noticed Nitro's eyes—or lack of eyes.

Like Miguel's, they were missing.

1957

She sank below the surface of the canal in a cloud of red until she came to rest on the rock-covered bottom. Unconscious, she wasn't holding her breath. Instead water gushed down her airway, filling her lungs, preventing the transfer of oxygen to her blood. There would be a feeling of tearing and burning inside her chest, though she wasn't aware of this. She was blissfully ignorant of any physical sensation.

Then her breathing stopped altogether, and she was in respiratory arrest.

Somewhere deep inside of her, however, in the womb of her mind where all thoughts were born and most dwelled without being spoken out loud or acted upon, she was wondering why this was happening to her, and this bewilderment was mixed with surprise that she was drowning, that she was dying.

And then the strangest thing happened. She experienced a kind of hiccup, and the part of her responsible for these thoughts was outside of her body. It was floating back up through the water, through the surface, and she could see her little body lying at the bottom of the canal, convulsing violently now, in the final stages of death, and she could see her father and mother already in the gondola, moving quickly away, her father's face a steely mask as he pushed the boat with the pole, her mother sobbing into her hands.

And as she watched them leaving her for a second time, abandoning her to her cruel fate, a hatred of frustration and despair roared through her, consuming her entirely, a banshee-like madness driven by a single purpose.

Revenge.

ELIZAVETA

1

Jesus blundered into the cabin, his face manic with fear, shouting in Spanish that Nitro's eyes were missing. Pita moaned miserably. Elizaveta felt sick. Whoever was out there—*Solano, it was only Solano, an old man*—took Nitro's eyes too? But why?

She clutched Rosa against her, covering her ears with her hands.

Jack returned next, pistol in hand. He seemed agitated.

"Did you hit him, Jack?" Elizaveta asked.

He shook his head. "He got away."

"What did you see?" Jesus demanded. "What did you shoot at?"

Elizaveta pointed at the knothole. "Solano was watching us through that."

"Watching you? Christ! For how long?"

"I don't know. Maybe five minutes? Maybe all night?"

Jesus whirled on Jack. "And you let him get away? How did he get away? You had a *gun*."

"The safety was on. I wasn't ready."

"Fuck, Jack!" Jesus exclaimed. "You could have killed him!"

"Whatever, he didn't do anything. Everybody's okay—"

"He took Nitro's eyes!"

"Did you see him, Jack?" Pita asked. Her hair was tousled and frizzy from the wind and rain, while mascara and dried tears streaked her cheeks, making her look zombie-like. "Solano? Did you actually see Solano?"

"I saw his eye watching us."

"But did you see *him*?"

"I know what you're going to say—"

"*Did you see him?*"

"He ran away when I fucking shot at him, Pita. Since when do ghosts run away from bullets? Wouldn't bullets go straight through them?"

She clamped her mouth shut.

Jesus said, "Maybe you should give the gun to me, Jack."

"Fuck no," he said.

"You blew your chance. Give me the gun."

"Blew my chance?"

"You weren't prepared! You let him get away!"

"And you've been super vigilant sleeping in the fucking bedroom—"

Jesus punched Jack, striking him directly in the nose. There was a sound like knuckles cracking. Jack spun away, dropping the pistol and cupping his nose. He examined his hands, which were bright red with blood. Jesus stood on the balls of his feet, holding his ground, ready to run. Jack charged him. Jesus made for Lucinda's room. Jack, however, caught him before he could barricade himself inside the room, hefting him off his feet and slamming him to the ground.

Pita leapt on Jack's back, wrapping her arms around his neck.

"Go to the bedroom!" Elizaveta told Rosa, shooing the girl away.

Rosa fled.

Elizaveta ran into the fray, wrapping her own arms around Pita's neck and pulling the smaller woman free. Pita shrieked and cursed. Elizaveta tripped and fell, dragging Pita with her.

"Bitch!" Pita yelled, flipping onto her front.

"Calm down!"

Pita didn't. She was possessed. She snagged fistfuls of Elizaveta's hair and yanked so hard Elizaveta rocked forward. She clawed blindly at Pita. She grabbed something soft—a breast? She squeezed. Pita screeched, then yanked Elizaveta's hair harder.

Scalp on fire, Elizaveta got hold of the throat of Pita's chambray shirt. She tugged with all her strength. Buttons popped. Pita screeched. Her left hand released Elizaveta's hair and went after her pink top, hooking her fingers around the collar and pulling. Fabric tore with a zipper-like sound.

Elizaveta shouted, more in frustration than anger or embarrassment. They were having a stupid catfight while Solano was outside somewhere. He might return, burst into the cabin wielding his knife while they were all distracted.

Elizaveta brought her knees to her chest and tried using her feet to push Pita away. Pita clutched Elizaveta's hair with both hands again, shaking as though she were trying to dislodge stubborn weeds from the ground.

Elizaveta kicked. Her foot struck Pita in the gut. Pita's grip loosened.

Elizaveta kicked again. This time her foot winged Pita's face.

The bitch finally released her.

Elizaveta tumbled away, the roots of her hair raw with pain. Pita lay on her side, panting, her bottom lip bleeding.

"Jesus!" Elizaveta said, pushing herself to her feet.

Somehow Jesus had gotten the better of Jack, and he now knelt on top of him, his hands around Jack's throat, strangling him.

He didn't show any signs of hearing her—or letting up.

The pistol lay on the floor a meter from her. She retrieved it, surprised by its cold, heavy weight. She aimed the barrel at the ceiling and squeezed the trigger.

The report boomed.

Jesus turned his head to look at her. His face was so twisted with hatred she barely recognized him.

"Get off him!" she said.

"Put that down!"

"Get off him!"

"Put—"

Jack bucked Jesus off him and rolled away, wheezing.

Jesus seemed ready to go for him again, while Pita was on all fours, spider-like, ready to come after her.

She fired a second round.

"Stop!" she shouted. "Everybody stop!"

2

Jack crab-scuttled farther away from Jesus. Blood smeared his chin. More blood soaked his tank top on the left side of his abdomen.

Had one of her bullets ricocheted off the ceiling and struck him there?

Elizaveta hurried to him, giving Pita a wide birth.

"Give me that," he said, holding a hand out for the pistol.

She hesitated only a moment before pressing the gun's grip into his palm.

He immediately swung the weapon at Jesus, who was bending over, picking up something.

A knife, she realized. A blood-drenched knife.

Had he stabbed Jack?

"Put it down," Jack told him.

"Put the gun down," Jesus retorted. The bangs of his usually slicked back hair hung in front of his face. His left shirt tail dangled from his pants. At some point he'd lost a penny loafer; one foot was bare.

"I don't think so, Jesus."

"What are you going to do, Jack? Shoot me?"

"I'm pretty tempted right now."

"Dammit, Jesus," Elizaveta said. "You *stabbed* him? Are you crazy?"

"Jesus...?" Pita said, appearing confused. She stood up. Her chambray shirt hung open to her sternum, revealing her breasts in a lacy bra a size too small so it acted like a corset, ballooning her cleavage.

"He attacked me," Jesus protested. "He was going insane."

"Where'd you get that knife, Jesus?" Jack asked. He pushed himself to his knees and grimaced, his free hand going to his bleeding abdomen.

Elizaveta helped him the rest of the way to his feet.

"Are you okay?" she asked, worried.

Ignoring her, he said to Jesus: "Where?"

He shrugged. "The kitchen. When you and Pita were outside, on watch."

"Where in the kitchen?"

"On the counter."

"Jack, stop pointing that gun," Pita said. "You're scaring me."

Jack ignored her too. "On the counter, huh?"

"So what?" Jesus said.

"Eliza, go see if there's a knife on the counter."

Elizaveta crossed the main room, wondering what was going on. Why did it matter where the knife was from? She poked her head in the kitchen, wrinkling her nose at the smell of something rotten. It was dark, no candles lit. Yet her eyes had long ago adjusted to the dim environment, and she could see well enough. A couple of bowls and plates rested on the counter. Next to them was a single fork. No knife.

She returned to the others. "No knife."

"See?" Jesus said. "Now stop pointing that fucking gun at me, Jack."

"I saw that knife earlier," Jack said. "When I was here by myself, when I first found Rosa."

"So what? I told you—"

"There wasn't any blood on it."

"Well, you shouldn't have attacked me, Jack. It was self-defense."

"There was blood on it before you stabbed me, Jesus."

A deep silenced ensured.

"What are you talking about, Jack?" Pita demanded.

Elizaveta frowned, trying to make sense of this. Where did the blood come from if it wasn't Jack's—

Her breath hitched in her throat.

"Nitro?" she said so quietly she wasn't sure she'd spoken out loud.

"Nitro?" Pita repeated, apparently hearing her. "Would someone please tell me what's going on?"

"Why'd you kill him?" Jack asked Jesus.

"Killed *who*?" Pita said. "*Nitro?*"

Jesus chuckled, shaking his head. "Are you listening to yourself, Jack?"

"What's he talking about, Jesus?" Pita asked him.

"Nothing. He doesn't know anything. This is bullshit."

"Why'd you kill him?" Jack repeated.

"Stop it, Jack!" Pita said. "Why are you saying this? Why would Jesus ever want to kill Nitro?" She glanced around the room, as if for answers. Her eyes paused on the empty vodka bottle on the floor, next to Elizaveta's forgotten garden claw and Jack's hay hook. "You've been drinking, Jack. Are you drunk?"

"He's not drunk," Elizaveta said.

Pita whirled on her, temper flaring. "Shut up, bitch! Jesus is your *boyfriend*. You should be on his side. Why are you listening to Jack?"

"Where's your jacket?" Jack asked Jesus.

He shrugged. "I took it off."

"Where is it?"

"In the other hut. I didn't bring it."

Elizaveta thought back. She couldn't remember whether

he'd worn his tweed jacket to the cabin or not. She'd had much more on her mind this night than trivialities such as clothing.

"Unroll your sleeves," Jack said.

Jesus had rolled the sleeves of his white button-down shirt to his elbows. "Fuck you, Jack," he said. "I've had enough of this."

"Me too, Jack," Pita said, going to Jesus's side. "You're acting like a lunatic."

"Eliza," Jack said, "check the bedrooms for his blazer."

"Jack…" Jesus said, taking a step forward.

Jack raised the pistol from Jesus's chest to his head.

Jesus stopped.

"Eliza, go."

Elizaveta checked Lucinda's room first, opening the dresser drawers, peeking beneath the bed. There was no jacket.

She was halfway to Pepper's room when the door opened. Rosa stood at the threshold, half in shadows, Jesus's tweed blazer balled against her chest. She had obviously been listening through the door.

"It was in the corner," she said.

"Give that to me," Jesus snapped, reaching for her.

She dodged his hand, then dashed across the room.

"Good girl," Jack said, taking the blazer. He shook it out, then held it up by the collar so everyone could see it.

Blood stained the left sleeve, from cuff to elbow.

3

Elizaveta felt hot and cold at the same time.

Could this be true?

Could Jesus have murdered Nitro?

No—there had to be a more mundane explanation for the blood.

"Let me guess," Jack said. "You're left-handed, Jesus?"

Jesus was shaking his head again, looking at the floor. He appeared to be smiling.

"Da," Elizaveta said. "He is."

Pita's saucer eyes bounced back and forth between Jesus and Jack. Finally they settled on Jack. "Why are you doing this, Jack?" she asked him. "You know Jesus wouldn't kill Nitro. So why are you doing this?"

"He has the murder weapon in his hand, Pita. Nitro's blood is on his jacket's sleeve. Maybe I'm wrong. I hope I am. But we're going to have to let the police figure that out. Jesus—put down the knife."

Jesus didn't.

Jack aimed the pistol at his legs. "You have three seconds."

"Jack!" Pita said.

"One..."

"Jack..." Elizaveta said.

"Two—"

"Okay!" Jesus set the knife on the floor.

"Kick it toward me."

Jesus hesitated, then kicked the knife. It clattered across the wooden planks, stopping several feet short of Jack. Rosa scooted from behind Jack's legs, retrieved the weapon, and returned to her refuge behind his legs.

"Tell me this isn't true, Jesus," Pita said.

"It's not. Of course it's not. It's bullshit."

"Then what about the blood...?"

"Jack's set me up."

"Oh, fuck off," Jack said.

"Nitro was my best friend, Pita," Jesus said. "We were like brothers. I loved the guy. Jack's the one who hated him."

"You were outside with him when he was killed!" Jack said. "I was inside. With Eliza and Rosa."

"It's true!" Rosa said.

It was true, Elizaveta thought, though her mind was spinning. She was suddenly more confused than ever.

"I'm not saying Jack actually slit Nitro's throat. But he organized it." Jesus paused. "He's working with whoever's out there in the storm."

Everyone looked at Jack, Elizaveta included. She didn't believe Jack put a hit on Nitro. It was absurd.

Wasn't it?

"Give me a fucking break, Jesus," Jack said.

"You had the chance to shoot him," Jesus said. "Whoever was outside watching you guys through that hole. You had a chance to shoot him but you didn't."

"And I suppose I murdered Miguel too, huh?"

"I don't know. Did you? I certainly didn't."

"I'm not listening to this shit." He wiggled the pistol at Jesus. "Get on your knees."

"Jack," Pita said. "I think you need to put down the gun."

"Get to your knees!"

"Jack, stop it!" Pita said.

"You hated Nitro!" Jesus shouted. "You set this up! You killed him!"

"I didn't even know he was coming until this fucking morning!"

"Give me the gun, Jack."

"Get to your knees!"

"Jack!" Pita screeched.

"Eliza," Jack said. "Go get me Pepper's belt."

"His belt? Why?" she asked. The air was thick with confusion. She didn't know what was going on, who to believe.

"I'm going to tie Jesus up."

"Eliza," Jesus said. "Don't listen to him."

She glanced from Jack to Jesus, frozen with indecision.

Rosa bolted to the bedroom, returning a moment later with Pepper's purple belt.

"Pita," Jack said, "move away from your brother."

"You can't tell me what to do."

"Move, or I swear to God I'll put a bullet in his knee."

Glowering, she moved away a few steps.

"Get down," Jack told Jesus, approaching him cautiously.

"You won't get away with this," he said.

"Get down!"

Jesus lowered himself to his knees.

"Put your arms out, wrists together."

"Fuck you."

Jack pistol-whipped him on the temple, though not very hard.

"Ow!" Jesus said.

"Jack!" Pita said.

"Do it!"

Jesus put his arms out.

"Rosa, you're going to need to—"

"No," Elizaveta said, getting hold of herself. She had to pick a side, and she knew in her heart Jack didn't have anything to do with Nitro's murder. "I will."

She took the belt from Rosa, then went to Jesus and bound his wrists together. She could feel Pita's eyes into her.

"Is it tight?" Jack asked.

"Yes."

Jack pressed his foot against Jesus's chest and pushed him, so he toppled backward onto his butt. "Stay," he said.

JACK

1

Rosa and Elizaveta and I sat against one wall inside the cabin, Jesus and Pita against another. I set the pistol on the floor next to me and peeled off my tank top. The knife wound was far to the left of my navel, deeper than it was wide. I could barely see the laceration beneath the fresh-flowing blood, but I could feel my heartbeat in it, steady and slow, an unwelcomed reminder of my mortality.

The stabbing played over again in my head, step by step. I'd prevented Jesus from escaping to one of the bedrooms and tossed him to the floor. Pita leapt on my back. Elizaveta pried her away. I hiked Jesus up by the collar of his shirt and slammed him into the wall. I slammed him a second time and heard Pita and Elizaveta scuffling behind me. I turned to check on them. That's when Jesus withdrew the knife from beneath his shirt and slid it into my side. I didn't feel any pain; I was too keyed up on adrenaline. But my first thoughts were: *He stabbed me. The fucker stabbed me.* I looked down, saw the blood, and stepped away from him. I figured the fight was over, but Jesus came at me, throwing his weight into me and knocking me down, knocking the pistol from my grip. Then he was on top of me, his hands around my throat, squeezing. My vision blurred, spun—then the gunshot. Jesus released my throat, and I bucked him off me to find Pita on her side with a bloody lip and Elizaveta standing a few yards away, holding the gun in her shaking hands.

"This is not good, Jack," Elizaveta said. She was kneeling next to me, examining the wound. Rosa stood by her, a serious expression on her face.

"Nice bedside manner," I said.

"What does that mean?"

I shook my head. "It's not as bad as it looks."

"It looks bad."

"It doesn't even hurt very much."

"Maybe you're in shock."

"I'm not in shock."

"Maybe you are bleeding inside."

"Seriously, Eliza, knock it off."

"I'm trying to help."

"It doesn't look very bad, Jack," Rosa said.

"Thank you, Rosa."

"It really doesn't," she added. "I cut my knee once, and it bled almost as much. But I didn't even have to go to the doctor's office. My mom just rinsed it with water, put some stuff on it that stung, and then a bandage."

"Do you have any vital organs in your knee?" Elizaveta asked her.

"What's a vital organ?"

I folded my tank top into a square and pressed it against the cut. I hissed with pain and closed my eyes. I could feel the shirt turn spongy with blood. When I opened my eyes, I was looking across the room. Pita was in front of Jesus, trying to free his hands. I snatched the pistol from the floor and pointed it at them.

"Get away from him!" I said.

Elizaveta and Rosa spun to look.

Pita and Jesus stiffened, both appearing very suspect.

"Move away from him, Pita."

"Why?" she said. "We were just talking."

"You were removing the belt."

"I was not."

"I saw you! Now move away from him."

"Or what, Jack?" Jesus said. "You going to call your accomplice? Have us killed too?"

"He'll beat you up!" Rosa said.

"Getting seven year olds to fight your fights, are you now, Jack?"

"I'm eight," Rosa said defiantly.

"Pita, last warning," I said. "Move away from him."

Her expression hovered somewhere between vexed and sulky. But after several long seconds of pointed insolence she moved away.

"We know why you killed him," she stated.

I was growing sick of this accusation, but since I had not killed Nitro, I was curious to hear what she might have to say. "Enlighten me," I said.

"You knew Nitro and I were having an affair."

It wasn't so much what she said—I'd known about the affair for the last couple of hours now—that pissed me off; it was the way she said it. She seemed proud of the fact she'd cheated on me.

"I've been meaning to talk to you about that," I said.

"So you *did* know!"

"I told him tonight," Elizaveta said.

"How did *you* know?"

"I saw you and Nitro on beach."

"You were spying on us?"

"I went for a walk. You were there."

"I can't believe you're taking Jack's side in all this, cariño," Jesus said. "You know me. You know I'd never murder anyone."

"I know you stabbed Jack."

"He *attacked* me."

"You *stabbed* him."

"Eliza, you're my partner. I care for you. Come over here, join Pita and me. I'll forget all this nonsense."

"I can't do that, Jesus."

"Yes you can. Get up and come over here. Now."

"No, Jesus."

"Don't say no to me."

"No."

"*You don't say no to me!*" Jesus roared. Then, collecting himself: "You know what you're doing, don't you? You're putting yourself on a one-way plane back to Russia."

Elizaveta clamped her jaw. I did too.

Jesus was back to his usual ways, playing cheap.

"A couple of calls," he went on. "That's all it will take. They'll revoke your visa and you'll be on a plane. Is that what you want? To be a schoolteacher making piss all in Russia for the rest of your life? I can offer you so much more."

I wanted to say something, to tell Jesus to shut his trap, to tell him he was full of it, but this wasn't my fight. It was Elizaveta's. She had to see through his ploy on her own.

"Offer me what?" she asked.

"Everything!" Jesus said. "As my wife, you'll have whatever you want."

"You'll never marry me."

"Of course I will. I love you."

"He does," Pita insisted.

"Don't you see how ridiculous this is?" Jesus said. "You sitting over there with Jack Goff? He's a loser. A has-been. He's an alcoholic and a murderer—"

"Quiet."

"Eliza—"

"Quiet!"

2

My head ached, my neck and shoulders ached, the wound in my side ached. My entire body, in fact, ached. I swallowed dryly. My throat felt mummified. But I was too buggered to get up and refill Elizaveta's bucket with rainwater. I glanced at my wristwatch through a film of gritty fatigue. It was 4:10 a.m., which meant another hour or so until dawn. Everyone had settled down, and for the last half hour they were either sleeping or pretending to sleep. I yawned silently and fought the urge to close my eyes myself, even for a moment, knowing I would be out as quickly as a man on an anesthesia drip. Whenever my eyelids began to droop, I pressed the tank top harder against the wound in my abdomen. The resulting pain functioned like an electric shock, zapping me awake.

I was getting worried about the gash. Aside from aching all over, I felt lightheaded and dizzy. I tried to recall what I'd learned about the human anatomy in high school biology, but back then filling my friends' pencil cases with fish eyes or frog legs during dissection classes had been more important than listening to the teacher or studying the textbook. Nevertheless, I was pretty sure my liver was on my right side, which meant it was safe. Kidneys were on both sides, which scared me a bit. I had no idea where my pancreas was, but I believed my spleen was on my left side too. So had the knife blade punctured a kidney? My pancreas, my spleen? Maybe it nicked an important vein or artery. Like Elizaveta said, I could be bleeding internally. This could explain the lightheadedness...

My eyelids were drooping. I applied pressure to the wound.

I inhaled sharply—but the pain was good. It kept me alert.

I glanced again at my wristwatch. 4:16.

Christ, the minutes were slugging by.

Another hour—an hour and a half, tops.

Yeah, until first light maybe. But what about the boatman? When was he going to show up?

This was something I'd spent a fair bit of time thinking about. Not if the boatman would return. I was sure he would. He knew we were out here, stranded. He also knew we had money. I wasn't sure whether Jesus paid him the full fee up front, but I didn't think so. That would have been stupid, and Jesus wasn't stupid. Which meant the guy would be back. So the question wasn't if the boatman would return, but when.

The worst of the storm had definitely moved on. I could still hear the rain falling against the corrugated iron roof, but it was no longer a full-on assault; more a steady drizzle. Come dawn I was hoping it would have ceased altogether, but even if it didn't, the canals should be navigable. And this was where it would boil down to the boatman's character. Was he the type of guy who would wake up bright and early to come get us? Or would he sleep in, go about his morning chores, fill his belly, and come get us when the moment suited him? I wanted to believe the former option, of course, but if I was being honest with myself, which I was, the latter option seemed more plausible. After all, he didn't know us, he didn't owe us. He warned us about going to the island. He might think leaving us stranded here for a while was a suitable punishment, a lesson learned.

A lesson learned.

Right. And what was that lesson?

Don't go snooping around creepy islands?

Don't trespass on private property?

This got me thinking about our reception when we returned to Xochimilco. One thing people couldn't get enough of was seeing the high and mighty fall, and Mexicans were no different. Jesus might not be a famous politician, or athlete, or movie star. But he ran one of the country's premiere breweries. He was a bigshot in his own right. Moreover, he was young and handsome, key ingredients for juicy scandal. Throw into the pot an island infested with dolls and supposedly haunted by the ghost of a little girl and you had nationwide headlines.

Would Jesus be convicted?

I wasn't sure. I knew he was guilty, but would a judge reach the same conclusion? After all, Jesus would surround himself with the best lawyers. He would have numerous connections to lean on. Not to mention the crime scene was a mess. We'd tramped through Nitro's blood, moved his body, handled the murder weapon.

And you're forgetting about Miguel and Lucinda and Mr. Peeping Tom. How did they all fit into this? Did I still believe the Peeping Tom was Solano? But if not him, who?

Nationwide headlines? This was going to be the story of the fucking year.

And to my chagrin I was going to be right in the center of all it.

3

4:24 a.m.

Nitro's missing eyes. Black, empty orbits in his bloodied face. I couldn't rid myself of the macabre image. Almost as bad was the thought of Solano sitting out there, nothing but a wall separating him from us, bent over Nitro's face, cutting, sawing, pulling.

4

4:35 a.m.

Elizaveta rotated her right shoulder, as if it were stiff. Then she reached her left arm beneath her right armpit and prodded the spot where the scorpion had stung her back with her fingers. She kept her eyes closed. I didn't think she was doing this in her sleep. She was awake, or at least semi-awake. Even so, I didn't say anything. I didn't ask her what was wrong, or how she was feeling. What was the point? She would either tell me she was fine, which would likely be a lie, or she would tell me she couldn't feel her shoulder, or something equally frightening. And there was nothing I could do about that. There was nothing any of us could do.

Except wait.

5

4:41 a.m.

Lucinda. Was she confused when she mentioned a doll? Delirious? Speaking through a dream? The doll on the table, gone, misappropriated somehow. Did Solano take it? But why? Because he was crazy? Wanted company? A grown man?

What was I missing?

6

4:50 a.m.

The ghost of the little girl. I hated myself for even contemplating this possibility. I felt like a kid at a sleepover being dared to look in the bathroom mirror at midnight to see Bloody Mary's reflection, sans scalp, which was said to have been torn away when she got her hair trapped in the doors of an elevator cab. Nonsense, of course. No grown adult could take it seriously. Just as no grown adult could—or at least should—take seriously the legend of a girl haunting an island in the middle of nowhere.

So why was I contemplating it?

I wasn't.

I couldn't help it if silly thoughts popped in my head.

Ghosts didn't exist.

Because if they did?

Well, if they did, I'd be more compelled to believe that my out of body experience hadn't been dead neurons firing, that I had indeed been crossing over to some other plane of existence, that the white light existed, along with whatever evil

dwelled within it—
  That was a dream.
  But was it?
  A dream—or a memory?
  Fuck, Jack. Stop it. You're going to drive yourself batshit crazy.
  Ghosts didn't exist.
  Devils didn't exist.
  Eternal suffering didn't exist.
  End of story.

7

5:01 a.m.

A humming had started in my skull, from fear or hunger or fatigue, I wasn't sure. My legs had gone numb from sitting in the same position for so long. I stretched the left one out in front of me, then the right, careful not to disturb Rosa, whose head was resting on it. Her eyes were closed, her mouth parted slightly. Her breathing was deep and regular.

Looking at her, a warmth bloomed in my chest. She was so small and innocent and beautiful. And brave. What other kid her age would cope with all the shit going on as well as she had? I certainly wouldn't have at her age. I wasn't really doing such a good job now at twenty-eight.

Her strength made her inexplicable affection for me all the more endearing. She'd even stood up for me, telling Jesus, "He'll beat you up!" I smiled to myself, but it was a smile of sadness. She shouldn't be here, going through this. She should be at home, in her bed, waking to her family and a warm breakfast, perhaps attending Sunday church, and later, playing jump rope and other games with her neighborhood friends.

Stroking her head affectionately with the back of my fingers, I vowed right then not to let her down, not to let any harm come to her. I would get her home safe and sound.

Even as I told myself this, however, I wondered whether it was true.

After all, how could I make such a promise when I didn't know for certain who or what was out there stalking us, hunting us, plotting our demise?

Who, Jack. Not what—who. No crazy Pita thinking, okay?

Okay.

Rosa's eyelids fluttered, then opened. Her brown eyes looked up at me. "Is it morning?"

"Not yet," I said.

She began to sit up.

"Go back to sleep," I told her.

"I can't. The floor's too hard."

"Come," Elizaveta said. As I'd suspected, she wasn't sleeping. Her eyes were open now, alert, and she held out her hand. "I'll take you to bed."

"I don't want to leave Jack."

"He'll be okay."

"He's hurt."

"I'm fine," I told her. "Go with Eliza."

Elizaveta and Rosa stood and crossed the room quietly, wraithlike in the candlelight and layered shadows.

Jesus, I noticed, raised his head and watched them until they disappeared into Pepper's room. Pita remained motionless on her side, sleeping.

"How does it feel, Jack?" Jesus asked me, speaking for the first time in a while.

"How does what feel?" I said, suspecting I was rising to some bait.

"Knowing Pita was fucking Nitro behind your back?"

I almost told him not so bad after I fucked Elizaveta behind his back. Instead I said, "How does it feel knowing you're going to be fucked six ways from Sunday in prison?"

"I'm not going to prison."

"I'm not so sure about that."

"I'm not. You know that. I know that."

"We'll see."

"Jack, Jack, Jack."

"Jesus, Jesus, Jesus."

"I don't like you, Jack. I never have. I think maybe it's time I make that perfectly clear."

"Oh, it's been clear for a while."

"I don't know what my father ever saw in you. But he was grossly mistaken."

"Not just your father, Jesus. Your sister too. Seems to me like your entire family was a Jack Goff fan. You're the odd one out."

"Seems to *me* like you didn't know how to satisfy a woman, otherwise Pita wouldn't have gone looking elsewhere for a real man."

"A real man? You've been reading too much *Cosmo*, pal."

"You know why I pulled support for you and your team?"

"Bad business sense?"

"Funny, Jack."

"No joke, Jesus. Your father built that brewery from nothing. He knew what he was doing. He knew the importance of breaking into the US market. He knew the returns would come. If he were alive today, the company would be worth five times its current value."

"You're dumber than you look, Jack."

"I'm not the only one who thinks this."

"What are you talking about?"

"I've followed the company, Jesus. And the pundits seem to agree with me. Pulling out of the US was a massive mistake, and nothing much has been going right for you since."

"Where do you get your news?" he snapped. "The *Gringo Gazette*?"

"Must be a pretty shitty feeling to know your entire board of directors is thinking about voting to oust you from your own company, huh?"

"You know nothing. *Nothing*. Dumping you was absolutely the right decision. Because you're a fuckup, Jack, a cocky, reckless, impulsive fuckup. I knew that from the moment I met you—"

"You let your personal feelings cloud your business judgment—"

"—before you crashed and ruined your career," he went on, speaking over me, "before you started drinking yourself to the gutter. I knew that, and I was right. *I was right*. Because look at you now. You're no longer just a fuckup. You've managed to become a drunk as well." He smiled mirthlessly. "You're a fucking joke, Jack. So congratulations—you've finally lived up to your name."

ELIZAVETA

1

Elizaveta helped Rosa into bed next to Pepper, who remained fast asleep, then pulled the sheet and rug up to her chin.

"What if I can't fall asleep?" Rosa asked.

"Huh?" Elizaveta said. Jesus and Jack were speaking to each other, and she was trying to hear what they were saying.

"What if I can't fall asleep?"

"Then you count sheep."

"That never works."

"Then imagine ice melting."

"What?"

"That is what children in Russia do. Trust me, it works."

"I don't know..."

"I will come back and wake you soon."

"Eliza?" she asked.

"Yes?"

"Will I see you and Jack again?"

"What do you mean?"

"After today?"

"Da, if you want to. If your mother lets you."

"Well, I'll probably be grounded for a month. But after that, maybe I can visit you and Jack? Maybe we can have a sleepover. Not like tonight. A fun one, with movies and stuff. I'm allowed sleepovers sometimes."

"Oooh. I don't know about that."

"Why not?"

"Jack and I don't live together."

"You don't?"

Elizaveta shook her head. "Jack lives with Pita."

"Who do you live with then?"

"I live by myself."

"That's great then! Jack and I can sleepover at your house."

Elizaveta smiled. "Go to sleep, Rosa."

2

Jack and Jesus had fallen silent. Elizaveta returned to her previous spot against the wall and sat down. She wanted to ask Jack what they were talking about—fighting about, more like it—and for a moment she wondered if it could have been her. Had Jack told Jesus what happened earlier? Instead of experiencing guilt over her infidelity and fear of Jesus's reaction, she felt strangely invigorated. *Had Jack been fighting over her?* No. This was a fantasy, her ego running away with itself. They'd had sex, that was all. And they'd only had sex because she'd instigated it. There was nothing more to it than carnal pleasure, a temporary escape. Why would there be? He was rich and famous and could have any woman in the world he wanted. She was just some displaced and disillusioned Russian schoolteacher with a closetful of skeletons and a headful of issues.

Jesus chose me.

But that was because he wanted a trophy girlfriend, something exotic to show off to his buddies. And that was all she ever was to him, wasn't it? Yes, it was. In their twelve months together he never told her he loved her. He never spoke of children. Marriage? The first she'd heard of it was earlier tonight, or this morning, and he'd only mentioned it to manipulate her like a pawn on a chessboard, to make her rebuke Jack and join his side. Ironically his efforts made her see the truth. He was simply using her to fulfill his needs and wants, to boost his self-esteem. Their relationship was a farce. It never stood a chance. She supposed, deep down, she always understood this, but she'd been so desperate for security and stability she'd refused to see what was right in front of her face. That was the double edge of hope: it made you weak, blind, foolish.

Elizaveta wondered whether Jesus would go through with his threat of getting her visa revoked. She knew he had the means to if he so pleased. If you had money in Mexico, and you were well-connected, you could do whatever you wanted, regardless of the law. Case in point, one night she and Jesus went to a trendy restaurant without a reservation and the owner refused to seat them. Furious and embarrassed, Jesus called a friend who ran the government's consumer protection agency, and the next day inspectors shut down the restaurant.

So if he wanted to get her visa revoked, he could do it. Not that she really cared. Her visa expired soon enough anyway. The bottom line was that she'd wasted her opportunity in Mexico, wasted it pursuing Jesus, pursuing a life that could never be, and now, whether it was sooner or later, she would inevitably be getting on a plane back to Russia.

3

Elizaveta was nodding off and tugged her head up. She was very lethargic. Keeping her eyes open took all her concentration. She wasn't sure whether this was a consequence of remaining awake all night, or whether it was a symptom of the scorpion's venom. She rotated her shoulder for the countless time. It had been stiff for a while now, the area around the puncture wound tingly and tender, almost as if a low-voltage current was running beneath her skin.

At least she hadn't suffered an allergic reaction. She wasn't drooling or twitching. She could still breathe and speak normally, which hopefully meant she wasn't going to drop dead from respiratory failure. Yet the scorpion sting still concerned her. She'd seen a picture of a young boy in a magazine once who'd been bitten on the ankle by a snake, and his entire lower leg had turned black and rotten, like something that belonged to an unwrapped mummy. And maybe, if she didn't receive anti-venom soon, that would happen to her shoulder. Her flesh would necrotize, spreading out from the puncture, consuming her shoulder, her arm, destroying cells and tissue, rendering her limb dead and useless, so the only medical option available (if they ever got off this island) would be amputation.

Jack reached over and took her hand in his, suddenly, unexpectedly. He shifted so he was facing her, then leaned toward her. His lips pressed against hers. Their mouths parted, their tongues explored.

Elizaveta's heart raced. In the back of her mind she wondered whether Jesus was watching them—and realized she didn't care.

Jack liked her after all!

His hands moved off her waist, down her back, slipping beneath her shirt. They were soft and warm on her bare skin. They moved up. His fingers unclipped her bra. Then his hands were moving down again, beneath the waistband at the back of her shorts, beneath the elastic band of her panties.

He kissed the side of her neck, gently, affectionately, his lips like butterfly wings. He nibbled her earlobe. Tremors of pleasure tickled down her spine.

"Jack..."

Then his lips were on hers again, silencing her. Her breasts, loose in her bra, pressed against his chest. Her groin pressed against. He was aroused.

His hands sank deeper down her shorts. They clutched the cleft of her rear, strong now, rough, pulling her tighter against him. One curled around the inside of her thigh, moving higher, brushing her—

A noise startled them apart.

Elizaveta opened her eyes. The room was cauldron-black. Someone had extinguished the candles while she'd had her eyes closed.

Jesus?

Where was he?

Her heart continued to race, though no longer from pleasure but fear.

She heard the noise again.

Rusty hinges?

"What was that?" she whispered.

"Trapdoor," Jack said.

Why would someone be going down into the crawlspace?

Or were they coming out?

"Jack—"

"Shhh."

A heavy crash. The hatch slapping the floor. Then scuffling. Someone climbing the ladder?

Elizaveta jammed a hand into the pocket of her shorts and produced her lighter. She clicked the button frantically. Metal struck the flint three times before a spark ignited the butane and a small flame whooshed into existence.

Holding the lighter high and in front of her, she gasped.

Two dolls stood before the trapdoor. They stared at her with their glass eyes and their furtive smiles. One wore a diaphanous tutu and nothing else, and its head seemed to have been transplanted onto its body from another doll, as it was much too large and a different skin tone. The other wore a dirty white infant bodysuit, its face and limbs charred black in a number of places.

They started toward her, their movement jerky, like clay

animation.

Their brows furrowed in anger. Their smiles turned to snarls.

"Shoot them!" she said, but no sound escaped her mouth.

The topless one with the transplanted head seized Jack by the hair and dragged him back toward the trap door. It disappeared down the hole, dragging Jack after it like prey into its lair.

The remaining doll cocked its head, studying her.

Its bodysuit, she noticed, was undulating. Something was beneath it. No, many things were beneath it, moving, squiggling.

A black scorpion scuttled out of the neck hole, up the doll's face, into its hair. Another one followed. More emerged, dozens, hundreds, spilling out from the short sleeves and where the Velcro extension closed over the crotch.

The plagued doll opened its arms for a hug.

4

Elizaveta jerked awake, momentarily disorientated, unbalanced, the tatters of the nightmare raw and disconcerting.

"You okay?" It was Jack. He spoke quietly.

She looked around the room. The candles still burned. Jesus and Pita appeared to be sleeping against the opposite wall. The trapdoor was shut.

She nodded. "Bad dream." She rubbed her forehead with her fingers. This made her aware of the stiffness in her shoulder. She rotated it experimentally.

"Still hurts?" Jack asked.

"A little," she said.

"It will be okay. If nothing bad happens in the first couple of hours after a sting, nothing will."

"So you are potato *and* scorpion expert?"

He imitated her voice. "Las Vegans know scorpions."

"Are you making fun of me?"

"Sort of."

"You can't do Russian accent."

"Da. It ees easy."

"No—you have to tighten throat. Seriously. And speak from bottom of mouth."

"I eem Boris. I vill conquer Yevrazia."

"Yevrazia?"

"Eurasia."

"Maybe you better keep practicing." She noticed him still holding his folded tank top against the wound in his side. She frowned. "Has it stopped bleeding?"

"Think so."

"Think?"

Grimacing, he peeled the shirt back. She leaned closer for a better look. The gash was lipless and filled with blackish-red blood, though it no longer seemed to be bleeding.

"It's fine," he said. He applied the shirt to it again.

"If we didn't drink all the vodka, we could disinfect it."

"It's fine."

"I can get some water, try to clean—"

"You said you had a bad dream," he said, changing topics. "What was it about?"

Elizaveta hesitated. She didn't like being dismissed. She was worried about him. But he clearly didn't want her fussing over the wound, and maybe that was for the best.

"Dolls," she said. "Two came out of trapdoor. One took you."

"Took me?"

"Down the hole, to crawlspace."

"Why?"

"I don't know, Jack. It was dream. Strange things happen in dreams."

"Didn't you go down to get me?"

"It was your fault. You didn't fight. You just let it drag you down."

He shook his head. "I would have fought it."

"You didn't," she said. "Anyway, I had my own problems. The other doll was covered in scorpions. It tried to hug me."

"Did *you* fight it?"

"Why are you so upset?"

"I'm not. I just wouldn't have gone down that hole without a fight."

"It was my dream, okay? In your dream, you can fight doll. You can fight one hundred dolls if it makes you feel like man."

"I actually did have a dream about a doll earlier," he said. "I heard a noise in Lucinda's room. I went in. There was a doll lighting a candle." He glanced across the room at Jesus and Pita. He lowered his voice further. "It was Pita."

"The doll?"

"She said Solano caught her and turned her into a doll."

"Da, that is something she would say."

"She said Solano caught you and Rosa too."

"And turned us into dolls?"

"Yeah."

Elizaveta thought about that. "Was I a cute doll?" she asked.

"I didn't see you. I woke up first."

"Oh." She smiled.

"What?" he said.

"You dreamed about me."

"I guess. Indirectly. You weren't actually in the dream."

"Do you dream about me often?"

He chuckled. "You dreamed about me too."

She almost told Jack what happened in her dream before the dolls arrived, but she didn't. Having a dream about someone was one thing; having an x-rated make-out session with them in the dream was something else entirely. She said, "Rosa asked me earlier if we would see her again."

"When we get off the island?"

She nodded.

"What did you tell her?"

"Maybe."

Jack shrugged. "Maybe we will."

"She wants to have a sleepover."

"A sleepover?"

"You, me, and her."

He didn't reply, and she couldn't read his face.

Then he said, "Where?"

"At my house."

"I heard you had a nice setup."

"It's a guesthouse."

"Are you allowed guests?"

"Of course."

"Maybe I can check it out sometime?"

Elizaveta's chest tightened. Her mouth went dry.

Was Jack asking her out?

"If you want," she said nonchalantly.

"Hey," he said, "there's something I've been thinking about."

She held his eyes. "Yes?"

"I'm wondering what you might think..."

"Yes?" she repeated.

"That newspaper clipping—the one about the firecracker explosion."

"Oh." She didn't let her disappointment show.

"We figured Solano caused it, killed all those people, came here to hide out and ended up staying. Well, what if his family didn't die in the explosion. What if he didn't leave them behind either? What if he brought them here, to the island with him?"

"Swiss Family Solano?"

"I'm serious, Eliza. It's possible."

"And nobody ever saw them?"

"If the cops were looking for Solano and his family, then it makes sense he would keep them out of sight. A single guy living as a recluse on an island is a lot less strange than an entire family living there."

"But keeping them hidden for fifty years?"

"This island's not exactly Times Square. Pepper said no-body even knew about it until the city council discovered it ten years ago. How hard would it be to keep his wife and daughters hidden from the occasional local who came by to trade dolls for produce?"

"So you're saying it's not just Solano after us? It's his entire family?"

"No, I'm saying maybe I was wrong. Maybe Solano really is dead. But his wife and kids are still here, or maybe his wife is dead too and just his kids are here."

"Why would they kill Miguel? Nitro?"

"Imagine you've lived most of your life in hiding. Then your father dies, the person who has protected you all that time. Then strangers begin showing up on your island. How would you react?"

She considered this in silence. Then she nodded. "You know, Jack, maybe you have solved the mystery a second time —"

Rosa screamed.

5

Bedlam ensued. Rosa continued screaming. Jesus and Pita were awake and on their feet and demanding to know what was happening. Jack was pointing the pistol at them, ordering them to stay put while telling Elizaveta to go check on Rosa.

She dashed into Pepper's room. Pepper remained fast asleep on the bed. Rosa sat bolt upright next to him, staring at the window.

She crouched next to the bed. "What is it, honey? What's wrong?"

Rosa turned her head. Her eyes were huge. "I saw it," she

said.

"Saw what?" she asked.

"It was looking in the window."

"What was, honey?"

"A doll," she said.

6

Elizaveta refused to accept this. For starters, the window was far too high off the ground for a doll to look through. Perhaps if five or six of them stood on each other's shoulders, the top one could peek in. Nevertheless, a troupe of acrobatic dolls was simply too farfetched to believe. Which meant Rosa had either seen someone or something else, or, more likely, she had imagined it. "What did it look like, honey?" she asked.

"A doll," she said.

"But...what else?"

"It had long hair."

"So it was female doll?"

"I don't know. Maybe."

"Did it say anything?"

"It waved at me."

"Waved?"

Rosa demonstrated using a princess wave, her little hand tilting left and right at the wrist.

"Then what happened?"

"You came in."

"And it went away?"

"Yes."

Elizaveta considered this, then said, "Maybe you were having nightmare?"

"No, I wasn't! I saw it."

"Maybe you thought you did. But sometimes when you dream, and you wake up, part of the dream comes with you. It can confuse you."

Rosa obviously wasn't happy with this explanation. She squared her jaw and stared at her lap. Elizaveta almost told her to go back to sleep, but what was the point? She likely wouldn't be able to. Plus, it was almost dawn. "Do you want to come with me to other room?" she asked.

Rosa's disposition immediately brightened, and she nodded.

Elizaveta offered the girl her hand, and they returned to the main room. Jack was still pointing the gun at Jesus and Pita. They were arguing but stopped when Elizaveta and Rosa appeared.

"She was having a bad dream," Elizaveta told them.

Pita's mouth turned down in a bow of disagreement. "She wasn't screaming like that because of a dream."

"She thought she saw something at her window."

"What!"

"A doll."

"A *doll*?"

"She was dreaming—"

"We have to go!" Pita snapped, everything about her changing in an instant, animated by fear: her posture, her expression, the sound of her voice. "This is too much. We have to go. We need to go. Right now. The storm's passed. We'll take the canoe. We can go right now—"

Jack shook his head. "We can't all fit in the canoe."

"Yes, we can, the four of us, we can fit—"

"What about Pepper and Lucinda? And Rosa?"

"Rosa can fit too. We'll send the police back for Pepper and Lucinda."

"We're not leaving them behind—"

"Nitro's *dead*, Jack!" Pita exclaimed. "Something got him! It got Miguel too! And now it's come for us. Whatever it is. Okay? Maybe it's a ghost, maybe it's not. I don't know anymore. But whatever's out there, whatever Rosa saw, it's *hunting* us. Don't you get that?"

"And you think you'll be safer out there in the dark than in here?"

"It's getting lighter."

"Stop trying to be a hero, Jack," Jesus said. "Think of the greater good—"

"No," Elizaveta said, shaking her head. As much as she wanted to leave the island too, she knew Jack was right. They couldn't leave anyone behind. "We can't go."

"Then stay," Pita said contemptuously. "Stay here and die. Jesus and I are taking the canoe." She turned to Rosa. "Do you want to come with us?"

"Well...I guess if Jack wants to wait...I guess I should wait."

"Do you want whatever was at your window to get you? Do you want to end up like Nitro? Do you want to end up dead?"

"Enough, Pita," Jack said.

"Because that's what's going to happen," she went on, her voice turning harsh. "You're going to end up dead, and whatever's out there is going to pull out your eyes. Is that what you want? *Is that what you—?*"

Elizaveta slapped Pita across the cheek. The sound was loud and flat, like a clap.

Jesus said, "Bitch!" and moved toward Elizaveta, as if to ram her with his shoulder. Jack stepped forward and cracked him across the temple with the butt of the pistol. His eyes rolled up in his head, so for a moment there was nothing showing but the whites, then he dropped to the floor like a felled tree.

Pita's right hand went to her cheek, which had already flushed red. Her bottom lip trembled. But instead of crying, she spat. A gob of saliva splattered against Elizaveta's chin.

While Elizaveta was wiping this away, Pita swung an overhead punch at Jack. It was easily telegraphed, and he batted it away.

"Stop it, Pita," he told her softly. "Stop this."

"Why are you doing this?" she said, and now she was crying.

"I'm trying to help us."

"You're not! You're getting us killed."

"It's still dark out there. It's dangerous. Wait twenty minutes, and we'll all go to the pier together."

"And do what? Sit there in the open?"

"In the light, on the pier, nobody can sneak up on us. The boatman will come. We'll all go back together."

Whether she believed what Jack was saying, or whether she realized he wasn't changing his mind, she gave up her arguing. She crouched next to Jesus, who was bleeding from the temple, and helped him into a sitting position.

Rosa went to Jack. Given he didn't have any free hands—one was holding his shirt to his wound, the other the pistol—she wrapped her arms around his legs and pressed her head into his stomach.

Elizaveta touched him on the shoulder reassuringly, and she was about to say something when there was as knock at the door.

1957

1

The fire cracked and popped and danced, an orange entity in an otherwise black and quiet night. Don Javier Solano sat on the hard-packed ground before it, the flames warm on his face, the photographs of his family held in his hands. The top one showed his wife, Paola, next to his two daughters, Carolina and Fátima. He and Paola married without either of their parents' permission when they were both nineteen years old. They eloped from Veracruz to Mexico City the following year and opened a tamale stand. It didn't make them rich, but it paid the bills and put food on the table, and they were happy. Solano knew he would have been happy even had they been dirt broke. Paola had that effect on him. She was pure and good, the kindest person he'd ever known—the last person in the world that deserved to be buried to death in the bed where she slept.

Carolina, his eldest, had inherited her mother's beauty, though she never had the chance to grow fully into it. She was fourteen when she too died in the bed where she slept. This was not only unfair, it was tragic. She had so much to live for, so much to give back to the world, so much joy to spread. She wanted to be a schoolteacher and eventually a principal. "But not like the mean principal at my school," she always added. "I would be a nice one. I would actually *listen* when students had a problem." She had a fantasy of living "down the block" so Javier and Paola could visit often, owning a dog and a cat and a rabbit, with a large kitchen so she could cook massive dinners for everyone.

She had been a great role model for her younger sister. In fact, Fátima had worshiped her, often imitating Carolina's hair styles and mannerisms and fashion. Fátima...always giggling, forever into mischief, innocent, angelic. The tears Solano had been fighting sprung to his eyes. She would be ten years old now. Ten years old and a triplegic, bed-ridden, nothing working but a head and an arm. Sometimes he thought it would have been better had she died with her mother and sister in the firecracker explosion. She would have been at peace.

The explosion occurred in the dead of night. There was a sound like thunder, and then the walls and ceiling were falling down all around him...then there was shouting and flashlights, firefighters lifting chunks of concrete off him, escorting him through the rubble of what had once been his bedroom, telling him not to look back. Barely conscious he did just that, looked back, and saw Paola—or what had become of his wife, for all that was visible beneath a slab of concrete was a blood-slicked arm and leg.

Solano must have blacked out, because the next thing he remembered was waking in a hospital bed, a doctor telling him Paola and Carolina were dead, but Fátima was alive, in critical condition. She was in a room on her own, hooked up to a machine, tubes going in and out of her. She didn't respond to his voice, but she was breathing on her own. He remained by her beside, praying for her throughout the night. In the morning she regained consciousness—and doctors were able to determine the extent of her injuries.

Finally Solano grieved, quietly and privately at first, but then his silent tears became racking sobs, and his sobs became howls of anguish, so loud and tortured two nurses escorted him from the building.

2

Solano spent the night in a bar drinking himself into an unthinking stupor. He woke in the morning on the street. He supposed the bar staff had carried him out there when they closed and realized he didn't have identification or money.

He knew he should return to the hospital. Fátima was alive. She needed him. But he couldn't bear to see her so fragile and helpless. He couldn't bear to tell her she would never walk again, never run, never ride her bicycle, never do anything on her own. Besides, what could he do for her? He couldn't give her back her legs, or her arm. All he could do was pity her. He wouldn't be able to help it. And she didn't need that. She would be better off without him.

He went to his apartment building. The police had cordoned it off, but an officer let him inside what remained of his unit to collect his wallet and pack some clothes into a bag. He tried not to look at the bloodstains shouting at him, but they were everywhere, and if he had a pistol right then, he might well have blown his brains out.

He spent the rest of the day wandering aimlessly around the city...and he kept right on wandering for the next year, sleeping in parks or alleyways, scrounging trashcans for food, panhandling for change to buy cheap tequila.

Eventually he ended up in Xochimilco. By then he'd pulled himself together enough to hold down a job as a dishwasher in a restaurant, and a few months after this, a job taking families through the old canals on a beat-up gondola. The gardens and greenery had a calming effect on him, the smog and noise and bustle of the city seemed a world away, and he began spending his free time exploring the waterways on his own. Sometimes he would disappear for days on end.

And then one day he never came back at all.

3

Solano had been living on the island on Teshuilo Lake for eight months when the family showed up. Until then he had not seen another soul so deep in the canal system. Frightened of being discovered, he kept hidden in the jungle, watching them in secret as they picnicked and went swimming. Then to Solano's horror the father struck the little girl with a rock and left her to drown in the shallow water.

As soon as the man and woman returned to the gondola and turned a bank out of sight, Solano collected the girl and brought her to shore, where he attempted to resuscitate her. Miraculously his efforts worked. She coughed and sputtered and opened her eyes. Then she looked at him and said, "My name's María."

"My name's Don Javier Solano."

"Where are my parents?"

"You don't remember what happened?"

She stared at him vacantly.

"Your parents left you here."

"They left me here."

"But it's okay. I'm going to take care of you."

"You're going to take care of me."

"Is that okay?"

She seemed to think about it. "Okay."

4

Solano slipped the photographs of his family back into the sleeve of his wallet, then he considered the wallet. It was time

271

to move on, he knew. He had to put his old family, his old life, behind him. María was his everything now. God had sent her to him. She was his redemption, his second chance to do right for someone in need, to make up for the wrong he had done to his own daughter.

He looked at the fire. No—he couldn't bring himself to burn the wallet. Perhaps he could bury it somewhere? That seemed more appropriate.

He got up and went to the hut he had been spending his days building. María lay on a straw mattress, sleeping soundly, the doll she called Angela, which he'd also rescued from the canal, clutched tightly in her hand. He knelt next to her and pulled the quilt to her chin.

Tomorrow he was going into the city to trade produce for matches and rice and sugar and other supplies. It would be the first time he left María alone, and he was terrified of something happening to her. But she told him she would be okay, and he believed she would be. Despite her mental shortcomings, she was resilient and capable of taking care of herself.

Smiling down at her, he decided he would get her something from the markets. She really liked that doll.

Maybe he could find her another one?

ELIZAVETA

1

Elizaveta watched as Jack opened the front door to the cabin cautiously. She didn't know who to expect—a hulking axe-wielding maniac?—but the woman in a poncho and torn jeans standing on the threshold definitely wasn't anything she had imagined. She was petite, perhaps Pita's height, but skinny as opposed to curvy. Her hair, like Pita's, was long and wavy, though it was not only wet and knotted from the storm but festooned with dead leaves and twigs. She wore some sort of mask, what appeared to be the face cut from a doll. It was strapped to her own face with twine. Where the doll's eye would have been were two holes through which a pair of very real eyes, brownish-red and intense, peered out.

In one hand the woman gripped a doll by its hair, and in the other, a long knife.

"Who the fuck are you?" Jesus blurted.

"My name's María," she replied in a shrill, clear voice, eerily mechanical. Elizaveta couldn't see her mouth moving behind the doll face, and she almost believed the voice to be a recording.

"She has a knife!" Pita said. "She killed Nitro! Shoot her!"

Jack, who had already taken a couple of steps backward, aimed the gun at the woman. She stared directly into the bore but showed no fear.

"Tell her to put down the knife," he said in English.

Elizaveta stepped beside him. Holding out her hand, she said, "Can you give me the knife, María?"

"It's my knife," she said.

"Yes, I know. But can you give it to me for now?"

"It's my knife!" she snapped viciously.

Elizaveta raised her hands, palms outward. "Okay, okay."

There was a brief lull. Then the woman—María—said, "I'm hungry." She sounded perfectly pleasant again.

"Jack, she's hungry," Elizaveta said, translating for him. "Give her some of your vegetables."

He dug a carrot from his pocket and held it out for her. "Last one."

She simply stared at it.

"Don't you want it?" Elizaveta asked her.

"Where should I put my doll?"

"Why don't you give her to me?"

"She's my doll!" That viciousness again.

Hands up, palms outward. "Okay, okay!" Elizaveta considered. "Why don't you put her on table then?"

María looked at the table. "I'll put her on the table." She went to it, moving in a flat-footed staggerstep, her back stooped, and set her doll in a chair. Then she returned, took the carrot from Jack, and stared at it for a long moment.

"Are you going to eat it?" Elizaveta asked.

María pushed the doll face up her forehead.

2

The woman was not horribly burned or mutilated. She did not

suffer from a disfiguring illness. She was in fact quite beautiful. The years had not been kind certainly—she must have been at least fifty, her leathery skin wind-burned and sun-creased—but her bone structure would be the envy of many women. The vertical marionette lines alongside her mouth were carved especially deep, giving her the hinged-jaw look of a ventriloquist's dummy.

She took a bite from the carrot, revealing a missing incisor. Then she chewed, staring myopically into space, apparently not bothered in the least that five strangers were staring at her with equal parts incredulity and confusion.

Elizaveta looked at the others. Pita and Jesus remained by the far wall, speaking quietly to one another. Rosa stood behind Jack, peeking around his legs.

"I don't think she's all there," Jack said softly.

"Shhh," Elizaveta whispered. "She can hear you."

"You think they have an English school out here on this island?"

Elizaveta watched María, but the woman showed no signs of understanding what they were saying. "Who do you think she is? Solano's daughter?"

Jack shrugged. "Must be."

"What about the other two in the photo then?"

"Ask her."

"She's dangerous," Pita hissed. "We have to at least tie her up."

Jack said, "You think she'll talk if you do that?"

"She has a knife!"

"I have a gun." Then, to Elizaveta: "Ask her."

Elizaveta cleared her throat. The woman looked at her.

"Hi, María," she said.

"Hi," she replied in her peculiar voice.

"I'm Eliza."

"My name's María."

"I know that, María. Do you live on this island?"

"Yeah," she said.

"Are you alone?"

She hesitated.

"Are you alone?"

"I don't know."

"You don't know?"

"I said I don't know!"

Elizaveta glanced at Jack. He was frowning, apparently having followed the gist of the questioning.

"She talks funny," Rosa said.

"I talk funny," the woman parroted.

Rosa giggled.

The woman smiled.

"I'm Rosa," she said.

"I'm María. My dad let me out of my room today."

"Your dad?" Elizaveta said.

She held out her hand, which gripped the partly eaten carrot. "I painted my nails today." Her fingernails were indeed a bright orange, though the paint was chipped. They clearly weren't done today; perhaps a week or so ago.

Rosa asked, "Did you paint them?"

"Yeah." She was still smiling.

"They're pretty."

"I have a spare finger."

Elizaveta didn't understand. She was wondering if María meant she had a mutated extra digit when she noticed that only three of the woman's four fingernails were painted orange. The index fingernail was untouched.

She said, "Is your father on the island, María?"

"He's gone to the city."

"When?"

"Yesterday."

Elizaveta was dubious. "Are you sure?"

"I said yesterday!"

"Okay—yesterday. What's his name?"

"He's gone to the city."

"But what's his name?"

"He's my father."

"Do you have a last name?"

"My name's María."

Elizaveta swallowed her frustration.

"She's got no bloody concept of time," Jesus said in English.

"Ask her a time question," Pita said.

"You ask her," Elizaveta said.

"She likes you."

"I'm not getting through to her."

Pita licked her lips.

"Go on, try," Jesus said.

She grinned at María a bit foolishly and said, "Hi, María. I'm Pita. Are you happy today?" She was trying to sound disarming but came across as more frightened than anything.

"My name's María."

"How old are you, María?"

"I'm ten years old."

"No you're not!" Rosa said.

"I'm ten years old."

"I think you're a bit older than that, María," Pita said.

María stared at her—*glared* at her, that switch inside her flipped to angry once again. Then she returned her attention to the carrot. After looking at it for a long moment, she took a bite.

"She's a fucking lunatic," Jesus whispered in English.

"Don't provoke her!" Pita said.

"She's clearly not making any sense. She thinks she's fucking ten years old! Jack, will you tie her up now so we can get the hell out of here."

"You want to leave her tied up here by herself?" he said.

"She killed Miguel and Nitro, man! Tie her up! We'll send the police back to get her."

Jack ignored him and said, "What's she been saying?"

Elizaveta shrugged. "Just...stuff. Jesus is right. She's not making any sense. She said her father went to the city yesterday, and she's ten years old. I don't think she's going to be much help—what?"

Jack was frowning at María. "What's she doing?"

Elizaveta looked at the woman. Her eyes were fixed on Jack, intense, unblinking.

"María?" Elizaveta said.

She didn't reply.

"María?"

No answer.

"Why's she just staring at me?" Jack asked.

Jesus smirked. "She's got the hots for you, Jack-o."

Jack tweaked the pistol back and forth.

María didn't react.

"María?" Elizaveta said.

Nothing.

"Maybe she's sleeping?" Rosa said.

"Her eyes are open," Jack said.

"*María?*" Elizaveta said.

She blinked. "My mom and dad had a baby."

"What did she say?" Jack asked.

"That her mom and dad had baby," Elizaveta said. "I think she just had seizure."

"What the hell do you know about seizures?" Jesus said.

"I've seen seizures before," she said, referring to the epileptic children she knew in the orphanage in which she'd grown up.

"Don't you shake and stuff?" Jack said.

"There are many different kinds of seizures."

"My mom and dad had a baby," María said again. "And her name is Salma."

Jack said, "Ask her about Miguel. Ask her if she knows what happened to him. Rosa," he added, "can you go into the bedroom with Pepper for a bit?"

She pouted. "But I want to stay with you."

"We're going to be talking about some adult stuff. It's best if you go in the bedroom. I'll call you when we're done."

She kicked at an imaginary object, scuffing the sole of her

shoe on the floorboards. But she obediently went to the room.

"Close the door!" Jack said.

She closed it behind her.

He gave Elizaveta a nod to begin.

"María?" she said.

"Yeah?"

"Who's that?" She pointed to the doll she was holding.

"That's my doll."

"Does she have a name?"

"Her name's Angela. She's my doll."

"Can I ask you a different question, María?"

"Yeah?"

"Did you see anyone on the island yesterday?"

She stared blankly.

"A man and a woman?" Elizaveta pressed. "Did you see a man and woman?"

"Yeah."

"You saw them?"

"Yeah."

"And the little girl who was just here. Did you see her too?"

"She was singing a song."

"A lullaby."

"Yeah."

"Were you watching her through that hole in the wall earlier?"

"She was singing a song. My mom sings me songs."

"She was singing the song today," Elizaveta agreed. "But did you see her yesterday—the little girl, Rosa?"

"Yeah."

"She's simply agreeing with you," Pita said in English.

"No, I think she understands," Jesus said.

"She said she saw Miguel and Lucinda?" Jack asked.

Elizaveta nodded. "But she just keeps saying *si, si, si*."

"Avoid yes/no questions then," Jack said.

"María," she said. "The man and woman you saw, what did they look like?"

279

"They were fighting."

"Why were they fighting?"

"I don't know what happened. They were fighting. The boy was hurting the girl. I stopped him."

"How did you stop him?"

Her eyes hardened. "I just stopped him."

"With that?" She pointed at the knife.

"Yeah."

"You stabbed him?"

"I stopped him."

"What happened to the woman?"

María stared blankly.

"María?"

"I stopped him with the knife."

"Did you stop the woman too?"

"I'm going to the city."

"María, the woman, she's hurt. She's in that room there." She motioned toward Lucinda's bedroom.

"That's my dad's room," she said.

"What about that one?" She indicated Pepper's bedroom.

"That's my room."

"Where's your dad, María?"

"He went to the city. He's going to bring me back a doll. He always brings me a doll."

"What's his name, María?"

"He's my dad."

Elizaveta gave up and explained to Jack: "She said Miguel was hurting Lucinda so she attacked him. I think. She won't say what happened to Lucinda. It's—I don't know."

"Can we agree this is a massive waste of time and go now?" Jesus said. "She's a fucking retard and a spaz. She stabbed Miguel and Lucinda, and she slit Nitro's throat. There's nothing more to it than that."

"You're not getting out of this so easily, Jesus," Jack said.

"What the hell are you talking about?"

"Maybe she killed Miguel, and maybe she stabbed Lucinda,

but Nitro's blood was on your jacket. You had a bloody knife hidden on you."

"Give it a fucking rest, Jack—"

"You're telling me this woman sneaked up on Nitro without him any the wiser and slit his throat?"

"Ask her about Miguel's eyes," Jesus said. "Do it!"

Elizaveta said, "María, the man you 'stopped' yesterday, he's missing his eyes." She pointed to her own eyes for emphasis. "Eyes. Do you know what happened to them?"

"Yeah."

"What?"

"I took them."

Elizaveta swallowed. Jesus crowed triumphantly.

"You took them?"

"I took them," she said. "My dad showed me how."

"Your dad showed you how?"

"With fish. He showed me how to eat them."

"Oh my God," Pita moaned.

"See!" Jesus said. "She killed Miguel and Nitro for their eyes! She just admitted it. Now would you fucking untie me, please?"

"What did she admit?" Jack demanded.

Before Elizaveta could explain, María dropped the half-eaten carrot on the floor and reached into the pocket of her jeans. She pulled her hand out. It was balled into a fist. She uncurled her fingers.

Resting in the center of her palm was a white eyeball, the iris and pupil gazing sightlessly at the ceiling.

3

Elizaveta gagged. Her stomach slid up her throat, and she dry heaved twice before uploading a mess of watery yellow gunk. She rode a hot wave of relief before her stomach revolted a second time and more gunk splashed to the floor.

"Hey," Jack said, kneeling beside her. He pulled back her hair so she didn't get sick on it. "You okay?"

She wasn't sure. She waited, her eyes tearing, her throat stinging.

Several seconds passed. Jack stroked her back. She started feeling better and raised her head, pushing her hair from her face—and saw Jesus sneaking up behind Jack. He held the post-hole digger with his bound hands like a baseball bat.

"Jack—!"

That's all she got out before Jesus swung the makeshift weapon. Jack turned, tried to duck. The long tube of iron caught him on the side of his head. He dropped to the floor. The pistol clattered out of his hand.

Elizaveta stared at it. She knew she should grab it, but she couldn't think clearly, couldn't move.

Then Jesus tossed the post-hole digger away and snatched up the pistol. He stepped backward and started using his teeth to free the belt securing his wrists.

Elizaveta snapped out of whatever had gripped her. She scooted next to Jack. She bent over him, examining his head. A massive, bleeding bump had already formed on the side of his skull. "Jack?" she said. "Jack?"

He didn't respond.

She checked the pulse in his neck. It was beating.

She whirled on Jesus, eyes raging. The belt lay next to his feet, coiled liked a snake. He was now aiming the pistol at Jack's limp body.

Pita was yelling at him: "Put the gun down, Jesus!"

"You don't understand!" he said.

"Put the gun down!"

"Shut up, Pita!"

"You can't shoot him!"

"There's no choice!"

"*What are you talking about?*"

"Eliza," Jesus said. "Get out of the way." His face was feverish. The pistol trembled in his grip.

"Stop this, Jesus!" she said. "What are you doing?"

"Eliza, move!"

"Jesus!" Pita shouted.

"He's going to rat me to the police!" Jesus snapped, glaring at her.

"So what! You didn't do anything. You didn't kill—" She bit off the rest of the sentence.

"You killed him," Elizaveta stated. "You really did kill him."

"Nitro?" Pita said.

"You don't understand." Jesus ran the back of his hand across his lips. He took aim at Jack again. "He was a cop."

"Nitro was a cop?" Elizaveta said, dumbstruck.

"Nitro was not a cop, Jesus," Pita said.

Jesus flourished the pistol in a declamatory way. "This gun! It's a Beretta 92. Marco has the same one. He told me it's his service gun from when he was a cop. They let him keep it."

Marco was one of Jesus's bodyguards: big, overweight, greased hair and a goatee.

Pita said, "That doesn't mean—"

"No, it doesn't, Pita," Jesus said. "But it got me thinking. What does Nitro actually do?"

She frowned. "He has his father's money—"

"His father who builds highways in Spain. Right. Convenient he's across the ocean. No way to run into someone in the Mexican construction industry who might know, or not know, of him. And did you ever see Nitro spend much of this money he supposedly had? He gets around on a fucking Honda motorcycle. Does he even have a car? Have you ever seen his car? And what about his place? Where does he live? Napoles? Conveniently across the city from me. Did you ever go to his place? All that time you were fucking him, did he ever invite you over?"

Pita glanced at Jack. He remained out cold. "No..." she said quietly.

Jesus shook his head. "It was a lie. Everything, a lie, so he would fit in with our crowd. Think about it, Pita—when did Nitro and I meet?"

"At Ana's birthday party," Elizaveta said.

"Ana's birthday, correct. Nitro came up to me. Said he was a friend of a friend. I figured he wanted something and brushed him off. He tried a few more times—and then that whole screen door episode with Jack. Everyone knows Jack and I don't get along. So what does Nitro do to get my attention?"

"Picks a fight with Jack..." Elizaveta said.

"And it worked," Jesus continued. "After you took him home, Pita, Nitro and I spent the rest of the night laughing about Jack. We hit it off because of our mutual dislike for Jack. I gave him my number, told him to ring me some time."

Elizaveta's mind was spinning in overdrive. She remembered perfectly well the next time Nitro called Jesus. It had been the following Saturday morning. He had tickets to a bullfight in the Plaza México and invited Jesus and Elizaveta to join him. Jesus, a huge bullfighting fan (this was no secret to anybody that knew him), promptly accepted the offer. "But *why*?" she said. "What was the big act for? What did he want?"

Jesus hesitated. Then: "He was investigating the company."

"What!" Pita said.

Jesus shrugged. "Some stuff's been going on—"

"What 'stuff,' Jesus? That bribery probe? Is that still going on? You said—"

"It doesn't matter, Pita. Everything's fine. Everything's taken care of. It will all work itself out—"

"So you killed him? You killed Nitro because he was *investigating* you? Oh my God, Jesus! Oh my God—"

Jesus's face transformed. "He used me!"

"You killed him!"

"He was a piece of shit, Pita! He used you too! Yeah, he did. Come on, why do you think he put the moves on you? He was undercover. He was going to start something up with the sister of the guy he's investigating because he's in love with her?"

Pita blinked, as if she had been slapped.

Elizaveta felt dizzy, surreal. The scope of the deception! And she'd never suspected a thing. "Okay, Jesus," she said quickly. "Maybe you are right. But we can work this out. We'll figure this out."

"There's nothing to figure out. Jack's going to tell the cops I killed Nitro. Proof or not, if they suspect me, they'll put it together."

"Shooting him won't make situation better."

"Of course it will," he snapped. "There's a bona fide killer on this island." He glanced over his shoulder at María, who stood statute still, watching them in silence. "She killed Miguel. She killed Nitro. She killed Jack—"

"I'll tell them, Jesus," Elizaveta said defiantly. "I'll tell the police everything."

"No you won't, cariño," he said. "Because she's going to kill you too."

4

The words flattened Elizaveta like a truck. She had been dating Jesus for twelve months. She had loved him—or thought she had. And he was not only a killer, he was a cold-blooded sociopath.

"Move away from him," Jesus told her. "Unless you want to die first."

"Jesus, please…"

"Move!"

"You can't do this, Jesus!" Pita said. "It's insane. You can't kill everybody—"

"It's either them or me, Pita."

"And Pepper, and Lucinda?"

"They don't know what's happened. They'll believe what I tell them."

Pita began wandering in a circle, mumbling, a hand to her head as if she might faint.

"Pita!" Jesus barked. "You have to be in this with me."

"I..." She shook her head. Her eyes were filled with questioning fear. "Jesus, you can't do this."

"There's no other way. If I go to prison, I can't fix what's happened at the company. It will all come out. We'll lose everything. You'll have nothing. You'll be *poor*."

"I'm not feeling very well."

"Pita, I need to hear you're in this with me."

"I can't—"

"Pita!"

"Fine," she said so softly it was barely audible.

"Fine what?"

"Fine! Just do it! Hurry up!"

Jesus returned his attention to Elizaveta. He did not smile or revel in his victory; he displayed no emotion at all, which terrified Elizaveta all the more. Her heart slammed inside her chest, and she found it difficult to breathe. It seemed impossible she was about to die. She had to teach the twins on Monday. She had a hair appointment Tuesday evening—

"Last warning, cariño," Jesus said. "Move away from Jack."

She almost asked him why he wanted her to move, but she knew the answer. He didn't want her and Jack's deaths to look like summary executions.

"Screw you, Jesus," she said.

Now his face filled with cold malevolence. With a brutish grunt, he stormed over and grabbed Elizaveta by the hair, yanking her away from Jack. She yelped, clawing and kicking him. He drove his knee into her face, stunning her. Light flowered across her vision. She tasted the calcified bits of a cracked tooth on her tongue.

Then he was hitting her over and over and over.

JACK

A commotion was happening around me, a sonic orgy of shouting and struggling, a million miles away. Pain flared in my head, and I remembered Jesus swinging the post-hole digger. Wondering whether a chunk of my skull and brain were missing—that's what it felt like—I raised my hand, touched the fiery spot above my ear. It was numb, pins and needles. But everything seemed intact.

Groaning, I sat up. The room focused though remained soaked in an underwater slow-motion quality. Jesus stood several feet away, bending over Elizaveta. For a moment I thought he was speaking to her, but in fact he was striking her with short, straight jabs.

And then, behind him, María was raising the knife she gripped in her hand. Her eyes flamed, her lips curled back to reveal her gums and teeth. She brought the blade down into his back.

Jesus went rigid, his arms shooting out to his sides, as if he had been electrocuted. He issued an unholy noise, more roar than shriek.

María plucked the knife free and stabbed him again.

Turning, Jesus swung the pistol toward her.

Juiced with adrenaline, I found my feet and sprang at him, slamming into his midsection, sending us both careening through the air.

ELIZAVETA

When Jack and Jesus crashed to the floor, Jesus released the pistol, which skidded across the floorboards. Although Elizaveta felt nauseous with pain from the whooping Jesus had delivered to her, this time she didn't hesitate. She scrambled toward the gun.

Her head snapped backward.

Pita had her hair!

The bitch shook Elizaveta's head from side to side, and Elizaveta felt déjà vu from their earlier fight. "Let go!" she said, kicking out blindly behind her.

The kick made contact. Pita, however, was too close for it to have much effect.

Elizaveta flipped onto her back. She raked her fingernails down Pita's furious face. Three parallel lines of blood appeared.

Pita yowled but didn't release her hair. Elizaveta grabbed Pita's right breast through her open shirt and squeezed as hard as she could. The yowl jumped an octave and she finally let go.

Still turtled on her back, Elizaveta brought her knee to her chest and kicked. Her foot sailed past Pita, who dodged left. Then Pita was on her feet, standing above Elizaveta. She produced the sickle, which had been tucked into the waistband of her jean shorts.

The curved blade grinned wickedly.

JACK

1

I landed on top of Jesus. He went for my throat, strangling me, inadvertently tilting my chin so I was looking at the ceiling. I shoved my right hand against his face, pressing it into the floor. My palm covered his nose and mouth. His lips were wet with saliva. Then a sharp bite.

The fucker bit me!

One of my legs was between his. I drove my knee into his groin. His teeth released their pinch. He bellowed. I kneed him again.

The pistol was a few feet away. I twisted off Jesus and grabbed it just as Elizaveta cried out. I'd been peripherally aware of Pita and Elizaveta fighting, but I'd been so focused in my struggle with Jesus I hadn't paid any attention.

Now I saw Pita standing above Elizaveta, the sickle raised.

"Pita!" I shouted, leveling the pistol at her. "Don't!"

She swung the curved blade.

I squeezed the trigger.

2

The shot struck Pita in the center of her chest, stopping her mid-swing. Her eyes widened, confused. They met mine. Then her legs gave out and she collapsed to the floor.

For a long moment I couldn't move. There was dead silence, but at the same time my ears rang with the gunshot. All I was thinking was: *I shot Pita I shot Pita I shot Pita...*

Elizaveta elbowed backward, away from Pita's body.

"Pita!" I said, scrambling forward. I tried not to look at the wound in her chest but couldn't help it. A small hole marked her skin directly between her breasts, an inch above the center gore of her bra. It was gushing blood.

Her eyes stared at me, accusing.

"Pita...?" I said, hearing my voice in stereo, the thickness of it. Time seemed to have slowed down, as if by some quirk of relativity.

"You shot me..." she said, a rill of blood trickling down her chin.

"Pita!" It was Jesus, rolling onto his knees. He crawled frantically toward her, shoving past me to take my place. He lowered his forehead to his sister's. He mumbled something in Spanish, his lips inches from hers.

I backed away. Elizaveta cupped her hand on my shoulder. I was aware of her doing this. I was aware of María standing against the wall, staring at the bloody knife in her hand. I was aware of Rosa peeking out of the bedroom.

I was aware of all this but none of it. I was trying to comprehend what I did, waiting for myself to react to the horror of it.

Then Jesus's shoulders began to shake as he sobbed. A moment later he reeled on me, wiping tears from his eyes, a clenched expression on his face. "She's dead, Jack! You killed her! You fucking killed her!"

This isn't happening, I thought. *It's wrong. It can't be happening. But it's done. It's been done.*

I opened my mouth but had nothing to say. The right words weren't there.

"She was going to kill me," Elizaveta said.

"Bullshit!" Jesus snarled.

"She was!" Rosa cried. "I saw her!"

"You did this," Jesus wailed at me. "*You killed her.*"

"You did!" I said, directing my anger and anguish at him. "You were going to shoot us! *You fucking caused all this.*"

"You bastard!" He grabbed the sickle.

I pointed the pistol at him. "Calm down."

"Calm down? You shot my sister!"

"Calm down!"

Jesus got to his feet. I did too.

"Get back down, Jesus," I said.

"Fuck you."

"Get down!"

He started backing toward the front door.

"Stop!"

"Shoot me, Jack. Shoot me like you shot Pita, you fucking piece of shit."

I took up the slack in the trigger.

"Jack..." Elizaveta said.

And I knew I couldn't do it. I couldn't shoot him.

I lowered the pistol.

Jesus opened the door and disappeared into the breaking dawn.

ELIZAVETA

1

It took some time, but they eventually woke Pepper, coaxed him out of bed, and told him to drink water until he had enough strength to stand. Then they moved Nitro's body inside so the animals on the island wouldn't get to it. They set it next to Pita's body, covering both with the sheet from Pepper's bed. Finally they went to Lucinda's room, to attempt to rouse her as well. A sour, yeasty smell permeated the air. The woman's skin was dire, her face possessed with an unnatural stillness, and Elizaveta feared the worst before Jack confirmed it a moment later.

"She's dead," he said.

2

They collected their packs—Jack carried Pepper's camera bag also—and they made their way to the pier. The sky was overcast, smudged with anvil-headed clouds. The air held that trapped-breath quality that often follows storms. A gloomy stillness hung over everything like a funeral shroud. Numerous plants were uprooted or broken, while severed branches littered the ground. Amazingly, however, most of the dolls remained dangling from the dripping trees just as they'd been the day before, only now rinsed clean of some of their grime and spider webs, their ragtag clothes soggy.

When they passed the hut with the shrine, Jack led María inside to the portrait of the Mexican man with the mustache and poncho hanging on the wall. "Do you know him?" he asked.

Her eyes shone. "That's my dad. He went to the market to get me a doll."

3

Unsurprisingly the canoe was gone. Jesus had taken it; he would likely be halfway back to Xochimilco by now. So they settled down on the pier and waited for the boatman to come.

4

At one point María wandered off into the woods without a word. They let her go. She'd survived on her own until now. The police could find her later.

JACK

1

The sky remained dreary for much of the morning, but gradually the sun burned away the depressing clouds. The cawing and screeching of birds greeted the new day. Then the flies and mosquitos returned, buzzing and biting, followed by the drone of the cicadas. I began to have my doubts that the boatman would come after all, but we had no option but to continue to wait and hope. For much of this time my mind was like a wheel caught in a muddy rut. It spun relentlessly on everything Pita, replaying the happy times we'd shared together. Nevertheless, this didn't lift my mood. Instead, it made me incredibly sad. Part of this was due to nostalgia, the sense that what was would never be again. But the other part, the big part, was because my thoughts kept coming back to her lying on the cabin floor, a bullet hole in her chest, dead.

I wanted to weep for her, to experience some sort of catharsis, but I couldn't. My eyes remained stone dry. I chalked this up to shock. When it abated, the floodgates would open, and the grief and darkness would come in torrents. But not now.

Occasionally I glanced at the dolls hanging from the surrounding trees, the dolls that had miraculously remained fixed in place during what had no doubt been hurricane-force winds and rain. Their eyes stared knowingly at me, their smiles as enigmatic as ever.

Watching and laughing, I thought. And then: *If it were up to me, I would burn the fucking island to the ground.*

2

I wondered about María. I had so many questions. Was she born with her intellectual disability? Or had her mind deteriorated over the years while she was held prisoner on the island? Had Solano treated her well, or had he abused her? She obviously harbored a strong affection toward him, but that was textbook Stockholm syndrome, wasn't it? And after he passed away, how had she survived on her own? She seemed capable physically. The vegetables in the root cellar came from a garden somewhere on the island. So had she simply lived off the land? And how had she avoided whoever discovered Solano's body, and the police who would have come to investigate? Had she hidden from them when they searched the island? Or had they not even bothered to do that? Had they known Solano lived alone, collected his body, and called it a day? And why had she "stopped" Miguel from hurting Lucinda? Given Miguel was naked, and Lucinda was too, my suspicion was that Miguel was not hurting Lucinda at all; more than likely they were having sex. María saw them, misinterpreted what was happening, and stabbed Miguel in the back. As for Lucinda, she was stabbed herself when she tried to stop María and fled in fear.

It seemed to fit. But then again, who knew?

"What's going to happen to her?" Elizaveta asked abruptly.

"Huh?" I said, blinking.

"María." Elizaveta sat with her knees pulled to her chest,

her arms wrapped around them. Her makeup was cracked, her eyeliner curdled. Her hair stuck up all over the place, as if someone had taken a leaf blower to it. She'd stopped rolling her shoulder, so I assumed the sting wasn't bothering her anymore.

I wished I could say that about the stab wound in my side. It still hurt like a son-of-a-bitch, and I had the sense I'd incurred some serious internal damage. Even so, I was alive. I wasn't going to complain about that.

"María?" I said, and shrugged.

"From everything you've told me," Pepper said, "I don't think she'll be going to prison."

"I hope not," Rosa said. "She was sort of nice."

As opposed to Elizaveta—and no doubt myself—Pepper and Rosa appeared none the worse for wear. Pepper wore his purple blazer draped over his shoulders again, and now that his bug was marching a hasty retreat, he almost seemed refreshed. He complained of being weak and tired, but you couldn't tell this by looking at him. And Rosa was, well, Rosa. She had the glow and resilience of youth. Her brother was dead, and she'd just survived a night of hell, but she seemed as though she could spring up and run a marathon, or bake a cake, at a moment's notice.

"I hope not too," Elizaveta said. "But she killed two people."

"She won't go to prison," I said, thinking even if it turned out she had indeed committed a double murder, forensic mental health professionals would almost certainly deem her mentally unfit to stand trial. "They'll make her plead guilty but insane," I added. "She'll end up in an asylum somewhere."

"I don't think those exist anymore," Elizaveta said.

"In Mexico they do," Pepper said. "I researched them for one of my shows—"

"You guys are as dumb as that retard bitch."

We all turned as one to see Jesus standing some ten feet away.

He gripped the pistol in his hand, which I'd left on the bank on top of our bags, and he was aiming it directly at me.

3

We stood very quickly. Jesus was bare-chested and scowling and watchful. He'd sliced up his white button-down shirt and used the material to bandage up his shoulder. His hair was greasy and messy, his once-fashionable stubble now slovenly beard shadow. He looked like a refugee that had escaped some third-world disaster.

"You didn't leave the island," I said.

"And leave behind witnesses to contradict my version of events?"

"Where's the canoe?" Elizaveta asked.

"In the reeds. Sunk in shallow water."

"You pull that trigger, Jesus," I said, "it's murder."

"You murdered Pita!"

"She was going to kill Eliza."

He shook his head. "I'm not here to talk, Jack. I'm here to kill you."

"You're not God!" Rosa said. "You're the devil!"

"The devil doesn't exist, cariño," he said. "Haven't you learned anything?" He returned his attention to me. "I'd tell you to say hi to Nitro for me, Jack. But fortunately for you, I don't think hell exists either."

He squeezed the trigger.

4

The pistol clicked. Jesus's eyes widened. He squeezed the trigger again and again.

I stuck my hand in the pocket of my shorts and produced

the cartridges I'd removed from the pistol's magazine earlier. I tossed them into the canal.

"Figured there was a chance you might have stuck around, Jesus," I said. "You know, to clean up your mess. And what better lure than a gun left serendipitously in the open."

His surprise metastasized into hatred. "You mother-fucker!"

Elizaveta passed me the string she'd scavenged from some of the hanging dolls, and I walked toward Jesus. "We can do this the easy way or the hard way," I told him, "and I'm sort of hoping you choose the hard way."

EPILOGUE

S eated in a Starbucks on Central Avenue in Los Angeles, I was sipping an espresso macchiato and reading the sports section of the *LA Times*.

It was early December, pleasantly cool. The forecast predicated light showers later in the afternoon. Elizaveta and I were staying at the Sheraton a couple of blocks away. We came to LA to see of all things a twenty-two-foot fiberglass sculpture called Chicken Boy. Elizaveta became obsessed with these so-called Muffler Men after I took her on a road trip along Route 66 a while back. I don't know what her fascination with them is, but we've traveled all over the country so she can snap pictures of herself with them. Some of her favorites so far include Paul Bunyan in Phoenix, The Casino Dude in Montana, The Gemini Giant in Illinois, and The Friendly Green Giant in Minnesota.

Elizaveta entered the United States on a fiancé visa almost ten years ago now. Two days after crossing the border we married in an Elvis-themed wedding chapel in Vegas, and she subsequently applied for a green card. Five years later she was granted citizenship, and all I can say is since then she's taken to the US with gusto. She asked me to install an American flag atop a pole in the front of our Tucson home, for instance. She knows every storyline and every devious subplot of every soap on daytime television. She's become the Phoenix Suns number one fan (we have tickets to a Suns-Clippers game at the Staples Center tomorrow evening). And perhaps most telling of all: the bumper sticker on her Audi reads "God Bless America." Sometimes her enthusiasm for her adopted country was a bit much, but I was happy she was happy.

So, yeah, things were pretty great between us. We rarely spoke about the night we spent on the Island of the Dolls. It was an experience both of us would like to forget, a horror story largely of our own creation in which we allowed our imaginations and fear of the unknown to overwhelm our better reason. Even so, although we might not speak about what happened, I still reflected on it every now and then, and when I did it seemed as though it all occurred only yesterday, and I suspect that's how it will always be.

The police had been waiting for us at the docks of Cuemanco. We'd called them in advance when our phones regained reception. Pepper, Elizaveta, and Rosa were taken to the local police station, while Jesus and I were taken to a hospital. As soon as the doctor fixed up the stab wound in my side, detectives were in and out of my room to question me. None were very friendly. They kept trying to get me to confess to an alternate version of reality—Jesus's version of reality—which led me to believe they were taking orders from someone deep in Jesus's pocket. The scenario went like this: when I discovered Pita was cheating on me with Nitro, I flew into a jealous rage, slit Nitro's throat, and shot Pita. The detectives told me Elizaveta and Rosa and Pepper had all confessed as much. I knew this was bullshit and pretty much told them to go fuck themselves. To be honest, though, for a day or two I had been worried they were somehow going to make the apocryphal accusations stick. But then the media caught wind of the story, and it became a national talking point that couldn't be contained or manipulated regardless of Jesus's money or connections. Consequently, he was arrested while still in his hospital bed and charged with the first-degree murder of Nitro, while I was allowed to walk free because Pita's death was ultimately considered a justifiable homicide as it prevented greater harm to innocents, namely Elizaveta.

I didn't attend Pita's funeral. I wanted to, but I couldn't. Her extended family and network of friends would have torn me apart. According to the rants they embarked on whenever a reporter put a microphone in front of them, I was the anti-Christ, a lying gringo, a spited lover hell bent on ruining Pita's reputation and framing Jesus for a crime he didn't commit.

I did, however, visit Pita's gravesite a few days after she was interred. That's when the floodgates opened and I finally grieved, crying until it hurt. I had loved Pita. We had a pretty amazing run until the last few months or so. She wasn't evil. I didn't blame her for the eleventh-hour betrayal. Jesus had manipulated her, just as he'd attempted to manipulate all of us.

Although I never saw Pepper or Rosa again, Elizaveta and I started spending a lot of time together. She was promptly fired from her position of governess—"No respectable family can continue to employ someone of your newfound notoriety," the Russian oligarch had explained to her—so I invited her to move into my place...and the intimacy that had developed between us that night on the island grew into something real and sustainable. At first I felt guilty courting her. But I told myself I wasn't doing anything wrong. Pita might have been Elizaveta's friend, but Pita was dead now. I couldn't change that. There was no reason her memory should stand between our happiness.

And the other side of the coin, the fact Elizaveta was Jesus's ex? Well, fuck that. I couldn't have cared less about his feelings. The guy would have happily put a bullet between my eyes if he had his way. He could rot in prison—which, incidentally, was exactly what he was doing. His trial had lasted one week. Given our testimony, along with the forensic evidence the police gathered from the cabin and Jesus's clothing, the eventual verdict of guilty had never really been in question. The judge fined him $300,000 and sentenced him to life in Altiplano, a maximum-security federal prison that housed some of the most infamous drug lords and murderers in Mexico.

For my part, after Elizaveta and I were married, and we bought the place in Tucson, I cut back on drinking. I didn't go cold turkey. I didn't think I could do that, or wanted to do that. But I became what I guess you would call a moderate drinker, preferring wine over spirits, eventually garnering a taste for some of the older nutty vintages. Moreover, during that first year back in the States, my migraines cleared up, I got back out on the track, and it wasn't long before I returned to top form.

Jump to the present, and I'd just capped the 2010 season with my fifth Cup series championship, and my overall numbers now stood at 68 wins, 301 Top 10s, and 25 pole positions.

Not too shabby for a guy whose career was supposed to be over before it really got started.

And this was why I didn't feel too bad about calling it quits at the end of next season. This wasn't a result of age or lassitude. I didn't think I would ever grow tired of racing. But I wanted to spend more time with my seven-year-old daughter, Alexa. She wasn't my biological child. Elizaveta and I tried to conceive for a while but eventually discovered we were infertile. That's when Elizaveta suggested adopting a foreign-born child, specifically one from Russia. This was not for nationalistic reasons. She simply knew what the conditions were like in Russian orphanages, and she wanted to give a Russian child the life and opportunities that had never been afforded to her.

So we went through the long adoption process, visited Moscow twice, and finally brought home Alexa two years ago —and she was proving to be everything we could have asked for and more.

I finished the *LA Times* story I was reading about the Clippers owner heckling his own player from his courtside seats, then looked away from the newspaper to give my eyes a break. The Starbucks had emptied out a little in the hour or so I'd been there. Across the café an attractive woman dressed in a pastel sweater, metallic mini skirt, and sneakers was seated at a round table, staring at me. I lowered my eyes to the paper again. I wasn't Nic Cage or anything. A race car driver was like the drummer in a rock 'n' roll band: people might know your name, but not your face, and you could walk down the street in complete anonymity. Having said that, every so often someone recognized you. It's happened to me on several occasions off the track, or away from the typical driver hangouts, and I always loathed it. Not that I minded signing an autograph. But when other people saw me doing this, they came over too. They'd ask me what movie I was in or something along those lines, I'd tell them I raced cars, and more often than not they'd be suitably unimpressed and wander off, cracking a joke or mumbling a derogatory remark to their friend.

I scanned the NBA and NHL standings, but couldn't concentrate. I had a feeling the woman was still staring at me, so I looked up, and sure enough she was, only now her lips had curled into a playful smirk.

I was wondering if I should continue to ignore her, or get up and leave, when the front door opened and Elizaveta strolled inside. She would be turning forty in February, but she looked ten years younger. She saw me and waved. I waved back. She came over and sat down, setting her leather jacket and shopping bags on the chair next to her.

"What did you buy?" I asked her.

"Christmas presents," she said, pushing her sunglasses up her forehead.

"For who?" I tilted open one of the bags.

She slapped my hand. "For you. So do not peek."

"What did you get me?"

"Why do you always want to ruin surprise?"

"Did you get Alexa something too?"

"Of course. One of those new iPads."

"Like she doesn't spend enough time on her iPhone already." I glanced past Elizaveta to the woman in the sweater and skirt. She was still staring at me.

"What?" Elizaveta asked, turning in her seat.

"Don't," I said quietly.

She turned back. "Don't what? Are you checking out that girl?"

"She has the hots for me."

"Has the hots for you?" Elizaveta laughed. "She's about half your age, Jack."

"I guess she's a fan or something. She's still staring at me."

"You're encouraging her. You keep looking at her."

"Not on purpose."

"You can't control your eyes?"

"It's weird having someone stare at you."

"She's very pretty, Jack. Perhaps I better go see what she wants."

"What are you talking about?"

"Maybe I better have a word with her." She stood.

"Eliza!"

She ignored me and crossed the room. She spoke with the woman briefly, then gestured to the spare chair at the table and sat down. She said something else, then pointed at me.

The woman smiled and waved.

Mortified, furious, I focused on the newspaper and waited for Elizaveta to return. What was she talking to the woman about? Was she telling her how I thought she had the hots for me? Probably. Elizaveta didn't have Pita's proclivity for jealously when it came to pit lizards and female fans, but that wasn't to say she didn't get jealous. She did. And she would sometimes do silly things like this to prove to me she wasn't jealous, which of course only underscored the fact that she was.

Abruptly Elizaveta stood. She pointed at me again. The woman nodded and stood also.

Then they were both coming over.

I set the paper aside and smiled pleasantly.

"Jack, I'd like you to meet my lovely friend," Elizaveta said. "You were right. She really is a big fan of yours."

I felt my cheeks redden. "I didn't say that."

"It's true though," the woman said. "I'm a huge fan of yours. I've been following your career for years."

"Please," Elizaveta said to her. "Have a seat."

"Actually," I said, "we probably should get going."

"Nonsense, Jack," Elizaveta said.

She and the woman sat. They exchanged amused glances, and I realized I was the butt of a joke I didn't understand.

"I didn't get your name," I said to the woman.

"Rosa," she said, holding out a delicate hand.

I shook. "You have an accent—" The words died on my lips. "*Rosa?*" I said. And it was. She looked completely different than she had when she was eight years old, but somehow she looked the same too.

"Hi, Jack," she said, appearing self-conscious for the first time.

"Surprise!" Elizaveta said.

"My God, Rosa, what are you doing here? In LA, I mean? Do you live here now?"

"Rosa has just started her freshman year at UCLA," Elizaveta explained. "I thought it would be the perfect opportunity to catch up."

"Catch up?" I said. "So you organized this? Today...the whole setup?"

"It wasn't a setup, Jack."

"Actually," Rosa said, "I was early. We weren't supposed to meet for another half hour. But I was too excited to see you, Jack. I didn't mean to go all *Fatal Attraction* on you. I just thought you might recognize me."

I looked at her more closely. Big almond eyes, nutmeg skin, svelte cheeks and chin. She wasn't attractive; she was beautiful—beautiful and, to be honest, sexy. I didn't want to think this. She was still eight years old in my mind. But I couldn't deny it.

She was, as Nitro might have said, a ten.

"Wow," I said. "This is blowing my mind. You used to be so

small, Rosa."

"That was a long time ago, Jack."

"Yeah, I know…" I looked at Elizaveta. "How did you guys get in touch?"

"Facebook, Jack. Ever hear of it? Maybe you should get an account."

"You never told me you and Rosa were Facebook friends."

"We weren't. Not until recently anyway."

"When I found out I was accepted to UCLA," Rosa explained, "I looked you up on Facebook, Jack. You know there are actually a bunch of other Jack Goffs in the world? I thought it was a one-off name. Anyway, there was a Jack Goff plumber, a Jack Goff accountant, a Jack Goff blogger. But no Jack Goff race car driver."

"Jack is too famous for Facebook," Elizaveta said. "He would have too many girls with the hots for him tracking him down."

"I've never said that," I said truthfully.

"You should see all the pit snakes that try to talk to him at races."

"Pit lizards."

"I went to your webpage, Jack," Rosa said. "But the only contact was for your publicist. She wouldn't give me your email address, so I searched for Eliza on Facebook. I didn't know her surname, but Pepper told me—"

"Pepper!" I said. "You still talk to him?"

"All the time. He's still doing *Mexico's Scariest Places*. It's really popular, and he's actually thinking of doing some episodes set in the US. There's this mansion in California with over a hundred rooms he was talking about. It was built by the widow of the guy who invented the Winchester rifle, and it's supposedly haunted by a bunch of ghosts. He wanted me to ask you if you would be in his show."

"No way in hell."

She laughed. "He said you would say that. But, yeah, he told me Eliza's last name. I did a search, and imagine my surprise when Elizaveta Grechko-Goff turned up!"

"Yeah, well..." I shrugged. "She was going to be sent back to Russia to work in a pre-World War Two ammunitions factory, so I decided to help her out with a green card."

Elizaveta glowered. "Funny, Jack."

"Anyway, she and I got in touch," Rosa said. "And I decided instead of her telling you I was moving to the States, maybe I would keep it a surprise. After all, it's been almost ten years. What's another few months?" She smiled. "So here I am."

"Here indeed," I said. "So how have you been? I mean, after Xochimilco, you just sort of disappeared. I asked about you. I asked the cops and stuff. But they wouldn't tell me anything."

"My mom didn't want me involved in the media circus that followed. She was really upset about my brother. We moved to France to be with my father, and we stayed there until I was fifteen."

I said, "I'm sorry about Miguel, Rosa."

She nodded. "Thank you, Jack. It's strange, you know. I was so young. I barely knew him. Sometimes now I can't even remember what he looks like. But at the same time, he's still such an important part of me. I think about him all the time. I just wish, you know, that I actually *did* know him, or could get the chance to..." She shook her head. "Anyway, I'm not here to talk about Miguel. I'm here to see you guys. And to...I never told you this...but I wanted to say thank you. That night on the island...it was pretty fucked up, pardon the language. I still remember you finding me under the bed, Jack. I was so scared. I thought you were a ghost at first."

"You seemed pretty brave."

"Because I was too young to know better. But if it weren't for you guys, both of you, I probably wouldn't be here right now. I mean, I don't think María would have done anything to me. But I was eight. I just don't think...I'm not sure I would have...coped for long." She wiped a tear that had sprung to her eye. "God, that was harder than I thought it would be!"

Elizaveta gave her an awkward hug.

I didn't want to offer up some platitude, so I said, "Speaking of María, did you ever hear what happened to her?"

Rosa nodded. "I've seen her a few times."

"You've *seen* her?"

"Yeah, she's in an institution. To tell you the truth, it's pretty damn depressing. Just the condition of the place, how the staff treat the patients. Some of them don't have shoes. And there was this one old woman I saw tied up in her wheelchair."

"Did she recognize you?"

"María?" Rosa shook her head. "I told her who I was, but she was completely out of it, all drugged up. She was just sitting in the common room with her doll—that same one she had on the island. I feel really bad for her. She doesn't have any family, no one to visit her."

"Poor woman," Elizaveta said. "I mean, what a terrible life. You know, I used to think my life in Russia was bad, but I guess there's always someone who has it worse off than you do."

"What about the island?" I asked. "You haven't by chance gone back to it?"

"Are you kidding?" Rosa said. "It's a freaking tourist trap now."

"What!"

"Don't you ever go on the internet, Jack?"

"Sure, but I've never...wanted to...I don't really google 'Island of the Dolls.'"

"Well, you should, you'll see what I mean. It's a tourist trap. Especially with foreigners. The legend is still the same: it's haunted by a ghost of a girl who died there fifty years ago. The locals want to keep it that way. A ghost brings more tourist bucks than a disabled woman wearing a doll face. By the way, you know it was Solano who made up the entire legend? Yeah, to keep people away from the island, and to explain María's presence if she was ever spotted." She glanced at her silver wristwatch. "Anyway, I don't want to keep you guys. I just wanted to say hi—and thank you for saving my life and everything. But we should definitely stay in touch. Next time you race in California, Jack, I'm going to be there, cheering you on."

"Let me know which race. I'll leave you tickets."

"For my girlfriends too? They think you're super sexy."

I raised my eyebrows at Elizaveta as she rolled her eyes.

We all stood, and I said, "Where are you heading, Rosa?"

"Back to my dorm on The Hill—the northwest edge of campus."

"We'll give you a lift."

"You sure—?"

"Positive. All we have planned for today is a big fiberglass chicken."

"Huh?"

"Never mind."

We left the Starbucks together and walked the half block to where my midnight-black '79 Monte Carlo was parked alongside the curb.

"Wow!" Rosa said, running her hand along the hood. "That's a pretty mean looking car, Jack."

"Don't tell him that," Elizaveta said. "It's older than me. I hate it."

"Can I give it a spin?" Rosa asked.

"Do you even have a license?"

"Come on, Jack."

"It's a manual transmission."

"So what?"

"That means it has three pedals."

She held out her hand for the keys.

Shrugging, I tossed them to her.

We got in, Rosa behind the wheel, me in shotgun (somewhat nervous), and Elizaveta in the backseat. Rosa turned the key in the ignition, and the engine gurgled to life.

I said, "Careful not to stall—"

Rosa clutch-shifted to first, rev-matched, and engaged the accelerator, swerving aggressively out of the parking spot onto the street. She upped to second gear, blipping the throttle to match the engine speed to the wheel speed, keeping the engine in the sweet spot of its powerband.

"Not bad," I said, impressed.

"Like I keep telling you, Jack." She glanced sidelong at me. "I'm not a little girl anymore."

"No," I said, slipping on my Wayfarers to cut the glare of the morning winter light. The sky was streaked with brush-strokes of pink and gray. "I guess you're not."